Finding Her Way

By Leah Banicki

Acknowledgements:

To my amazing family who cheered me on for many years, I thank you. My parents for letting me read anything I could get my hands on when I was young. You both are so creative in your own ways.
I love you both!

For my Mom, her endless support and shared love of writing. Thanks for all the help! Dad, thanks for the tech and graphics support, your insight made a big difference along the journey.

To those who helped me clean up the multitude of grammatical issues, I pray a blessing over all of you. You were such a blessing and help to me.

For my husband Jeff, for encouraging me and helping me make sure that a guy would really say what I wrote. I love you!

For my daughter Emma, for always believing and telling me that I am nothing less than a superstar. I pray you reach for your dreams with tenacity and vigor!

For my sister Rachel, your light shines in my heart so bright. Thank you for everything. I can see you dancing and worshipping in heaven in my dreams.

Wildflowers Book 1 ~

Corinne ~ like a lavender blossom.
A simple pretty flower to the eye but inside
hides strength and healing.

Part One:

Chapter One
Feb 22, 1848 – Boston, Massachusetts

She had married a stranger.

Corinne Temple had accepted and wholeheartedly agreed to marry a man she had not known. An arranged marriage, of sorts. So far, Corinne had not liked him much.

The morning had been chaotic. Corinne nerves were frayed. She went back and forth on her decision a hundred times. Lingering thoughts repeated through her mind.

Am I being wise? Is this marriage a huge mistake?

It seemed like such a strange thing to agree to, Corinne knew this. She had not been able to express it aloud very well, her words locked behind her tongue when it came to her choices. She felt defensive and vulnerable.

But that day, above any other, she would have said what she felt. If anyone would have asked her. Corinne would have said she was ashamed. Ashamed of the girl she had been three years ago. The loud and petulant child she had been.

She thought about the last few years, the agony she had gone through, and the regret. Her father's first letter from Oregon had arrived, in the fall two years ago. She had read it a thousand times and she had reacted immediately to it. She had made so many decisions based on his words.

Dearest Daughter,

The journey across this land was certainly more difficult than I ever could have imagined. But the long trail gave me days on end to think of our last conversations. I regret so badly how we left things. I love you dearly and miss your smiles.

Oregon is splendid, with the mountain air and freedom to spread out. I spent a few months getting the cabin and the first barn built, with the help of the neighbors. Such a community feeling here. We all are grasping at the will to concur the rugged land and make a new world here.

I can see you here. You are so much like your mother and grandmother, with your love of green and growing things. The woods and mountains are in the bloom of summer. The great Willamette River is alive with fish, and the woods are full of wildlife.

My healing heart is coming back to life again, after losing your mother. My one regret is that we are so far apart.

Sending my love across the miles,

Your father ~ John Harpole

His letter made her realize that she belonged with him in Oregon.

Corinne was seventeen years old. She knew she was naïve, but not as naïve as she had been. Her choices back then had proven that to her. She had this terrifying tendency to realize her mistakes, only after the decision had been made. She knew her choices that day could easily backfire, but she stiffened her spine and determined herself to endure through.

She reviewed her choices. No woman, at any age, could travel west without a husband or guardian. It was impossible. She would never be safe without protection. So, Andrew Temple was the compromise. He had sworn to keep her safe. Her father had put his trust in him. The fact that she did not know Andrew, was giving her more than some moment's pause. Choices were so limited. She could easily have lost her sanity, if she had let herself get riled up. But after countless days and nights, and countless tears, she had found a solution. Andrew Temple was her way west.

Her new husband, Andrew Temple, was a good friend of her father, but mostly unknown to her. He had recently graduated from Harvard Veterinary Medical School. His tall blond good looks were a front though, Corinne quickly realized. After one brief visit, and a letter of introduction from her father, she still wasn't sure about Andrew's true disposition. Corinne was clueless how to handle him.

Her inner fire was snuffed out when he stood near. She was not sure if her immature wit could stand up to his ill-tempered condescension.

Andrew's stiff and formal facial expressions were unreadable. And if Corinne allowed herself an opinion, his demeanor was still a bit chilly. She had always heard glowing accounts of the Temple family from her father. But in his conversations from years past, he had only mentioned the parents. Corinne was going off old conversations and her remembrance was probably way off, she mused.

Who can remember exact conversations from years ago? she wondered. *I was a child at the time.*

It was true that her first impressions of Andrew were not stellar. She found him rather cautious and gruff. She would have preferred to glimpse into his thoughts, but he was well guarded. Just one smile, or kind word would have done wonders to ease her fears. In their short meeting months before, he had barely acknowledged her. Instead, he only spoke to her guardian, Aunt Rose. Corinne felt like a child standing there, with a thousand questions. His demeanor had been so solid, not to be interrupted.

No matter what her opinion, she had little choice. Andrew was her ticket to Oregon. So she packed her objections in her satchel and focused on reuniting with her father. He waited for her in Oregon City. Her father was wise, hardworking and kind to a fault. He certainly would not have trusted Andrew if he was undeserving.

Corinne waited in her Aunt's fashionable 12th street Boston home. For her own sanity, she was determined to think about anything except that man. She fidgeted with the plain silver band on her finger. The simplicity of it contrasted with everything in her environment. The opulence surrounding her, this mansion where her Aunt lived. The walls were gilded in pinks and golds. Great drops of crystal cascaded from the chandeliers. The grand staircase wrapped elegantly around the back, and majestically descended into the great hall. Halfway down the stairs, there was a great view of the parlor on one side, and the ballroom on the other. Artisans from Italy and France laid the exquisite marble floor. The fireplaces were designed by a famous stonemason. The iron grates and tools were imported from the best artists and craftsmen around the world. Few houses in Boston boasted of finer rooms or impressive displays of wealth. It had been a long while since it even fazed Corinne. This place had not looked like a prison, but Corinne had lost her freedom a few years ago, when she tied her first whalebone corset around her petite frame. The grandeur came at a price.

The servants scurried around her as she followed the strict orders of Auntie Rose. Corinne's secret name for her was the *General*. Auntie Rose threw orders at Corinne and the servants, as well as any military man did with his platoon. Corinne grew impatient with waiting and tried to help a few hours earlier. She was reprimanded instantly.

"Oh Corinne! You dishonor the place I have given you in my home, when you insist on acting like the common scullery," her Aunt said, in her usual volume--loud!

Corinne stopped helping with the bag organization and resumed her brainless position by the door. Feeling useless, she watched her Aunt belittle the help. She looked about for her lady's maid, Angela Fahey, for encouragement. Instead, she found disappointment. Her Aunt had put her lady's maid to work.

Within the hour, she was leaving her temporary Boston home. She would be heading out toward the great West, with this stranger who was her husband. The Oregon Trail would be months of grueling travel, far removed from her momentary comfort. Corinne was eager to start though. She could not have stayed here any longer. This gilded prison was not where she belonged.

She held her mother's book of psalms. Though she did not dare read them in front of her Aunt, she felt a comfort in knowing their words in her heart. The wisdom she gained, daily, helped her. She said a prayer of thanks, again and again. To Corinne, it was a miracle that her father had forgiven her outburst from three years before, and was willing to make arrangements for their reunion. She reread the short message from her father, which she received in September. It was placed between the pages of her psalms.

Arranged for travel to Oregon. Andrew Temple can marry and escort you. He will contact you.

Andrew sent his calling card the third week of September 1847. He arrived with a long letter from her father. It proposed a plan of Andrew marrying Corinne and bringing her West. Andrew's parents were already there. He was going to work with her father, John Harpole, on his ranch.

Corrine was not interested in the mundane details about breeding stock and ranch issues, but was comforted in seeing her father's strong, bold handwriting. She ran her fingers over his words, trying to remember every detail about the last moments she had spent with him. Even with the harsh words between them, he had said farewell, with love and an embrace. She missed her father and would go to impossible lengths to see him again. She would deal with a husband to make amends.

I am sure Andrew's attitude will improve once he gets to know me, she thought.

A part of her knew that having married a stranger was foolish. But she had known of no other way to see her father again. She had known of many people who married for convenience or arranged by a family member. It was still a common practice in many ways. Even with that logic though, the negative consequences would sneak back into her mind. What if they never got along? What if they could not eventually have a loving marriage? After weeks of struggling with doubts, she set aside all her negative thoughts and made up her mind. She was going West, and a husband of her father's choosing was the only way.

Andrew had stoically agreed to see to her safety and marry her in February, before they left. After the short meeting in September, he left, claiming to have classes to attend. After five months of no word, Andrew sent a telegram saying the wedding was arranged for February 22, at nine a.m. He had made all the arrangements.

The *General* had been outraged to have a wedding with no fuss or guests, but Corinne stood up to her Aunt. Corinne made her Aunt realize that this was not a 'social event', but a simple ceremony. Corinne boldly told her Aunt that it did not concern her.

"Our train will be leaving at two in the afternoon. There is no time for wedding nonsense."

For the entire week, words had been strained between her and Auntie Rose.

During the short ceremony, she glanced Andrew's way a few times. His height reached over six foot, and it made her feel tiny. His dark blond curls were peppered with light blond highlights. His lips were pressed firmly in a tight line through the entire morning. He barely spoke a word beyond what was necessary. Corinne felt that the awkward silences were just encouraging all her doubts. She felt like a silly and anxious girl all morning.

The judge came to her Aunt's home and efficiently performed the service. Corinne wore her traveling clothes and Andrew was in a common tweed suit. There was no kiss-the-bride moment.

Corinne was certain it was her wild imagination, but Andrew seemed agitated with her already. She had no idea what he could be so annoyed about, in such a short acquaintance. *Certainly not the joy of a groom on his wedding day.* She nearly laughed at her own thoughts, but kept her face composed, as her Aunt and husband were glaring at her. It was very disconcerting.

Corinne pulled herself back to the present. She began to watch the repacking of her precious medicinal plant oils. Several small wooden boxes held her medicines and healing balms to take on the journey. Her lady's maid, Angela, clearly expressed to the footmen, Corinne's desire that the oils and balms be well packed. The packing was being double-checked. Suddenly a small vial of peppermint oil was dropped and broken, by a servant who would remain nameless, for his own protection from her Aunt. It soaked immediately into the Oriental rug in the grand foyer. Within minutes, the smell of peppermint was strong. It made Corinne's eyes water a little, but it wasn't too unpleasant. There were worse smells, Corinne thought, amusing herself.

Auntie Rose was instantly mortified. She declared that the stench was giving her fits and a migraine. Auntie Rose's goodbyes were brief, as she rushed her well-corseted frame up the stairs and into her wing of the house.

If Corinne hadn't left that day, she was confident she would have seen Auntie Rose in a shrieking rage. Auntie would have stirred the staff into a flurry of activity, taking her away to her country home, for a stay of a week or more. The oriental rug was certainly doomed. Corinne was certain to never know, but the scene played out humorously in her imagination.

With a glance at the hall mirror, Corinne made sure she was put together. When she looked at her young face, she heard Auntie's voice in her head. "You look like a child with a woman's body." Auntie had a way of saying things that kept you guessing whether it was an insult or not. Corinne shrugged at her own reflection. Her long brown hair was swept back neatly, and her bonnet was simple but fashionable. She would not embarrass herself, but cared little about being elaborate for traveling.

Corinne clutched her green silk satchel close to her. "It's the latest fashion!" Auntie Rose would say in her high-pitched voice. Corinne learned long ago to hide her expressions from her Aunt. So many times, she wanted to smirk, or roll her eyes at the ridiculous pursuit of what others deemed fashionable. She may have looked the part of the fashion plate right then, but she was still a rancher's daughter at heart. She knew how to ride horses well, tie knots, and break a horse, if necessary. She wasn't a tomboy but had her rough and tumble moments in life. She knew the calluses had faded away over the last three years, but the knowledge was still there. Corinne enjoyed dressing up sometimes. Feeling pretty was always pleasant, but she didn't care for fashion the way the Boston crowd did. It made her head swim keeping up with 12th Street crowd. They were all about parties, flirting, smoking cigarettes, and gossip mongering. She allowed them their pursuits, but she had her own goals. She had wondered more than a few times if she had already changed too much, being under the strict influence of her Aunt.

She had never had a strong Kentucky accent, probably because her parents did not. Her Aunt declared even Corinne's slight accent to be vulgar. Within months, Auntie had scolded her enough to force her to watch every word. She had learned to never speak her mind or opinions, because they also were unacceptable. This world was so closed and judgmental. The longer she stayed in this society, the more she wanted to be away. If she stayed, she knew the path that lay ahead for her. The *General* had a plan for Corinne. She wanted no part of society life, and being a debutante was not one of her plans. There had been countless arguments about that topic, between her and Auntie Rose. The plans for the marriage and journey west, had finally put a stop to the society dreams of Auntie Rose. The mountains and woods of the Oregon valley were calling to Corinne. She had dreams of her own. The cobblestone streets of Boston were not a part of them.

Corinne's true passion was botany. She learned botany from her mother, and she loved it still. During her three years in Boston, she spent as much time as possible in the greenhouses, learning and volunteering with the experts. Auntie Rose had taken her there on a whim, in the early days when Corinne would cry from home sickness. Corinne had spoken of her mother's garden and the blooming plants. Auntie had thought that being around the plants might revitalize Corinne. It did in a way. It again gave Corinne a taste of her love for nature. It gave Corinne a reason to get up in the morning again. It vexed Auntie greatly when Corinne demanded to go back again and again. She had learned a lot from the staff at the greenhouse. She absorbed everything they taught her. She made some lasting relationships there. She promised to write to them about everything she would discover in Oregon, and along the trail. As a parting gift, the greenhouse staff gave her a beautiful leather-bound journal. They had been so pleased when she shared her heart for plants, and the power the plant's had within them.

So much of what they had taught her would be going along the trail with her. Her mother and grandmother's journals were also coming with her. They were her most prized possessions. Her grandmother, Trudie, had studied with the Indian women of the Smoky Mountains. After earning their trust, she learned many healing secrets from their women. Corinne secretly hoped to do that in the West. She hoped to find plants and ointments to help future generations, and maybe even publish her journals. Corinne smiled to herself. It was a lovely dream.

"Miss Fahey." Corinne spotted her companion. Despite their cultural and social differences, they were the dearest of friends. But they kept it behind closed doors, for the sake of 'house rules', and the taboos of polite society. Auntie was quite stern about any endearments between the two girls. Corinne knew she would never do anything to cause Angela Fahey to lose her good position in the household staff. Corinne secretly hoped the barrier of propriety would lift once they left Boston. She was certain that the road west held many different types of freedom.

"Is everything at the ready, Miss Fahey?" Corinne smiled, and reached for the fair-skinned maid. They shared the same excitement, after so many hours together, hidden in her room. For months, they shared their dreams, and hopes for freedom.

"It is, Mrs. Temple."

The new title made Corinne squirm a little, but she nodded at her friend.

"At this moment, the trunks and surplus supplies are being loaded on your travel car. Your personal items and trunks are to be packed into our coach. I have called for it twice. I shall send a footman to see about the delay." Angela's voice was tired, and with only the slightest hint of her Irish birth. Most of the time she could hide her accent, but Corinne could tell how Angela was nearly done in from the workload. Corinne said a silent prayer for her friend, as they waited impatiently for their time to go.

Corinne stayed silent and watched the door. There was nothing left to do but wait.

<hr/>

Angela's own expectations and need for perfection, pushed her hard this week. Angela was nearly at her end, with the wedding this morning, and all the packing for today's trip, as well. Her nerves were weary to the breaking point. Without the head housekeeper in attendance the last three days, Angela managed the entire household. Additionally, the trip planning was also put under Angela's leadership. Corinne's Aunt was more than a little unmerciful, expecting Angela to handle the packing, wedding, and daily chores. Angela should have anticipated it though. The head housekeeper had a delightful habit of catching her "death-of-something," when huge events came around. Angela was certain that the housekeeper would rally from her illness, just in time for the afternoon train departure. Twenty-hour days put the fifteen-year-old Angela into an emotional daze. Last night after a quick prayer, and a long cry, Angela slept like a baby. After only a few short hours, she was up and going again. She had a beautiful vision of herself on the train, taking a long nap, on a cot. At this point, surely a blanket and the floor would have worked for her.

Angela took a quick moment to secure her bonnet over her red hair and headed out the front door. She heard the crunch of carriage wheels as they traveled up the stone road, stopping close to the front door. She joined Corinne in the carriage seat and let the footmen do their job loading everything. Angela and Corinne shared a hand squeeze when the carriage finally moved forward. Forward toward their future.

Angela only had a few bags herself. She owned so very little. But leaving Rose Capron's house was a good feeling. When she felt the heaviness lift from being in the Capron house, Angela's joy was complete. She would relish every moment of it.

⬥•⦿•⬥ ⬥•⦿•⬥

The train station was crowded, and the footmen struggled to get through the crowds with Corinne's luggage. The fancy train station was a modern wonder, with tall brick pillars and a shaded area to block the cool rain that had begun to fall. After several minutes of jockeying around the station, they found Andrew and joined him near the end of the train. His cowboy hat sat on his brow, and he looked like he was ready to take on the world.

Corinne took a moment to look around. The luggage footmen were holding the bags and trunks, awaiting her instructions. She heard a frustrated sigh from a man, and realized it was probably her husband. She snapped her head around. Corinne tried to appear friendly when she made eye contact, but he looked away. Andrew wanted to her to say something. She was tongue-tied.

Then it seemed like he changed his mind, and spoke, "Hello wife."

Andrew's bright smile greeted Corinne, as she gestured her footmen forward. Andrew made a striking figure, with his dark blond curls and cowboy hat. But his green eyes had a look in them that she just didn't understand. He was intimidating and confident, and he did not seem to be interested in her at all. Corinne told herself to stop being fearful, and just keep thinking about making a good impression.

She smiled, but did not know what to say, her mind empty. A thin man with short brown hair and a serious face, walked up silently and stood next to Andrew. Corinne wondered why he was there.

Andrew noticed her perusal. "This is my man, Reggie. If you need me and can't find me, tell him. He will always know where I am." He gave Reggie's shoulder a tap and pointed. Reggie took the satchels sitting on the ground and headed into the traveling car next to them. Corinne wondered if his job was also to be mute.

Well, she mused, *I am a mute too today it seems.*

Corinne's luggage was loaded. She checked inside her handbag with a sweep of her hand. Everything was there. Money, mints, a small brown bottle of lavender, a pocket watch, and a small sewing kit. She had plenty of money sewn into her clothing, hidden in her luggage, and stuffed into book pages. Andrew insisted that she need for nothing and should not buy anything. He had said as much in the morning. Her Aunt had agreed. Corinne was in the complete care of Andrew. She thought that was foolish. She had her own money to spend, but she acknowledged his thoughts, to make peace at the time. Her mother taught her that a woman should always be prepared for the worst, though. 'A girl should have the means to support herself, in case there was trouble.'

Corinne thought about the long days ahead. Andrew kept busy, ordering everyone about. Corinne retreated within herself, thinking of how unknown her future was. She longed to see her father again, but almost dreaded it, too. Three years was a long separation. She had changed a lot since her days on the ranch in Kentucky.

His letter said he wanted to meet her in Oregon, but she wondered if the disappointment would still linger between them. It would be months before she would know. *I should focus on getting the first part of the trip traveled successfully,* Corinne thought.
It would take four weeks or more of train and coach rides to reach the Missouri River. *Four weeks with a stranger.* Corinne had no idea what she would discuss with Andrew, but she would work on being friendly. *I should try to stop being intimidated. Foolish girl!* Corinne then stopped her inner dialogue.

With a great blast, the train whistle blew, and the conductor yelled for the passengers to board. She let the golden-haired Andrew lead her up the stairs to the traveling car. Andrew had her arm and helped her up the steps. She was very aware of his hand on her arm. She glanced his way briefly, and he looked at her distractedly. Maybe he also was nervous about spending the long ride with a stranger. *Do men get nervous, too?* She looked back at her feet, but her grin was hard to hide.

The train car was comfortable, with soft seats, a dining car and two separate rooms with beds. He arranged for everything. He obviously got what he wanted. He acted like a force to be reckoned with. She tried not to think about the wifely expectations, but was ready to face that reality, if need be. She was secretly hoping to first get to know him a little better. Inside her head, she whispered a prayer for strength. Then she stared out the window, seeing nothing for a while.

The newly married couple sat quietly for nearly an hour, as they watched the train leave the station, and then the city rushing by. Andrew rang the bell and within a moment, he ordered tea.

The tea was served a few minutes later. Corinne desperately searched her mind for something to discuss with Andrew. The landscape out the window was unremarkable. With their own private car, they were not able to see the other passengers. That would have been a lovely distraction. Corinne absently wondered if reading a book during tea was rude. Her manners finally kicked in, and she did what had to be done. She stopped avoiding her husband and thought of a question to ask.

"Andrew, I was wondering if you have any hobbies?" Corinne sipped her tea and put on her bravest smile. It sounded silly to her once it was said, but there was no taking it back. She just tilted her head and looked him in the eye.

Andrew met her gaze and smiled. "Well, I do believe college was my hobby, I suppose." He laughed, and his green eyes looked bright for a second. "I still feel a little strange after these last three months, to be actually finished. Six years of my life was spent at Harvard." He paused and stopped smiling. "Well child, I suppose you can't understand. Six years ago, you were eleven." He took a sip of tea himself and reached for a pastry.

Corinne blinked, wondering what just happened. She tried again. "Do you plan on opening a vet clinic in Oregon City?" Corinne felt good for making a second effort toward conversation.

"I will help your father with his breeding stock and perhaps head to California to see what the competition is up to. I know you have your 'prodigal daughter' plans, but some of us must work. I may or may not settle in Oregon at all."

She had to work hard at not rolling her eyes. She felt like a stranger was scolding her, and she tried not to resent it. *He wasn't playing nice*, she thought.

"I want to be clear on my intentions towards you. I have married you as a favor to your father. His influence over my getting into Harvard was the best gift anyone ever gave me. I will gladly help you reunite with him in Oregon, but," he took a breath. "I will be getting an annulment when we arrive. I have no intentions of us being in a marriage in any other way than in name only. I have no need for marriage now in my life. I do not mean to be impertinent." Halfway through the speech he stopped looking at her, opened a newspaper, and began idly flipping through pages.

An annulment… Corinne's mind jumbled with the implications. No long-term plan, no stuck in a loveless marriage. She was trying to keep her face impassive, but she wanted to cheer. She almost laughed. This was joyful news. She had to use every ounce of restraint to keep her countenance composed.

She found Andrew staring at her, trying to gauge her reaction. He seemed so grumpy. Perhaps he wanted a response.

"I understand. Once we are across, you will file for an annulment," Corinne said simply, hoping her voice wouldn't crack. Or, that she would break into childish giggles.

"Good girl." Andrew said, and then continued reading his paper.

Corinne realized she couldn't be insecure with this man, or he would run over her. He was a *General*, too. As her mother used to tell her, 'Out of the frying pan, then eaten by the dog!'

<hr />

In the next room, Angela was busily preparing the sleeping car. It had two beds. It would be her and Corinne's quarters for two weeks. The beds looked soft and comfortable. She could feel the softness and the rest calling to her. She tucked her own bags into a cupboard, glad to know that her few precious belongings were safe and secure.

Angela's mind was thick from exhaustion, but she pushed herself just a little while more. She still had many duties to attend to. Angela would need to find out whether Corinne preferred the top bunk or bottom bunk. Angela then put three traveling suits in the tiny wardrobe, and hung the rest of Corinne's dresses in the next car, where the luggage, trunks, and supplies were stored. There were hanging racks, space for a washtub, and all the cleaning supplies Angela would need these on this trip. Traveling and keeping Corinne's clothes clean was her duty. She did not intend to let her mistress be shamed in front of her new husband.

Angela was certain, by the strong set of his jaw, that Andrew would expect things to be perfect. She would do everything within her power to make Corinne look respectful in his eyes.

Chapter Two
February 23, 1848

"I want to see the complete inventory of Corinne's bags this instant." Andrew's young stern voice pierced through the tired haze in Angela's skull. Too many long days and late nights had her exhausted beyond bearing. At that point, her body seemed to have shut down.

She spent the first day aboard the train in the storage car, making sure Corinne's things were accounted for and easy to get to. As dusk approached, Corinne sent for her and they got ready for bed. At ten p.m., Corinne headed to bed but there was a knock at the door. Angela grabbed a robe and cracked the door open a sliver.

"Why are you dressed in your night clothes?" Andrew's harsh whisper dashed Angela's hopes of rest. Angela muttered an apology and closed the door. She was back into her work clothes and ready for duty by 10:05 p.m.

Corinne protested, but Andrew claimed it was important that Angela follow his instructions. Angela gave Corinne a pointed look, communicating that she needed to get off on the right foot with Andrew. Frowning, Corinne silently agreed.

His demand for the inventory list was easy to fulfill, but she cringed when he wanted to go over her expected duties. Andrew did not share Corinne's idea of how to treat servants. Auntie Rose was hard on her servants, also. Corinne was raised to treat them like family. Common courtesy had no class lines in Corinne's way of thinking.

Angela was ordered to awaken at five a.m., to stoke the coal stove for a hot, eight a.m. breakfast. It was a moot point that three hours was not needed to load coal into a heating stove. But with her new master, she was never allowed to have that opinion.

Angela spent two hours going over inventory with Reggie. She then retired, but woke up before the sun came up. Reggie was quiet and polite. Angela saw that she would have no problem working with him. He smiled a few times while they worked together. Angela was hoping for a pleasant camaraderie between them. It had taken a lot of will power to wake up so early. She used the tried and true method to get up. She drank two full glasses of water before she went to sleep. She knew her body would handle the rest.

She completed the stove duties quickly. The room felt toasty warm by ten past six a.m. She sat on a stool and fell back into an exhausted sleep, while holding onto a nearby railing. She felt a swift soft kick to her boot. She stood to attention just in time to see her new master, Andrew Temple, enter the dining room. Reggie stood next to her. He must have been the source of the wake-up kick. She looked down at her pendent watch and saw that it was seven forty.

"You look disheveled, Ms. Fahey. I expect professionalism when working for me. I see some discipline will be in order." Andrew gave her a dismissive wave. Angela rushed to the storage room for a mirror.

She saw a few tendrils had escaped her tight bun at the nape of her neck. It probably happened as she slept. She brushed her copper tendrils into place and used a white cap to solve the issue. She would wear it daily to prevent receiving any further 'discipline' from her new master. Angela prayed, asking God to give her humility and strength for the job. She was so tired. She wanted to cry, but she pulled her pain inward and resumed her work. Her early life at the work orphanage prepared her for the reality of her servitude. Then, at only 12 years old, she was sold into the Boston home of Mrs. Rose Capron. As payment, Mrs. Capron sent Angela's first-year wages directly to the orphanage.

She met Corinne several weeks after joining the household. Corinne was very sad after the first month. In a hasty moment of sympathy, Angela stopped her chores and gave comfort to the grieving girl. Corinne and Angela were fast friends after that. Angela was there to comfort Corinne after her regrettable decision to stay with her aunt, when her father went west. Corinne was there for Angela throughout her trials in Auntie Rose's household. They both were separated from a family member, and talked often about reuniting with each of them. Angela's own brother was in the west. Sean Fahey ran away from the work orphanage several years back and worked recently with a trapper along the Snake River. Angela daydreamed about her brother, as she worked to stay awake. Her prayer was that he was happy and free.

Her work kept her busy for long days, but eventually the late nights did her in. Three days into the trip Angela Fahey was sick, burning with fever and a chest-rattling cough.

◆•◆•◆———◆•◆•◆

Corinne informed Andrew of her maid's illness. "She has a fever and she coughed all night. She is a tough girl and I am certain with a few days rest she will be fine. I told her to go back to bed." Corinne sipped her tea as a breakfast tray was handed to her.

"I have a feeling Ms. Fahey is a worthless servant," Andrew said with certainty. "She will probably be a run-away once we land in Iowa. We should withhold pay until the trip is concluded."

"That is possibly the most insensitive remark I have ever heard. You have no idea how hard Angela works. She is fifteen years old and has an excellent work record in my aunt's household. She has a great mind and work ethic. She fought me like a tiger this morning when I sent her back to her bunk." Corinne huffed and puffed but could see Andrew wasn't listening. Talking to him was useless.

Really, what could I possibly need so desperately over the next few days? I can dress myself, thought Corinne. *Well, the simpler frocks anyway.*

After sleeping for two days, Angela improved. She went back to work even though the fever persisted.

The train moved along, and the Temple car chugged on its way. The only joy shared was a few precious moments allowed between Corinne and Angela behind closed doors.

Corinne rarely spoke to Andrew and he was happier for it. Angela obeyed her orders and almost never spoke to him, only saying 'yes sir' when appropriate. She was the perfect servant, busy and quiet.

Chapter Three
March 29, 1848

Corinne fought off an anger headache. Her husband Andrew was being impossible. He could make any situation miserable with his glaring and shushing. So far, marriage had not been such a pleasant endeavor. He was only happy when people were silent.

The coach was stuffed to capacity and instead of being able to make the situation bearable, he refused to allow any talking. If some brave soul did try to speak, Andrew used his condescension to mock the person who spoke, until they were shamed into silence.

Corinne was trying to imagine how any person her father was acquainted with, could act in such a manner. Her father was always one to encourage conversation and welcome opinions of all kinds. It would have made the journey seem faster to her. Andrew would not allow it. Along with everyone else, she was forced to stare out the coach's dingy windows and simply think.

Corinne pulled out her journals. Her headache and the bumpy roads were making her stomach ill, which made it difficult to read them. She stared at her mother's name on the front of the journal instead.

Lillian Harpole was printed in her mother's artistic handwriting. Corinne traced the name hundreds of times as she rolled along in the silence of the smelly coach.

Corinne could still remember her mother's face, but she was starting to forget the sound of her voice. She died only three years before, sending Corinne's life in a new direction.

Her father had been devastated, naturally. His soul mate had died of a fever, so suddenly. There was nothing that could have been done. No doctor could have been found in time. The fever took many in the town and spread until it had run its course.

Only months after her mother's death, Corinne's father had decided to sell out and leave Kentucky. Corinne's heart broke at the thought of leaving behind her mother's home and garden. She didn't understand. How could her father want to leave it all behind?

Corinne lashed out in the last days. The ranch sold, and the horses were transported to the West, first by train, then by trail.

Corinne picked a fight with her father, declaring herself unwilling to travel with him. Instead, she chose to to move to Boston to be with her wealthy aunt. Only briefly did her father plead for her to leave with him. His heart was set on escaping the home that contained so many memories of his departed wife.

Her mood slipped into melancholy as the miles passed, and she spent time praying to be able to move past her regrets.

———◆·◎·◆———◆·◎·◆———

"How mighty and beautiful!" Corinne said to herself.

She was in awe of the Missouri River. Its wide birth seemed so much larger than any five rivers combined. The month of travel hadn't been easy, especially with very little conversation. The train ride had been dull yet comfortable, but the stagecoach in Iowa was brutal. Andrew procured a private coach but ultimately, they had to use a regularly scheduled coach due to a sick driver. Two young men joined the coach with Andrew, Corinne, Angela and Reggie. The smell of these young men was enough to make anyone want to walk, rather than ride the rest of the journey. Corinne told Angela that they should be prepared for the jostling of the wagon from the carriage ride, but Andrew hushed her with a glare. Corinne figured out why Andrew's servant Reggie was nearly a mute. It was a survival instinct.

She spent most of her journey reading her botany journals whenever possible. Her mother, Lillian, began Corinne's interest in herbs, and how to get medicinal oils from them. Corinne spent many years of her childhood learning the scents and uses of many common plants in Kentucky. She helped grow a large garden with her mother. The scent of lavender still made Corinne remember how much she missed her mother.

Corinne stood on the ticket platform on the dock and waited patiently for Andrew to tell her where she was needed. She avoided speaking to him as much as she could, to keep him from using his 'insult me with a friendly voice' trick. She would have plenty of opportunities to get to know him better on the trail. She hoped he would improve as they got better acquainted. She bit back any sarcastic thoughts she had, that doubted Andrew had any positive attributes.

St. Louis was a bustling city. Corinne felt a bit like she had in Boston, overwhelmed. She missed the smell of sweet grass and watching the rolling prairie. *Oh, why did I ever leave my Father?* Corinne tried not to beat herself up every day for her mistakes, but the city reminded her of what she had lost.

"Are you daydreaming Corinne?" Andrew grabbed her arm and made her jump.

"Why yes, just missing Kentucky a little. I am not a city girl." Corinne was startled but being honest with him had felt natural. She prepared herself to receive a snide remark.

"I guess I knew you grew up in Kentucky on your father's ranch, but I lost sight of that after seeing you in Boston. Your clothes and manners were pure Boston society." Andrew had a confidence that intimidated her, but he was being nice, at least.

"Yes, my aunt was a powerful influence over me in Boston. She had high expectations concerning my every move. Secretly I called her *The General*." Corinne grinned at her own joke and was shocked when Andrew laughed. It was a nice sound.

"I had an aunt like that growing up. She scared me to death." He chuckled again and looked at Corinne warmly. His laugh relaxed her. She felt they had crossed a threshold.

"Well Corinne, I can't take you back to Kentucky, but I can take you on a ferry boat ride." His charm was a delicious change. She latched onto his arm and let herself be led away.

The ferry was an awesome spectacle! Corinne was positive that the massive structure would never stay above the water, but it did. There were five stories, two decks and scores of people. The elegant carvings on every corner made the ferry both beautiful and frightful. The paddle wheel was enormous, and Corinne secretly thrilled in her anticipation of watching it forcefully push the craft through the great river.

The baggage was handled, and Andrew led Corinne to the loading dock. Andrew let out another laugh as they walked up the plank to the boat.

"Corinne, you look like a five-year-old child at Christmas. I can tell you've never been on a ferry boat." His smile was genuine, but she tried to disregard the child-like reference. She swallowed her disappointment and continued her adventure with her best smile.

Corinne loved her room aboard the steamship. With red and white calico pillows and curtains, a small vanity table, and a breakfast nook, it was all southern elegance. The lace pillow shams and a small desk with stationary, made her feel like it was her own little home. She could see Angela had been there and had already unpacked her belongings. She sat down in an overstuffed armchair for a few minutes. She felt free to be herself there. Her mask was slipping away. She knew she had a lot to offer, but felt stunted by this marriage to a stranger. She had not wanted to become a mousy anxious woman, with no opinion or abilities. She desperately wanted to reunite with her father, but the cost was wearing her down.

Angela bustled in carrying a hatbox and two bags hanging off her shoulders. Corinne jumped to her feet, grabbed the items away from her friend, and forced her to sit.

"Oh Angela, please sit. Andrew has you running around doesn't he?" She watched Angela's sweet creamy skin relax around her eyes and Angela gave a little grin with a nod.

"You are such a hard worker and I know that Andrew treats you poorly. He is constantly trying to find more work for you. You have already done so much. Please let me finish, like I used to at my aunt's house. I'll block the door with a chair and do your chores like before."

Angela could not hold back a girlish giggle. For a few minutes while she caught her breath, Angela felt young again. She watched her dearest friend act like a clown dancing around the room, hanging clothes and hats in the wardrobe.

"Let me help too, Cori." Angela plopped on the ground and opened the first bag. Within a moment, she tossed things across the room at Corinne. Catching each item with a flourish, Corinne filled her vanity table. They laughed and enjoyed a sweet moment just being together, forgetting for a moment the roles they played.

The bags now emptied and stuck on the top shelf of the wardrobe, they removed the chair from under the door handle and resumed all appearances of normalcy.

"Angela, tell me again where your brother is. Did you get any more letters? Before we left Boston, I was so busy, as were you. We never had time to talk." Corinne settled into the chair and patted it for her friend to sit next to her.

"Sean's last letter was months ago. He had been trapping near the Snake River with a friend named Old Willie. He has no idea that I am going to be on that side of the world. I wonder how I will ever hear from him again. Once we are settled, I do hope your aunt forwards any letters I receive. I have nightmares about her just throwing them out." Angela tried not to be concerned and took a deep breath to clear away sad thoughts. "I am so glad he is happy though. He longed so much to be free and wild. I just hope someday I will see him again. Like you with your father." Angela felt a tear slip without permission and quickly hugged her friend as emotion overtook her.

Corinne hugged back and worried along with her. These were hard days of questions without answers. Corinne and Angela were traveling towards an unknown future, and at the mercy of the men leading the way. Corinne was grateful, but felt a churning in her middle about what her role would be, when the path to the west became more difficult.

Chapter Four
April 1848

The days aboard the steamship were primarily spent indoors because, according to Andrew Temple, 'A lady should never associate with the riffraff aboard such a vessel.' Corinne kept her opinion to herself. She enjoyed many hours of cribbage and backgammon in her quarters with Angela. She wasn't quite sure what her husband did with himself, but twice a day he would drop into her room and make sure everything was as it should be. Corinne was always happy when he left, then felt guilty about it for at least an hour. Once every evening, she was allowed into the elegant dining room for dinner. Afterwards, Andrew and she would take a casual stroll on the top deck. He rarely said anything and would soon deposit her to her quarters for the rest of the night. Corinne was grateful when Reggie came to the room on day twelve.

"We are landing in the morning, Mrs. Temple." Reggie was a man of few words. He always got straight to the point. "Tomorrow morning, we will port at Independence, Missouri." Angela and Corinne reacted in a traditional girlish manner by squealing and embracing each other. Shaking his head, Reggie left, a friendly smile on his face.

Corinne was thrilled, and with a joyous abandon, helped Angela pack everything that night. Corinne was on the floor, elbow-deep in a bag of toiletries when Andrew knocked, and entered before she could respond.

"Mrs. Temple, what are you doing?"

Corinne thought it was obvious, but she managed to answer without smiling.

"I'm packing toiletries, Mr. Temple. I hear we are landing tomorrow. I was too excited to sit still anymore." Corinne stood up and straightened her skirts. She wished he would go away. With a sinking feeling, she knew that the strange battle brewing between them was getting ready to surface.

"I do recall that you have a lady's maid. She is paid to handle these kinds of jobs. She is, isn't she?" Andrew's tone crossed over into condescension with the ease of breathing.

"Yes, Angela has been packing all evening." Corinne felt threatened suddenly. *He cannot harm Angela, can he? Or take her away?*

Angela stood nearby, holding on to Corinne's traveling suits that she had been brushing.

"Sir, I am glad for the work. I do believe Corinne is just getting anxious." Angela smiled her little subservient smile and curtsied.

"Miss Fahey, you are to call her Mrs. Temple at all times. You're on thin ice with me. Do not speak again unless I ask for you to speak!" Andrew's face turned a slight shade of pink, but Angela never wavered. She nodded and resumed her work. Corinne was amazed, silenced and a little bit afraid.

"Corinne, I would like to talk with you at breakfast about what is expected of you as a lady. As your husband, even just in name, I am your guardian and keeper. The disregard of your station and relationship to the staff has caused me some concern. We will discuss this before we disembark tomorrow. Goodnight." He delivered his speech then departed, leaving behind two upset females.

"Angela, I don't know what to do. I have prayed and thought so much about our friendship. I know it's not wrong, but why..." Corinne was at a loss to finish her thought. She was so angry with Andrew and the world of rules, that she could have fallen in despair right there. Angela, with her sweet face surrounded by red gold curls, came up to her and held her hand.

"I know, Corinne. I know. We must resume our jobs, my dear friend. I think I know what he will do, and we will not like it. We are going to be separated somehow. We must be careful to be indifferent to each other from now on. I know your friendship is strong, and you know how I feel. No one else can know until we arrive at your father's home," Angela said gravely. It was one of the few times Corinne had ever seen her frowning.

" As a woman, freedom doesn't come easy. Maybe in heaven, it will be better," Corinne stated quietly. Her eyes had dried. Her heart determined itself to take life as it came. She desperately wanted to put up a wall between her and her husband. Maybe even men, in general. She fought it down like a bitter elixir, then found peace. That night, her prayers were long and pitted. Her young heart questioned how to handle her husband. She purged her own guilt over a few unforgiving thoughts she had thrown his way.

The next morning Angela found herself amid a lecture, after her early morning fire duties. She usually kept herself awake with sewing projects by the fire. She tried to think positive that at least she was warm, even if sleep was elusive.

"Miss Fahey!" Andrew's tone was curt and intimidating. "Your behavior is bordering on incorrigible. I can only guess lack of breeding has to be the case, that allows you to feel you can address Mrs. Temple as your equal. If you want to keep your position, I expect you to work harder and behave more appropriately." He saw her nod. Then he turned and walked away.

Angela stood still, as emotions washed over her. She had feared the worst. She thought she would have been left behind. She needed this job to help her into her new life. Corinne was an amazing friend and had promised to help her reconnect with her only surviving family. Sean, her spirited brother, was out west. She had to find him. Her friendship had nearly cost her the dream. She swallowed her fearful tears and got back to work. Corinne had to be awakened. Cori was certain to get her own lecture this morning.

Corinne handled herself gracefully through a long painful lecture.

She would not see her friend abused or hurt in any way. Legally, Andrew was her husband. Angela belonged to him and could easily be fired.

Breakfast was served after the 'meeting' and Corinne ate it in an emotionally frozen state. No one spoke except for Reggie, who also seemed on edge. He asked a few questions, all pertaining to the arrival on shore in Independence. The questions succeeded as a distraction for Corinne's mind.

One more lecture and my head might pop. Corinne wondered if there would ever be a day in her life when she felt free to be herself, without a rulebook being opened in her face.

She didn't lie or cheat. She had never been immodest and had always tried to be open and kind to people. Corinne believed in God and genuinely loved helping people and learning about the world around her. What in the world was wrong with her that people in authority over her always wanted her to change and be like them? Corinne nibbled on her breakfast while contemplating her troubles.

Chapter Five
Independence, Missouri - April 10, 1848

Corinne's shoes made a hollow thump down the bridge connecting the steamship to the shore. She felt like a child again as her brown eyes took in the surroundings. She reached the land and felt its steadiness. It felt good. She was now in the West, well, the start of it anyway. The great river had been crossed, and she suddenly realized her childhood was over. She wasn't sure why she felt that way now. She'd been married for over a month, but the journey had turned in her mind. In all the awkward moments of silence, she learned to talk to her Maker. God's peace was settling in her. It kept her moving forward, when she wanted to hide from the scary new challenges she faced.

The world bustled around her in a flurry and tempo of another world. The weather was beautiful, and the sun shone down on the wagons and shops that lined the streets of Independence. Horses, oxen and mules were in corrals wherever there wasn't a building. The city was growing, but in that haphazard way of a boomtown. There wasn't much structure just a lot of madness. Corinne wanted desperately to share with someone about all she could see, but knew it was impossible. She sighed and continued to watch her surroundings.

She felt lead by her husband, as he barked orders to everyone around him. Corinne was silent and observant. There were vendors standing next to the dock. They screamed over each other about animals, wagons, and foodstuffs. It reminded Corinne of an orchestra warming up, a beautiful noise.

Andrew and his all-important list led them to a hotel where Corinne and Angela would stay for one night. Reggie and Andrew were gone for the rest of the day. The many trunks, bags, and items all had to be loaded somewhere and the wagon outfit had to be assembled.

Corinne was too anxious to sleep knowing within days they would be on the open road. Should would be traveling the same path as her father did just three years ago. She knew his road had been more difficult. Trail blazing was hard work with many unknown variables. Which mountain path to take? What part of the river was safe to cross? There were maps now that gave more clues on the safest passages. She tried to keep trail horror stories out of her mind. She was in God's hands now.

"The forts along the trail are now better prepared with supplies, although very expensive," Andrew told her earlier, when she had been open about her fears. She made conversation with him. Sometimes it went well. She started to get a sense about when she could talk and when to stay silent. Reading his moods was her new profession. She found that he responded better if she asked about things that interested him. He liked instructing her, she reasoned. He rarely looked at her while he did it though. He kept an impassive face and lips pressed together tightly whenever he was annoyed with her speaking. He was still very impersonal.

Without an audience, Corinne and Angela had a chance to talk. The strains of the morning were gone soon after, and they enjoyed talking about their experiences. They were both impressed by the downtown area of Independence and even the hotel was bigger than they both expected.

Angela and Corinne finally slept. They woke early as the morning sun shone bright in the window. They dressed and tidied the room, anxious for a long day of hard work and preparations. A knock at the door came at 7:30 am and Angela answered. Andrew was at the door, frowning.

"I expected to be cross, but you are both ready. Wonderful." He let out a deep breath, like he had been prepared to yell, then changed his mind. He kept talking without looking at Angela. "We have our wagons and teams at the west end of town. I have found everything we need here. Reggie will escort you ladies after you eat breakfast downstairs in the dining room. It will be your last meal sitting at a table for a long while." Andrew was smiling. He seemed even a little happy. Corinne was surprised. Angela and Reggie carried the little bit of luggage downstairs to load on a wagon taken to the staging area. They worked well together, with as little communication as possible. The way Andrew liked it.

The dining room wasn't fancy, but the food was good and filling. Corinne had a million questions and finally could not hold them anymore.

"Reggie, how many wagons do we have?" Corinne tried to use her friendly smile to win him over.

"You will be in the main wagon. We hired a Cookie and he will have his own chuck wagon. He was a grump, but his cooking last night was good. Andrew and I will be the third wagon. Angela, I think you will be traveling with the chuck wagon."

"The **chuck wagon**! She is my maid and traveling companion. What a pompous, insensitive..." Corinne was sure if Andrew had been nearby, she would have thrown her fork at him. She calmed herself quickly though. Having a tantrum today would not help anyone. With two cleansing breaths and a silent prayer, she found her calm voice. "Reggie, you will make sure she is safe? Impropriety or not, I treat my staff like family. I will not tolerate anyone getting unnecessarily hurt on my watch." Corinne swallowed and was bold for another second. "Andrew may be your boss, but I also have some fears about this journey. His concern, or lack of it, about certain people, is causing me more than my fair share of stress. I do hope that we can be friends, Reggie. The intimacy of travel dictates that we all should be on the same team. Feel free to be open to communicate with me, and your reward from me will be generous." Corinne saw the respect grow in Reggie's eyes and his walls came down.

"I agree wholeheartedly, Mrs. Temple. I appreciate your frankness and pledge to you I will keep you and your companion safe. I have the greatest respect for your sincerity. I will not take advantage of that." Reggie blushed a little and nodded respectfully. Corinne could see the humanity in him and was glad she had been bold. She may have been a mouse around her husband, but she still had some fire inside. She hoped it would not get her into any more trouble. She nibbled her breakfast and found the silence calming. Her thoughts slowed down, and she daydreamed pleasantly of Oregon and her father's home. She noticed a few minutes later everyone had cleaned their plates.

"Well, I say we go. I'm ready to start. Reggie, lead the way." They stood together and began a half-mile walk to the wagon staging area. They passed all the stores in town. The early morning dew made the walk rather pleasant. There was no dust on the roads and the air was fresh like spring. A chill remained in the air and Corinne enjoyed the breeze on her cheeks. She thought of her father walking down this same street watching the wagons and animals go by. Her father loading his wagons with flour and bacon, and buying extra shirts for the journey. She wondered how his trip went. What sights had he seen? Had they fought any Indians, or traded for provisions?

Corinne realized she was sharing something with him now. The journey across the wilderness could be the new starting place for them. Her own adventure was under way.

Corinne was not prepared for the crammed staging area. Every inch was full of wagons, animals and bodies. The smell of all those things combined took a few moments to get used to. Both Angela and Corinne covered their noses for several minutes, as they wound their way through the maze of humanity to their wagon outfit. Everyone's mood seemed excited and rushed. When Reggie stopped Corinne and Angela, they were pleasantly surprised. Their wagons were a beautiful golden brown. Their gleaming white canvas bonnets were striking in contrast. The chuck wagon was shorter but had a gleaming sheet-iron cooking stove on the side. It was truly a great invention for cooking on the trail. A short, square-shouldered man was hustling in and around the chuck wagon. Immediately, Corinne and Angela went to introduce themselves.

"Just call me Cookie and stay out of my way. You can make requests but don't make a habit of it. I know my way around the chuck wagon and what's needed to survive on the trail. Mrs. Temple if you wanna make the coffee and campfire each mornin', I can focus on the food." Cookie finished talking and headed back to his duties.

"Absolutely, Cookie. Be glad to," she said loud enough for him to hear, as he walked away. She turned to Angela. "At least I'll have something to do. I'm sure Andrew will truly think it most undignified for me to make breakfast, though every other woman out here will be pulling their weight." Angela nodded but she was silent. Her face clouded over with emotion and something else. "Angela, are you feeling well?" Corinne said. For the first time, she realized that Angela had barely spoken. She had been very distant. Corinne grabbed her friend by the shoulder and looked into her eyes. Her green eyes looked away and suddenly Corinne knew why. They dreamed of coming West together as friends, free to be themselves and help each other. Now Angela was under the power of someone else who may decide to leave her behind. But, if they got separated, Corinne had already secreted away enough money into Angela's things, for her to start her own life. Polite society's opinion mattered little now. Angela had enough rough breaks in her life. Being Corinne's friend shouldn't have been counted as one of them.

"Angela come to my wagon and see if you can help me get it organized." Corinne needed a private moment with her friend. They both made their way to Corinne's wagon. The wagon's rear flap was open. There were steps and handles for the short women to grab and pull their way up. The trunks and bags were lying about in no sense of order. Within a minute, they both were strategizing on how to make the best layout for a sleeping area. As they worked, Corinne spoke softly.

"Angela, one night several months ago, I had a nightmare that we got separated on the trail and you were stranded without money and friends. I woke up that morning with a resolve to take care of you as you have taken care of me. I know you are a hard worker and will never accept charity, so I devised a plan to help you." Corinne kept moving bags but stopped upon hearing a sniffle behind her. Angela had two fat tears running down her cheek. "Don't cry friend. God will watch out for us."

"You are my dearest friend Cori. Three years ago, when I began to work for your aunt after the work orphanage, I was sure that my life would forever be as a servant. When you came to the house, it was the best day of my life. I know if God can find me a friend in a mansion, as a servant, He can make my life better. I will walk to the ends of the earth for you, friend. And I know you will for me, too." Angela usually refrained, but today, on the eve of this great unknown, she reached out and embraced her friend. They felt the pressure release, and after the briefest minute, they were back to work.

Corinne and her friend both saw the large trunk and lifted it together. The girls slowly moved it to the front of the wagon near the jockey box. They both grunted as they lowered it, then sat down on the trunk using it like a comfortable bench. Corinne peeked out of the small round opening at the front of the bonnet. No one she knew was around, so she decided to divulge her plan.

"In your luggage are several hiding places. A book I gave you as a gift has two pages glued together in the middle. Also, the medicine pouch has several things that will help you; there are remedies for an upset stomach and several vials of oils for scrapes and bug bites. In the bottom there is a pocket with two buttons. Inside, you will find some paper money. Your stocking may have a surprise or two, as well. I have hidden enough money for you to purchase passage on a wagon train and support yourself for a long time. I know you want to say no, but before you protest, let me explain. I know that money can help buy safety for a woman. If something were to happen to me, you will be taken care of. Or, Lord forbid, if we get separated. This is a dangerous and long journey. If for some reason you need the money, it's there for you. If we reach the end of this journey and you have no need for it, you can return what you haven't earned with your duties as my companion. My wish is that you are safe and happy. My Aunt would call me foolish and Andrew would probably flog me if he found out about this but in all sincerity, I will sleep better knowing you have provisions." Corinne reached her hand out for Angela to strike the deal.

"Corinne, if I do need the money, how can I pay off the debt?" Angela's look was comical, her eyebrow rose. She doubted Corinne had a plan for that.

"Well I will hire you of course. I have my own plans, Angela. Somehow, we will make it work. Ok, let's get back to work before Andrew arrives." Corinne looked for something to move around. She stood up straight as she remembered another detail. "Oh yes, I have stashed two of my altered dresses for you. You will enter your new life in the West dressed as my equal. Because, in my opinion, it's true." Corinne got back to work moving bags and Angela sniffed again a time or too, but Corinne let her be. Sometimes a girl needed a moment to cry alone.

Andrew's booming voice sounded about twenty minutes later. Corinne and Angela made their way to the back of the wagon and opened the flap. The morning was bright and crisp, and the wagon was dusty from them moving the bags around.

"Lunch will be in an hour. Miss Fahey, you are under Reggie's charge now, and Mrs. Temple..." he paused with an annoyance in his tone "You will talk to me if you need her services. Otherwise, her daily duties will include tending your needs, as well as what is needed by Cookie and Reggie."

Angela quickly jumped down from the wagon and joined Reggie over by the chuck wagon, her head down in perfect submission. Corinne's heart broke for her.

<hr />

"Mrs. Temple, come meet our team handlers." Andrew called her down from the wagon. Corinne just wished he would stop calling her *Mrs. Temple*. The way he said it made her feel like he owned her. Her memory recalled him saying this was only a marriage of convenience, to be annulled at the end of the journey. She started to believe he enjoyed bossing her around. She thanked her good fortune lately that he didn't want to stay married to her, for she would truly be miserable then. She admitted he was handsome in looks. And, he was charming, but only for those he deemed worthy. Everyone else was just an unlucky soul in his path. A sudden fear shot through her. *What if he changed his mind about the annulment? Forever with Andrew would be ... a nightmare.*

"This is Jimmy Blake and his brother Joe. They are the drivers. You have six oxen for your wagon." Andrew pointed them out.

They were both healthy, thin young men. They both bowed and said, "Howdy ma'am," in unison. They were definitely twins.

"I will be in charge of all the men, so you needn't worry about a thing. Just stay out of the way. They know how to keep you and the wagon safe. I hired Jim and Joe in September when I got word from your father. I sent them ahead to get us fortified with wagons and oxen. They did a great job." Corinne knew he wasn't really talking to her anymore, just talking to himself. Andrew patted them on the back then returned his gaze to her.

"Come along." Corinne followed him like the puppy dog he wanted her to be. Andrew introduced her to a nut-brown mare tied to the back of her wagon, complete with a glossy saddle.

"I will want you to ride most of the day. I know growing up in Kentucky you know how to take care of her. Joe and Jimmy will assist you, too. I don't want you walking on foot unless your horse needs a rest. You are a lady, I expect you to be an example of that even in the wilderness."

"Riding every day is not what I expected. I will need to adjust my wardrobe. I am glad I won't be traveling sidesaddle, at least. Thank you for sparing me that." Corinne knew she probably didn't sound very grateful, but she was frustrated at him barking orders, expecting her to just accept everything he said as the 'gospel'.

"The wardrobe issue should be easy to figure out. Mrs. Temple, please don't make me figure it out for you." Andrew sighed and held his head in his hands. Corinne paused and looked at him slowly, contemplating a way to knock him down a peg or two. Her mind drew a blank, so she kept her angry glare short. He looked at her as though her existence caused his head to ache.

If I give him a headache now, just wait until I smack him silly. Corinne thought to herself. She realized violence was inappropriate and wrong, but the visual made her feel better.

"I will be bothering Reggie for an escort into Independence then. I will need a few more petticoats. I have enough dresses for the journey, but the adjustments will require a few more layers. I have only one riding gown. I suppose I am boring you with my dreary life details." His look said it all.

Within a few minutes, Corinne was escorted back to town. After a short shopping trip, she was ready to go. She finished arranging the wagon box to her liking and made a pleasant sleeping area and working area. She examined her traveling garments and picked a few to make the necessary adjustments. She also checked the chuck wagon to make certain that Andrew had provided a proper place for Angela to sleep as well. She was pleased to make eye contact with Reggie. He had known why she was looking. With a wordless exchange, she knew that he had taken care of everything for Angela's comfort. That was one worry from Corinne's mind. There were many others to take its place though.

The night passed quickly. Masses of people around her were doing the same preparations for their outfits as well. Cookie announced dinner and Corinne was given a plate. She saw Angela sitting by the fire with Reggie and Andrew. Everyone quietly eating. Corinne saw two empty stools and sat in one.

"Corinne, I will need you to join me this evening for the train meeting. Your signature will be needed for the train agreement. Our boss will be Mr. Corbin Walters. He is a levelheaded man who has made the journey six times. This will be a large group of over a hundred wagons. We will be safe in this large a group."

"Just let me know when we need to go. I'll be ready." Corinne ate and watched the sky. She thought of a few things to discuss with Reggie and proceeded to ask him about the laundry and chore schedule. She needed to know when she was expected to help. Andrew quickly chimed in.

"Corinne, you will not be doing laundry or any chores, besides starting the fire in the morning and making coffee. Reggie will have the firewood and kindling stored in the wood box of the chuck wagon." Andrew said it very matter-of-factly. He finished his plate and sat back down on his stool and waited for Corinne to finish.

"Mr. Temple," Corinne said calmly. "I am not a China doll. I was raised to not be a burden to my household. My father was wealthy, but I learned a strong work ethic from him. I will not burden the staff when my hands are fully capable of helping the wagon outfit." Corinne was proud she had spoken to him as an adult, without her nerves failing her.

"Mrs. Temple, you are not in your father's house now, are you? This is my outfit and you are my wife until I say otherwise. You pick herbs and draw pictures to your heart's content, but I will not endure you doing the staff's work. I hope I am understood." Andrew stood and removed his hat, shook it out and placed it back on his head. He seemed annoyed that he had to converse with her at all. Corinne felt like a disobedient child.

"Finish up your meal Corinne. We need to go." Andrew watched her eat her last few bites. She considered tossing her plate into his hands but calmly returned it to the chuck wagon. Corinne resumed her position behind him as she followed him through the crowd.

The wagon boss wasn't handsome, but he appeared agreeable enough to Corinne. She read through the wagon train rules. The train was a well-oiled machine, with the scouts and captain and his assigned leaders who made the final decisions about which paths they would take. The contract they had to sign was simple. They agreed to let the wagon boss and his assigned leaders make the decisions. Any disagreements would be decided by the wagon boss. If you disagreed you would be removed from the wagon train. Any game killed by scouts would be distributed with a fair system. Fighting and large consumptions of liquor would not be tolerated. Corinne smiled as she read through the rules. They were all things she could live with easily. The leadership was experienced and that was all she needed. She was putting her life in their hands. After a quick prayer in her head, she signed the contract.

She and Andrew headed back to camp. "Andrew, could I please talk to Angela this evening? I won't keep her long. She is my companion and I was hoping she could stay with me in the wagon." Corinne used her sweetest voice.

"I am sorry Corinne, but your aunt warned me about the attachment you have for your maid. While in my outfit she is in my charge. She will sleep in the chuck wagon. Cookie and Reggie will be in a tent next to it. I do not want to see you speaking with her. Otherwise, I will have her sent back to Independence, or hire her out to another family. I will tell her so tonight as well. Sometimes young people do not understand the differences between the classes. It's my job, as your husband, to better educate you." Andrew's word was final.

I am completely alone and under the rule of a snobbish dictator.

As dusk fell, Corinne's thoughts were with her friend. In the morning they would be leaving. Her only duties were to make a fire and coffee. This would be followed by long days in the saddle with no one to talk to. Her friend Angela no longer had her protection. If Corinne even tried, she was certain Andrew would not hesitate to fire Angela. He had no real need for her besides an extra hand to do laundry and help if anyone fell ill along the trail. Corinne would have to work at keeping her spirits up. As the sky grew, dark she headed into her wagon. She was still awkward at changing inside the wagon. It rocked a little as she stepped out of her petticoats. She set out her riding clothes for the morning and put on her warmest nightshirt.

The night's temperature was falling fast under the clear sky above. Corinne crawled into her bedding and had fitful prayers. She fell asleep after a few tears.

Chapter Six
April 12, 1848

Corinne awoke early and dressed in minutes. She felt freer without her required corset and reveled in her traveling clothes. It was impractical and dangerous to wear a corset while in the wilds so Corinne had all her practical clothes made to fit her natural form. She knew Andrew would have had a fit if she attempted this on the ferry or train, but he could not have a fit now as they were leaving in a few hours. Corinne grabbed her long wool coat, scarf, and bonnet and climbed out of the wagon. Andrew already had a fire going and the coffee pot was settled on the grate over the fire.

Drat. One point to Andrew. "It's not even six a.m. Andrew. I thought I was to get the fire started." Corinne's only job for the whole day was already done. She wanted to growl.

"I was excited and woke early. It was no trouble." Andrew pointed at the stool next to him. He seemed in good spirits. Corinne took a deep breath to calm down and convince herself to behave. The breakfast routine started. Everyone gathered around the chuck wagon at seven a.m. and wordlessly got their plates. They ate their meals either sitting or standing near the fire. Jimmy and Joe gathered the animals from their grazing spot and got them prepared to leave.

Corinne's horse was delivered to her saddled and ready. Yesterday, while in town getting more petticoats, Corinne purchased some dried apples, stowing the large bag of fruit in her wagon. She shared a piece of dried apple and stroked her horse calmly. Corinne cooed and talked to the brown mare for a few minutes. "I will call you Clover. I hope we will be friends." Corinne tied Clover to the back of the wagon and warmed herself by the fire until it was time to pull out. She listened to the sounds around her. Sounds of harnesses jingling, complaining animals, a few shouts and women instructing children.

Angela approached Corinne with a simple request. "Your laundry, miss?" Corinne nearly cried. They were reduced to master and servant again. This was worse than at her Aunt's. In Boston, there were doors and privacy. At night, they would hide in her room for hours at a time.

Corinne gathered her dirty laundry and handed it over to her friend. Corinne grabbed her hand under the pile, gave it the briefest squeeze, and felt her friend squeeze back. It was all they had. Corinne returned to her spot by the dying fire and wiped away a few stray tears. No one seemed to notice her there, until Reggie came by a few minutes later to inform her they were pulling out soon. He handed her a bundle to tie behind the saddle.

Corinne examined her bundle, a rubber tarpaulin, and tied it neatly behind the saddle. They were leaving! Her heart flipped, and she pulled up images in her mind of her father. He was waiting for her.

Jimmy helped her into the saddle and Corinne clicked a bit to get Clover's attention. Corinne and Clover were a good team. Clover was a responsive but gentle mount. Corinne watched Reggie kill the fire, and Angela put away any last second items Cookie had left behind. The sound of wagon harnesses jingling, and wagons creaking filled the air. Yells and hoots were ahead of them as the team handlers got the oxen moving. Within ten minutes, the Temple outfit was rolling. The sun was out, the day was new, and the adventure had begun.

Andrew rode in next to Corinne, as the wagons pulled out. "Are you comfortable on your mount, Mrs. Temple?" Andrew smiled at her. Corinne grinned her society smile. It was the best she could do after the last few days of bickering with him.

"Why yes, Clover and I get along well." She gave Clover a loving pat and turned to her husband. "And how are you fairing? Are you ready for a long day in the saddle?"

He nodded affirmatively. Somehow, she knew he would be fine.

"Yes, Drake and I will make do. I will be checking in with the scouts during the day today. I want to learn as much as I can from them. Stay near the outfit and if you have any trouble, Jimmy and Joe will be able to help you, I'm sure." Andrew smiled and waved as he rode off. Corinne smirked again at his back, as he rode away. At least she would not have to deal with him today. She took a deep breath and concentrated on her mount and her surroundings, as the morning rolled by. Noon came and the wagon boss, Mr. Walters, rode by. Corinne noticed all the wagons were halting ahead. Mr. Walters's gruff voice announced that they were breaking for lunch. Cookie had bread and cheese prepared, with a cool mug full of water to wash it down. One o'clock came, and the wagons were on the move again. Once the wagons were stretched out, Corinne rode over to Reggie, who was driving the jockey box of Andrew's wagon.

"I will be checking on the local flora nearby, to see if there is anything to add to my collection. I'll be within shouting range."

She rode past Angela who was walking behind the wagon. She gave her a wink and a wave. Angela smiled back, then moved her eyes forward and continued her walk. Corinne knew everyone would be sore from all the traveling tonight, including herself. She felt several muscles starting to mildly protest, having not been in the saddle this long for years.

She was still living with her father, the last day she had spent in the saddle. No time to be sad now. With the shade of a tree behind her, Corinne dismounted long enough to relieve herself behind a large bush. It was the best she could for now. The lack of privacy was a growing concern. The land here was lush with trees and the ground covered in rocks, but several hundred miles would change that. Corinne would deal with that when the time came.

Clover nibbled the green grass shoots. Corinne held her lead while walking for a few minutes, looking for anything useful on the ground. This reminded her of times spent with her mother and grandmother hunting through the woods for mushrooms or wildflowers. She learned so much about nature from them. She was so grateful for those years and memories.

She came upon a few young children playing nearby. Corinne looked up and realized the wagon train spread out sideways rather far. She was only a few hundred feet away from them now.

"Whatcha looking for, ma'am?" asked a young lady, blond braids sticking out from under her bonnet. All the children kept glancing at the wagons to make sure they stayed within a safe distance.

"I am looking for good healthy plants. I make medicine out of certain ones." Corinne smiled and picked a nearby thistle. "See this thistle. This is a pretty common flower. But its cousin, Milk Thistle, grows in Europe and is a wonderful medicine." She thought for a second and continued. "If someone gets poisoned, milk thistle seeds or parts of the plant can be used to make them better." Corinne gave the thistle to the girl with the braids.

"Well what kind of plants grow here that make medicine?" The girl's interest was real, Corinne could tell.

"There are hundreds of plants that make medicine here. Even some we haven't discovered, yet. That's why I'm looking around. I will draw pictures of the plants I don't know and send them to Boston or maybe show them to Indians we might run into. Indians know a lot about making medicines, too." Corinne watched all the children grow wide-eyed when she mentioned the Indians.

"Can we help you, miss? I can look for plants too. That will be fun." A little boy's shy voice finally spoke. Corinne guessed him to be around eight years old.

"That's sounds like a deal. I am Mrs. Temple. You know how to find the Temple wagons?" All the kids nodded. "Then bring me plants that look different than the normal thistle, clover and grass that grow around here. I have peppermint candies and hay-pennies for really good plant samples." The smiles were broad at the mention of candy and money.

The blond with braids raised her hand as if she were in school. Corinne nearly giggled at their enthusiasm. She nodded at the girl to speak. "Can we tell our brothers and sisters, too?"

"Yes, you may. Just tell them to get me the whole plant if they can. I don't need any poison ivy, either." They all giggled. Corinne's heart melted a little. "You need to be careful of wasps and snakes, too, okay?"

"Okay." They all spoke at once.

"My wagon outfit is near the creek today. I had better head back. You children be careful." They all nodded and then spread out looking through the bushes. They were her little treasure hunters. Corinne mounted up, rode back to the creek, and found the wagon with no trouble. Andrew had purchased large wagons and Corinne's was very prominent as it rolled along. Smiling, Corinne wondered how long it would be before she had fresh plant samples from her little angels. The miles passed quickly for her. She imagined her young botany crew busily hunting through the green grass as they made their way to the great unknown.

Ahead, Corinne could see the wagons were slowing down. The long stretch of wagons were pulling in near the creek. Mr. Walters rode by, pointing out a few things to Jimmy and Joe, as they slowly moved into a small half circle near the creek. Corinne rode up to Joe as they stopped to take her mount. She would gladly care for Clover herself, but she knew it was pointless to try.

"How far did we go today, Joe?" Corinne wanted to have a pleasant working relationship with the team handlers. Joe reached under the wagon to reset the odometer gearbox attached to the wheels.

"We did sixteen miles the first day. I am glad we are stopping though. It will take a few days to get used to the jarring of the wagon. I will make my brother sit up here tomorrow." Joe's laugh was refreshing. He climbed down, and Corinne handed over Clover's reins. Corinne stretched out for a minute and then took in her surroundings. The world around her worked industriously to make camp. Animals were set to pasture, riders carefully watching them. As the animals fed off the new spring grass, every man would take their turn to keep the them safe. Women and men prepped fires. The lucky few who had sheet stoves were constantly poking the fires to get them hot and ready for dinner for several hundred people. This was a traveling village. Corinne knew she was the oddity. Fully able but banned from doing work. What a strange problem she had. She sighed and walked to her wagon to get her journals. She would read while she waited for dinner.

It was twenty minutes later that a little voice broke through the sounds around her. Corinne saw the girl with braids approaching her. "Hello, Plant Lady." The girl thrust forward a flour sack, her offering for the day.

"Oh my, were you able to find me some treasures?" Corinne was flattered by the nickname, 'Plant Lady'. She looked in the bag and saw mushrooms of different varieties, some edible. She saw several ferns, and a few mysteries. "Amazing, did your friends come too?" She glanced and saw them hiding behind the wagon.

"We all put them in the bag. We didn't want to crush the mushrooms." The blond girl was the leader of the operation.

"Well, good thinking." Corinne reached into the wagon and grabbed her small handbag. Each child lined up and Corinne put a mint in each hand. She watched each of them put the peppermint in their mouths. Then she dropped a half-cent into each of their warm, dirty hands. "Thank you, children. Be sure to tell the other children, too." Smiling, they headed out of the campsite. Corinne felt useful, at last. She carried her wares over to Cookie. She won some favor with him by presenting a few morel mushrooms, to do with as he wished.

"Thank you, Mrs. Temple. Did those kids pick these?" Surprisingly, Cookie spoke to her. She nodded, and he laughed, shaking his head. He washed the mushrooms well and sliced them into the stew he was cooking.

"It will add some great flavor," claimed Cookie. His approval meant a lot to Corinne.

Andrew rode up within an hour. He seemed to be in a good mood while waiting for the stew. Tired muscles and the long first day made everyone quiet, as they finished up any chores. By seven p.m., Cookie called everyone to get a plate of stew. Andrew commented on the morels. Cookie gave credit to Corinne and her band of herb hunters. Corinne was certain that her friendship with Cookie was growing.

Dusk came quickly, and the temperature dropped. While sitting around the fire, Corinne yawned until she could not take it anymore. She excused herself and headed into her wagon. She was exhausted. She didn't lay there long before she fell asleep. Everyone followed her example and headed to their beds early, too.

Chapter Seven
April 13, 1848

The morning was cold. Corinne curled under the warm blankets and turned to find the best sleeping spot. The air was crisp, and the night was still dark around her. She drifted back into a soft sleep...

The startling clunk pulled her from her peaceful moment. A second and third clunk, and the unmistakable sound of dirt drifting to the ground brought her out of slumber, straight into terror. Corinne sat up quickly and looked around. The night was black as pitch. There had to be an animal outside the wagon. Corinne's thoughts usually leaned to the worst possible scenario. Corinne's heart jumped in her chest. She held the blanket close to her, as she leaned into the darkness to hear if the creature had left. The wagon train was only sixteen miles outside of Independence. Corinne wondered what kind of animal made such a racket?

The shuffling continued, several footsteps and then pans rattled. Corinne's heart dropped as the wagon suddenly moved under her. As Corinne's eyes grew accustomed to the darkness, she moved slowly, on her knees, toward the front of the wagon bed. Reaching it, she felt for the rope that held down the flap. Conveniently next to the wagon's flap was a small bench and she sat on it to peek thru the tiny opening she had made. With an exasperated sigh, she recognized the situation. Andrew was prepping the fire. Corinne quickly found a lantern and lit it with the nearby matches. She dressed hastily. She had a pendant watch that she was going to pin onto her coat. She leaned closer to the lantern and glanced at the time. It was 3:45 a.m.!

Corinne wanted to scream. Wagon train rules were to have fires started at six a.m. and breakfast ready by seven. Why had Andrew risen so early? Did he expect her to make coffee before dawn?

She climbed out of the wagon. She marched over to her husband. "Do you know the time?" He barely looked at her.

"You are making a huge racket while everyone is sleeping. It's 3:45 a.m., Mr. Temple." Corinne wondered if he had any

47

common decency. He glanced at her, and by lantern light, checked his own pocket watch. He grunted and stopped his activity.

"I suppose you are right. I am an early riser," Andrew admitted. He sat down on a stool. "I think I'll start the fire anyway. I'll wait for the coffee." Andrew grabbed the fire pot from the chuck wagon and started stacking the sticks in the fire pit from last night. *Another point to Andrew.*

"I'm going back to bed. Andrew, the people here will not have patience for you banging around this early. Respect is good, but sleep is more important. If I were you, I'd keep it silent." Corinne marched back to her wagon.

Corinne heard every movement he made for the next hour. She fell back asleep eventually, but woke up at 5:45, when Cookie began puttering around in the chuck wagon. Corinne was in her makeshift bedroom, thinking about Angela sharing space with Cookie. She hoped for a reason to convince Andrew that Angela and her sharing a wagon would be beneficial. She had not come up with a good excuse yet.

Corinne started the morning with a mug of black coffee that Andrew prepared, ate biscuits and fruit jam that Cookie made, and gave all her laundry to Angela. Joe saddled and prepared her horse. Corinne got a boost onto her mount by Reggie. She was pretty sure she was the most useless adult on the wagon train.

Before they left, the only useful thing she had done was spend some time in her wagon drying out the plants from her treasure hunters the day before. With the cunning use of string and a few knots, she secured her finds under the bonnet and upside down to the wagon bow. They would hang there until she was ready to draw them with detail.

Corinne rode Clover all alone. She tried to slow down and allow Angela to walk next to her, but Andrew was hanging around the wagon outfit and Corinne didn't want to risk it.

The morning sun became hidden behind some gray clouds by mid-morning. Soon after that, they got their first taste of rain. Corinne used her rubber tarp over her head. She was happy to see Reggie stopped the last wagon, making Angela jump in. The rain came down with a wind that was cold. It bit into Corinne's cheeks and took her breath away at certain points. She steered Clover behind the wagon to block some of the wind. They stopped at lunchtime and ate some brown bread and rehydrated peas that Cookie had soaked overnight. The sheet-iron cook stove was handy for cooking in this kind of weather, if the rain wasn't too heavy.

The wagon train moved along that afternoon as the rain slowed to a drizzle. By nightfall, the rain had cleared and the air was mild. Corinne ate in silence but listened as the sound of other wagon outfits drifted their way. Someone played a fiddle, sweet and soft. It reminded Corinne that the world still had gentleness. Angela made eye contact across the fire. Corinne smiled. They enjoyed the music together before they went to their beds.

Chapter Eight
April 15, 1848

The sun was fresh in the morning sky. Corinne was up and tending the fire before she started the breakfast coffee, the one job she was allowed to do. With a long stick in her hand and sitting on a short stool, she absently watched the sparks fly out of the fire and float up to the sky. From her side vision, she saw three little heads peek around the backside of the wagon. She pretended not to notice them, to see what they would do.

There was a scuffle and the hushed tone of children, doing what they believed, was quiet.

Corinne could not resist and finally turned to peek at them. She saw three very dusty children clasping various types of plant life in their little arms.

"Jessie told us to...to bring you plants and...and you would give us sweets and money," the boldest one said. He was a disheveled eight-year-old lad with a mop of brown hair and smiling eyes. The other two children were younger and stayed close to his back, shuffling near him. With a quick gesture from Corinne, they all came forward with huge grinning faces.

Corinne "oooed" and "aaahed" at their offerings and gave them each a peppermint candy. She split the proceeds equally between all of them for their donations to her plant collection. She gave them an age appropriate plant lesson on what kind of plants she wanted most and how to pick them. As they watched her, their little nodding heads were enough to nearly melt her heart completely. She could not resist patting their little shoulders in a hug-like fashion. She sent them home to their wagons with coins in their pockets, but she was the one who felt the most blessed. Her job as 'plant lady' felt truly inspirational today. She knew the money would help their families. And, her stocks of plant life were kept full. She sorted through the the plants each evening before she slept.

Andrew strolled into camp a few minutes later. He watched her bundle the plants to put in her wagon. He shook his head. "I can't believe you pay the children to pick plants for you. You will probably end up with more junk than you can ever use," he laughed.

Corinne was certain he enjoyed hearing himself speak. She got a mug and poured coffee for him, as he plopped down on the stool. "Knowing you, your wagon will be half full of scrub bushes before the month is out. What does that heal, plant lady?" Corinne was well rehearsed at not responding with anything but a smile and nod, when appropriate.

"What are your plans for today? Riding with the wagons, or something else?" Corinne hoped for 'something else' but tried desperately to hide her own wish. It was rude to ask him to stay away from his own wagon outfit all day, but she really liked it better when she didn't have him underfoot, and his mouth nearby.

"I think I'll ride along with the horse wranglers today and see what the scouts are doing later. I do enjoy seeing the lay of the land, away from all the wagon traffic." Andrew sipped his coffee and headed over to Cookie's tent for a plate of vittles, and to visit with the men folk. Corinne followed him silently, got a plate, and headed back to her own little fire and stool. She was glad for Andrew's absence but was lonely for her friend, Angela. So far, this trip had not started the way she had hoped. She worked through her breakfast plate and returned it to a grumpy Cookie, who snatched the plate without a word. Unless, of course, the grunt he uttered was a language she didn't understand. She wandered around her campsite looking for something to do, while she waited until it was time for the wagons to start rolling. Her heart was aching for a friend or companion, something to fill the lonely hours. She got an idea and climbed into her wagon. Within fifteen minutes, she had out a charcoal pencil and sketchpad. She enjoyed drawing plant life and decided to document her journey with some drawings. This would be a great way to pass the time since she wasn't allowed to do any chores.

Corinne thought herself a decent drawing student, as long as she was looking at her subject. She knew some people could invent a picture and draw it from their memory, but Corinne was limited to what she could see in the here and now. She grabbed a small hanging plant from the wagon and began drawing it. "It's not fine art, but it will have to do," she said to herself.

After busying herself for almost an hour, the small fire died down. The sky was bright with sunlight. Corinne looked up from her page when the sound of horse hoofs pounding near her wagon startled her.

"Are you Mrs. Temple?" A tall man on an enormous horse hovered over her. Corinne's neck could have practically broken, from the angle she had to look at him.

"Um...yes. How can I help you?" He just about scared the breakfast coffee out of her, when he jumped off and motioned her to get on his horse. She had no thoughts in her head before he explained. "A small boy was burned, just a few hours ago, and we heard that you make plant medicines and ointments. Can you help?" He watched her face carefully. She nodded quickly and saw his instant relief.

"He is in terrible pain and cries out from it most unspeakably. He is only two years of age and..." Corinne hushed him.

"Silence, I know what to do. Give me one moment." Corinne's heart was pounding in her chest with a strange sadness and excitement. The terrible ache of knowing a child was in pain and the thrill of knowing how to help, truly a mysterious combination of emotions. In mere moments, Corinne was in and out of her wagon with a small bag. The tall man helped her mount onto the dark horse.

"We must tell someone where I am going, sir," she shouted, as he tried to gallop away from the area.

He did a quick turn and signaled the first person he saw. The driver, Joe, was walking by. The tall man shouted, "Mrs. Temple will be with the Grant outfit. There has been an injury. We will return her shortly. Can you tell her husband?" The tall man didn't even wait for a response as they flew across the ground moments later.

Corinne knew only a few children and women since their trip started. She wondered how her reputation had spread to strangers so far from her wagon. It was a large wagon train and she was not allowed to venture out to visit people, due to Andrew's strict propriety 'rules'.

It was only minutes later that the horse slowed. The tall man got down and gently helped her from the animal. The nearby cries of a child were loud and pierced her heart with distress.

"I am so sorry, Mrs. Temple. I am Lucas Grant. My nephew is this way." He led her through several wagons until the crying was very close. A wagon flap opened and Corinne saw a mother, lost and grief stricken from the pain of a child.

"I know what to do. I will ease his pain." Corinne climbed into the wagon in a second. "What's his name?"

"Brody," the mother spoke softly. Fresh tears of unexplainable relief washed over her. She had hope for her son.

Corinne crawled through the small space, to the boy who was thrashing about. The space was dark, understandably, keeping the burn wound out of the warm sunlight. "Hello, Brody." Her voice was sweet but with a little bit of no-nonsense about it. She needed him to listen. She saw his arm had a two-inch circle burned into it. The color was a fiery red that Corinne knew would hurt excruciatingly. She almost choked out a sympathetic sob. She stopped her own emotions and continued to do her job.

"I have something to put on your sore arm, Brody. It got burned. Is that true?" Corinne hovered over him and watched his face while she rifled through her bags for the needed supplies.

Brody opened his crying eyes and slowed his thrashing at the sound of a new voice. He looked scared and his cries continued. He snatched his arm away from the strange woman and cried even louder.

"Brody, I know it hurts, little man. Can I put some medicine on it? It will make it feel lots better." Corinne gently smiled and showed him the small bottle of lavender oil. She opened it, put one drop on her finger. Its sweet floral scent wafted quickly through the wagon's enclosure. Its calming effect worked on Corinne's beating heart. She hoped it would also calm his fears. She took the drop of lavender, touched it to her cheek, and rubbed it in a little. "It doesn't hurt at all. See Brody." Corinne bravely touched the finger to his cheek. His eyes went wide but his cry was softer now, with his curiosity. He relaxed his body and slowly laid his arm back down. With gentle hands, Corinne held his arm. Drop-by-drop, she poured the healing lavender oil over the entire surface of the red and blistered skin.

"My name is Corinne. Some of the kids call me the Plant Lady. You and I are gonna be such close friends. I think you should call me Corinne. What do you think Brody?" His eyes held tears, but he wasn't crying now. He nodded in response to her question.

"Doesn't that feel a little better?" Corinne watched him nod again. "I'm almost done Brody. Let me put some more of this medicine on it, then you can go to your Ma." Corinne liberally applied another layer of oil and watched it soak into the skin. The scent in the air was thick and its effect on the young boy would do wonders to help him sleep.

"You are such a good boy Brody." Corinne helped him sit up and then handed him over to his mother. She finally realized she had a large audience staring into the wagon. She felt herself blush and could not stop the heat from rising through her face.

"Mrs. Grant, is it?" Corinne met the woman's eyes and saw gratitude. Mrs. Grant nodded. "You will need to pour the oil on again later. Do not cover the wound until after the wound has dried up into a crusty layer. The lavender oil helps it heal fast and takes away a large amount of the pain. No bandage is needed. Keep him in long sleeves after today, whenever he is in the sun. The heat will make the pain return." She handed the small bottle to the mother and smiled at the young copper haired child who looked like he was recovering from his morning ordeal. "The lavender aroma will help him and others nearby to sleep. It is such a great healing oil. Any oil you have left can be used on any wounds or scratches on adults and children. It does help some at keeping away infection." Corinne realized she was rambling. So, she shut her mouth and left the wagon.

"I cannot thank you enough, Mrs. Temple." Mrs. Grant cried again. Her dark brown hair fell around her shoulders. Her tear-filled eyes endeared her into Corinne's heart.

"Please call me Corinne. I am so pleased to be able to help." She saw how young this mother was and knew she needed a female friend.

"Then please call me Chelsea. My husband is Russell." Chelsea gestured to the tall handsome man beside her. "My brother-in-law brought you here. His name is Lucas." Chelsea handed her sleepy child to his father and he headed over to a shady spot. She grabbed another stool, set it next to hers already near the fire, and motioned for Corinne to sit. "How did you learn about making medicines?" Chelsea seemed to be without embarrassment, as she pulled all her pins loose, braided her hair and wrapped it around her head with surprising skill.

"My mother taught me all she knew. I also learned from the Boston Greenhouse about the healing properties of plants and oils. My grandmother had the knowledge of a healer, as well. Her journals still teach me things every time I read them." Corinne missed them.

She grew quiet. Chelsea sensed Corinne's moment of sadness, stood up, and checked on her son. There was yelling nearby that sounded like the wagon boss preparing people for the day's run. Corinne thought she should get back to her own outfit soon. Andrew would not be pleased. Chelsea had a sleeping child in her arms and thanked Corinne again. Lucas Grant brought the horse around and carried the bag she had left inside the wagon.

"Can we pay you for the medicine, Mrs. Temple?" Lucas held paper bills in his hand. Chelsea stood near him nodding and looking at her with gratitude.

"Please don't, I have plenty of lavender oil. However, I will accept your friendship. Chelsea, I am in great need of a friend out here in the wilderness." Corinne held a smile on her face. Inside though, her heart was close to breaking. She needed this. Chelsea reached out and squeezed her hand. Two tears escaped from Corinne's eyes and they struck a deal. Corinne felt foolish for crying. She hopped back up on the tall dark horse. As she held on, Lucas plotted his way through the bustling village of wagons, back to Corinne's own little home.

Chapter Nine
April 15, 1848

With a scowl and frown aimed at his wife, Andrew impatiently waited next to Corinne's wagon. She was so grateful that Lucas took charge the moment they stopped to dismount.

"Mr. Temple, please forgive our interruption. The Grant outfit has extreme gratitude for you loaning us your wife's healing skills." Lucas reached for Andrew's hand. He shook it warmly, grabbing with both hands, almost bowing to Andrew as he stood there. Andrew's response was instantaneous, a near preening look.

Oh, how he loves to be admired, Corinne thought, stifling a laugh.

"My young nephew was burned this morning. We heard there was a healer in the wagon train and had to see if she knew how to ease his pain. We are abundantly grateful and wish to invite you and your wife to be a guest for dinner and music at our fire tonight. The best we can offer on a journey such as ours. Please say yes. It will be an honor." Lucas' speech was brilliant, Andrew rewarded him with an agreement and another handshake. He could hardly deny Lucas, who seemed educated, and had a gift for flattering him.

"Mrs. Temple, thank you again." nodded and was gone.

Corinne made herself useful, tidying up the camp and putting everything where it belonged. Jimmy hooked up the oxen and got ready for the ride. Joe brought Corinne's horse around and hitched it to the back of the wagon. Andrew stood quietly watching her.

"Well, good work, Mrs. Temple. I can see, maybe, I was a bit harsh about you and your work with plants. Maybe, you do know a thing or two. Perhaps flower picking, and medicine is a good job for women. Well, at least when they have the acumen for it," Andrew said to her and perhaps his imaginary audience. Then he wandered off to get his horse while Corinne put away the coffee pot and drawing utensils. She then untied her mare and prepared herself for a long day in the saddle. Within twenty minutes, the train was moving forward. The long morning was forgotten as they traveled across the land toward the next 'x' on the map.

Fifteen miles came and went, and Corinne was admittedly saddle sore. She thought all day about dinner with the Grant family.

Little Brody had been in her prayers as she rode beside her wagon. His sweet face and cries stayed with her for a long time. Corinne was relieved she was able to help him but had concerns about his suffering as he healed.

The wagons ahead were beginning to form groups. Corinne noticed several turning back and heading towards spots along the trickling creek. The wagon boss rode through the wagon train giving his orders for the day. About five minutes later, he stopped at her wagon informing them that they should stop, also. Tomorrow there would be a river crossing. A scout said it was less than two feet deep where they needed to cross. He glanced at the wagon and told Joe and Jim that the wheels needed a good soaking. The boys nodded. The train boss moved on, tipping his hat to Corinne, before he passed.

Jimmy and Joe were grunting and smacking the oxen to get them in position. Lucas Grant rode up on his big black horse.

"We were hoping to have you join us. Our outfit is about two hundred yards ahead. We cleared enough space, and Chelsea has already got a fire going. Looks like a dry night. We would like your crew, Mrs. Temple, and your husband, as our guests of honor." His smile was infectious. Jimmy and Joe followed his lead as they joined the Temple outfit to the party. Corinne rode next to Lucas, admiring his stallion.

"Wow. Mr. Grant, he is beautiful! My father would pay handsomely for breeding rights, I bet. My Father is John Harpole. His ranch is in Willamette Valley, Oregon country," she said emphatically.

Lucas brought his animal closer to give her a better look.

"Well, that will be grand. I say, after what you did for Brody today, it's a done deal. He has been sleeping peacefully in his mother's arms on the wagon bed all day. A good healing sleep, thanks to you!" Though his eyes were focused forward, Corinne could see that Lucas was still haunted by Brody's earlier cries. As was she.

"Mr. Grant, it is a valuable offer but payment will certainly be necessary. Breeding rights for a stallion that magnificent would be a small fortune. If I may ask, where did you get such a creature?"

Corinne was certain the stud was at least 17 hands high. She was more than impressed.

"His name is Solomon. Well, actually, I call him Solo. He is a gift from my fiancé, Sarah Ballentine. I'm sure Solo was essentially from her father, Nicholas Ballentine." Lucas patted Solo on the neck as they walked along.

"Ah yes, I have heard of them. The Ballentine's reputation is excellent in the breeding circles. My father did business with them before going west." Her eyes were still on the horseflesh when she heard her husband ride up on his mount.

"Lucas, are we headed for your outfit tonight? I've been looking forward to it all day," Andrew said. He could be so charming and polite to others.

Corinne wondered what it was about her that made him irritable or regard her as such a bother. She hadn't figured it out yet.

"Yes, Mr. Temple. We have a full night of dinner and music planned. My brother shot some venison yesterday, so we will feast tonight." Lucas moved away from Corinne to give Andrew space to be near his wife. He was surprised when Andrew went all the way around to the opposite side. It almost looked as if he was avoiding her.

"Your wife has been making arrangements for breeding rights to my horse, Solo, with her father's horse ranch. After her amazing care for my nephew Brody today, it's settled! Perhaps we could work out a deal that the first foal goes to her." Lucas gave Corinne a friendly grin.

"He is a stunning creature, but that offer is too generous. That mount, Solo, you say. He is worth more than whatever simple trick she used today with her flowers and ointments. You cannot be held to a silly promise to her. Her father is my benefactor. He will pay handsomely. How many hands? Sixteen?" Andrew gave his speech just as always, unaware that condescension dripped from his words like rain.

"He reached seventeen hands this spring. He is five years old and may still grow a bit more," replied Lucas, a bit dryly. Mr. Temple was more than a little insulting to his wife. Lucas owed her a lot but didn't want to be inhospitable. "Here we are up ahead. I am hoping supper will be soon. I'm hungry. Thanks for coming, Mr. and Mrs. Temple." Lucas dismounted and led the way for Jimmy and Joe to get the wagons in position for the night, the oxen unhitched and the animals grazing. Andrew joined him. Corinne made her way to the middle of camp looking for Chelsea and little Brody.

"Corinne, over here," hollered Chelsea, waving her over to the fire. Chelsea was busy peeling potatoes. Brody was sitting in his father's lap. They both looked comfortable napping in the shade.

"Let me help," Corinne offered, and was handed a small knife. "My husband does not allow me to cook at our camp. Maybe I can be useful here." Corinne sat on a stool and started peeling. It felt good to have her hands busy. "How is Brody doing?"

"Oh, he has had a few fits today but that's expected. Mostly, he napped and kept one of us busy holding him today. The redness has improved since the morning and the edges are already looking healthier. The oozing is gone completely, thanks to you." Chelsea was smiling and continued peeling. "This morning is still such a blur. Brody was nowhere near the fire. From the first day we left Independence, he had learned that the fire is off-limits. We heard a dog barking nearby. People were yelling. I was sitting next to Brody when this small dog ran through camp. The dog clipped the edge of the tripod holding the boiling water pot. I had started it early this morning to wash some of the men's laundry. The water pot fell into the fire and sent a large coal flying through the air. It landed on poor Brody's arm. I was inches away and grabbed him right up. The burning piece of log fell off his arm, but the damage was so bad." At the memory, a tear fell down Chelsea's cheek. Her hands were both busy, so it rolled down to the edge of her face and disappeared into the collar of her dress. "I have been wishing all day that the coal would have hit me instead. I was only inches away." Chelsea took her large container of peeled potatoes, started cutting them into little pieces and then plopped them into the boiling water on the fire.

"I am so sorry, Chelsea. It must be hard to have a little one out here. There are so many dangers everywhere." Corinne knew the sacrifices women made to follow the men, 'wherever they went.'

"I just pray we will stay safe after this. But I will take one day at a time. As God wills it," Chelsea said, with all sincerity. She had such a great attitude. Her face was full of resolve. "Thanks for helping here. This is the last of the potatoes. I saved them in the root cellar and now they are gone. Mashed potatoes with butter sounded like such a luxury. The butter is easy enough with the jostling wagon.

It's just feeding the cow that will get tricky. For now, the land is lush with grass. I know better than to believe that it will always be so." Chelsea stood up and stretched, after the potatoes were happily boiling. "Russell darling, keep an eye on the pot. Corinne and I need to stretch our legs."

"Let's grab our neighbor Susannah and then we can have real privacy." Chelsea headed on a winding path through the wagons. Corinne had no idea what Chelsea meant by privacy but followed behind her. Corinne grateful for a distraction, after the long day of no one to talk to.

"Susannah, come, let's stretch our legs." Chelsea waved to an older woman, who grabbed a young woman by the shoulder, and led her to them. After a minute, they all headed away from the wagons into a section with grass and bushes. Corinne could see no reason to stop. She watched Chelsea to see what she was doing.

"Who's first?" Chelsea questioned. Corinne was about to ask a question but was interrupted by Susannah.

"Please let it be me. I haven't had a chance in a while and I'm near to bursting." She hustled forward. Chelsea corralled the other woman around her. They all grabbed their skirts and turned around.

"Like this Corinne, dear." Chelsea held her skirts out in a huge bell at each side, creating a very private wall for Susannah. In a split-second, Corinne understood. Female privacy for when... things were necessary. Nature called and the girls gave each other privacy. Corinne had been riding out during the day to find the largest tree or bush possible to relieve herself. Now, this was better and would take less time than traveling so far. Corinne could not help but giggle a little when it was her 'turn' in the circle of ladies.

"I can't tell you how much better this is compared to the way I was doing it." Corinne heard the other ladies tell their stories, too. She would try to convince Andrew that Angela could join in, *for propriety's sake.* He would like it if she worded it like that.

They walked swiftly back to their wagons and said quick goodbyes, as they all had jobs to do and dinners to make.

"Thank you, Chelsea. That was educational." Corinne laughed again, heading to the fire and boiling potatoes they had left behind. Corinne brought over a bucket of cold water. They washed the day's trail grime from their hands and then their faces. Corinne felt like a new woman. The evening had turned out beautifully. So far, the spring weather had been mild since they began the trip. Corinne wondered how long it would last.

Dinner was delicious. Cookie even contributed with a dried apple pie. He really outdid himself. Andrew, Lucas, and Russell got along well, and the fire was a place of warm laughter and stories. After all the food and dishes were cleared away, Corinne peeked at Brody's arm and applied more oil. She was pleased with the way the skin looked. It would be tender for a few weeks, but the danger of infection had decreased considerably. Brody was a dear little man and very shy. After she gave him a peppermint candy, he offered a big hug as payment.

An old-timer was sitting by the fire when Corinne and Chelsea returned after tucking Brody into the wagon. Silver was peppered throughout his dark black hair and his smile was infectious. His clothes made him look like a trapper. He held a coonskin cap in his lap that Corinne thought confirmed his profession. She took an instant liking to the man. He had kind, wise eyes.

"Let me introduce you to our new friends." Russell smiled and pointed to the Temples. "This is Andrew and Corinne Temple. This is Clive Quackenbush."

"Please just call me Clive. My Ma called me 'sonny.' My brother called me crazy, and my Pa called me names I can't repeat in front of the ladies present." Clive reached for Corinne's hand and gave it a genteel kiss. She responded with a grand curtsy.

"Mrs. Temple here is a natural healer. She helped us out with Brody this morning. She is the main reason for this gathering." Russell saw she was blushing and gestured them all to sit. Every stool and crate they had available was around the fire.

"Well let's enjoy the evening. I say we have some music." Russell grabbed a guitar, Lucas a violin, and Clive had a harmonica. With a flourish, the music started. Nearby wagons joined in the fun and added a few more instruments. The wagon boss, Mr. Walters, brought a washboard and the band was complete.

Corinne had missed her childhood days of singing and dancing. When a song started that she knew, she sang right along with everyone.

Tell me the tales that to me were so dear,
Long, long ago, long, long ago,
Sing me the songs I delighted to hear,
Long, long ago, long, long ago,
Now you are come all my grief is removed,
Let me forget that so long you have roved.
Let me believe that you love as you loved,
Long, long ago, long, long ago.

After they all sang sweetly, the fiddler started a reel, *Old Dan Tucker*. Her new friend Clive invited Corinne to dance and she joined him with vigor. The crowd was clapping and stomping, and a large group were dancing. Corinne lost all her sadness. She saw Angela dancing with Cookie. She could not help but laugh at Reggie who seemed to have trouble keeping time as he clapped. Even Andrew was smiling and clapping.

The night passed with many more songs. They danced and sang every song they could think of. After a few of the adults started heading back to their wagons, the men agreed that the Temple and the Grant outfits would travel together.

Clive was thrilled at the idea. Somehow, he and Corinne struck an interesting friendship. Her mama would have called them kindred souls. Corinne had a sweet memory of her mama's voice. 'Sometimes you just connect with somebody. Don't need a good reason.' That was probably why Corinne questioned society rules about befriending Angela. She was raised to respect people of all backgrounds.

Corinne went to bed smiling and with more than a few good memories of the night.

Chapter Ten
April 17, 1848

"River crossing ahead," Corinne heard Jimmy say, as they moved along slowly. Mr. Walters rode by earlier, but Corinne had ridden off by then. After an early morning rain, she went looking for plant life. She had just made her way back to the wagon outfit when Jimmy informed her of the bad news. She didn't like river crossings one bit. So far, the small streams they had crossed had not given them any trouble, but she knew the Wakarusa River was going to be more difficult. They had received news that there was a safer way across. One never knew, however, if the rumors were true or not, until you were already across. With the last several days of rain the current could be strong. She said more than a few prayers for the safety of the whole wagon train. Corinne rode ahead and saw Chelsea walking behind her own wagon, with little Brody next to her.

"Chelsea, I hear there's a river crossing." Corinne tried to be friendly and calm. She dismounted and walked a few minutes with her friend. She tied Clover to Chelsea's wagon.

"Yes, the Wakarusa... I've heard, it can be tricky. Though I try to trust the men, I do get nervous. You look a bit nervous, too." Chelsea smiled and gave her young friend a squeeze across the shoulders. "Our husbands will take good care of us, no worries my dear." Chelsea saw a strange look cross Corinne's face. She wanted to question Corinne about it, but some yelling ahead distracted her.

Corinne's heart began to pound as she heard a woman screaming. The words were too jumbled to understand. The tone and inflection brought an instant dread, the way that only bad news could bring. The crying continued, and gasps were heard ahead. Chelsea reached down, grabbed her boy, picked him up, and held him against her chest. His face looked sleepy. He willingly snuggled against her. Corinne saw the look on Chelsea's face. It was pale and fearful, like she felt. Russell mounted up and rode toward the sound to see if he could help. The wagons stopped rolling. Confusing voices surrounded them as everyone tried to figure out what was happening. Within a few minutes, Russell rode back to them, grief painted on his face.

"A six-month old baby girl fell out of a wagon and was crushed beneath the wheels," he spoke softly. "The Hagan family," he added. It sounded like he had more to say but could not speak anymore. Russell dismounted. He walked to his wife and held her and his son. Chelsea cried quietly. Corinne quickly wiped her own tears away. She had not met the Hagan family. They were strangers, yet the tragedy was so close. The woman's cries lingered in the air. The sound cut through Corinne like a dull blade. Mr. Walters rode by a few minutes later and said they were camping there.

We are crossing the Wakarusa tomorrow, she thought.

Corinne watched Russell and Chelsea as they tucked in their son for his afternoon nap. She didn't realize it, but she had wrapped her own arms around herself like an embrace. She could see the Grants had a good marriage. Russell was supportive and strong without dominating his wife. He treated her with respect. For the first time in her life she recognized how wonderful that must be. In a moment of chaos and tragedy, they were quietly supporting each other.

"I think I will go and see if Cookie needs me." Corinne knew that statement was ridiculous but wanted to leave the Grant family alone for a while. The events of the day were overwhelming her. She needed a place to cry.

She took Clover back to their wagon outfit and handed the reins over to Jimmy. Usually, they did their duties in silence. It left Corinne missing her younger days on the ranch where everyone was boisterous, and had a word to say or a song to sing. Everyone in her world now was so silent and afraid. Corinne was desperate for some joy. Angela was next to the chuck wagon scrubbing on some laundry. Corinne wanted to help. But, of course, she turned away making herself useless but obedient. Boredom was eating away at her, as well as this looming sadness. She needed a task.

After spending an hour in her wagon sorting through her journals and trunks, she decided to walk toward the Wakarusa to see what the river situation was all about. Dinner was going to be a few hours wait. The men were all busy with their wagon repairs and wheel soaking.

Corinne headed toward the west edge of the camp. She followed the sounds of the men chopping trees. Corinne tried to understand the mens' general hubbub. She picked up a few phrases as she walked by. "The chains will be attached to the pulleys." "The limestone will make the drop more difficult." The phrases confused her more, however, rather than helping her to understand.

Everything around her was very green and lush with spring growth. There was an area that was clear of trees, wide enough for at least two wagons to fit through side by side. Corinne could not see the water, but she was certain she was heading in the right direction.

"Mrs. Temple!" an unmistakable voice called to her. She smiled even before she saw him.

"Clive!" Corinne saw the old man headed her way. "I was hoping to run into you." She wanted to adopt him as her grandfather, if she was honest with herself.

"Howdy, young beautiful thing. You heading to take a gander at the river we is crossin' tomorra?" His eyes were a stunning ice blue. Today, he had on a wide brim hat that had seen a few years of rain and weather. He had a spring in his step. Corinne fought the urge to hug him as he came closer.

"Yes, I need a distraction. I cannot do any chores..." Corinne knew she should stop. She shouldn't be sharing her troubles with anyone. She sighed instead.

"Your husband laid down the law, huh?" laughed Clive. "Young men will never understand women." He laughed again. It sounded so rich and heavenly that Corinne joined in. What a terrible, ridiculous situation. Corinne felt a little freer after laughing with her new friend.

"I can't stand to be idle. Let's just say I need a walk," she said. Clive offered his arm and together they walked through the trees.

The river wasn't deep and it was perfectly calm. The steep sides were going to be a problem. Corinne could see that. The flat land next to the river dropped off about five to six feet before it hit water. Basically a stony ledge. *How can we cross that?* she thought.

On the opposite side, there was one small sandy section that was nearly flat. It had the potential to climb up with a wagon but then dropped off. Corinne could not wrap her brain around it. *After one hundred wagons, would that pleasant sandy beach turn into a bog where wagons could sink or break the oxen's legs?*

"This sure is a pretty spot. I would've come here to fish when I was a youngin." Clive surveyed the spot, too. He had made this journey several times and he knew what backbreaking work was ahead. "Though we may scare the fish away permanently tomorrow. It will be quite a ruckus, I imagine." Clive glanced at Corinne and saw her concerned face.

"Now, don't get yourself all tied up in knots. I saw the wagon boss talkin' to some local Shawnee. They have been doing this a few years. They use chains and pulleys and get the wagons and animals safely across. There are always risks but we will get through this my dear, Lord willin." Clive gave her a chin up gesture. "I will get you and your young maid friend across safely myself." Clive grabbed her arm and they turned back.

Without her telling him, Corinne was surprised that he knew so much about her.

Clive seemed to have read her mind and had answered her unasked question. "I could see you watching her, with the concern of a friend. The other night with the music and dancing, you could not enjoy yourself until you saw she was having a good time herself."

Corinne just smiled and gave his arm a squeeze. She didn't know what to say.

They walked arm-in-arm back to her camp. She passed on having dinner and went to her bed before the sun went down. She used the light in the wagon to read her journals and be alone.

Chapter Eleven
April 18, 1848

The morning dawned cold with a light drizzle. Their six-a.m. start announcement was given the night before. Though many of them were up and ready, they knew it could be hours or perhaps, even the next day, before their turn to cross would come. Clive came by right at six and told Andrew his plan to take "the girls". His excuse was they were jittery women that got nervous watching their wagons being handled. He whispered something in Andrew's ear, making Andrew laugh and nodding in agreement.

After a breakfast of coffee and johnnycakes, Clive escorted Angela and Corinne to the edge of the Wakarusa. He disappeared for a few minutes. Corinne and Angela chatted nervously as a low whistle got their attention.

Clive was on horseback. His thin frame was straight as an arrow. He wasn't brawny, but he had a strong, wise presence. He needed a haircut and Corinne decided she would take care of that for him later today. She started to feel possessive about him, as she did with Angela. She wanted them both to be near and safe. She had lost so many people when she was young that she felt unnerved when she started to care about people. If she started loving them too much, she somehow thought they might be taken away or harmed.

"You want me to join you, should I jump in?" Corinne stood on the edge of the Wakarusa. The drop was about five feet to the water. She had seen a few people jump and most went well, but one girl sprained her ankle. Corinne had no desire to hurt herself. *Andrew would love that.* She could hear his thoughts about how foolish she was.

Clive stood below her on his mount. "Just sit on the edge and put one foot on my horse. He's gentle. He is steady and don't scare so easy."

Corinne sat down on the edge. She scooted herself until her foot landed on the saddle behind Clive. Clive coached her along with 'there you go'. She grabbed his hand, and then slowly turned her body to stand up. She moved her other leg over and slowly slid down to ride behind Clive.

"Your turn next, Angela." He returned for her, after dropping off Corinne safely on the other shore. Angela looked unsure.

"I'm a little nervous. I'm not as good around horses as Corinne. She grew up around them. They seem to smell my fear." Angela smiled nervously but did as Clive instructed. She nearly slipped when she stood up, but Clive's strong grip held her until she slid into place behind him. Clive worked his way through the shallow, calm water. He deposited Angela safely with her friend.

———◆•◉•◆———◆•◉•◆———

Clive tied his horse on a close tree and walked with the girls to the wagon crossing area. It was quite a spectacle. Many men gathered around a large apparatus. The Shawnee men were wearing very little clothing. There was a group of white men with them, wearing just pants. Angela and Corinne took turns blushing.

Several very large logs were sticking out of the ground. Under the them, there was a structure with ropes and chains, and taut muscled men with purpose, handling the logs roughly. Yelling seemed the thing to do. The chains would attach to a wagon, stripped of all its wheels and harness equipment. The front and back of a wagon attached to the large pulley chains. Then, with brute force and more guttural yelling, along with recognizable words, the wagon slowly swung up to the top of the pulley. It was then lowered to the water and hung just a foot above getting wet. On the other side, the pulley was put to work attaching chains and ropes. The wagon was then pulled up and nearer to that bank.

As she watched, Corinne felt her stomach drop every time she saw a wagon box swinging freely. One false move and a man could get crushed. It shook up her nerves.

"Angela, let's find Chelsea." Angela nodded in agreement. They followed the edge of the river to the Grant outfit.

———◆•◉•◆———◆•◉•◆———

In the morning, Corinne kept busy with Chelsea Grant and Angela. They went downstream a few hundred yards and placed a few young teen girls on guard in shifts.

The women prepared to bathe. There were no class systems that could safe guard you from one of the hazards of real trail life... Grime! Cleanliness was almost impossible. Every woman did their best, but the lack of privacy and long hours spent walking or riding, didn't afford them much opportunity to wash. The women carried stools with them and made a nice area to have a bathing party. The sun was warm, soap was shared, and the atmosphere was jovial. Several women even started singing. This was one of the best days they had on the journey so far.

Corinne felt so good having clean skin and hair again. Chelsea helped brush and braid Corinne's hair. She admired her Swedish braid using Chelsea's small hand mirror. The braid looked like a complete circle around her head. It suited her well. Chelsea then braided Angela's hair the same way. They all felt fresh and energized.

By noon, the Grant's wagons were put back together after their river crossing. Mr. Waters told Corinne when her wagon would be crossing the river. She was tempted to not watch. She would be devastated if her wagon fell or hurt someone. Or if all her oils and journals were potentially harmed. She shuddered at the thought. She watched her wagon being handled for several minutes, then decided to head back to the Grant outfit again. She could not watch anymore. Her heart was in her throat. She pushed up her sleeves and helped Chelsea prepare dinner for the Grant and Temple outfits, since not all the three wagons had crossed the river yet.

"Cori, come tell Chelsea about your grandmother, Trudie. I was just telling her how your grandmother was welcomed into the Cherokee Indian camps and even stayed with them for weeks at a time." Angela smiled and beckoned to Corinne.

"I need to hear this, my dear girl. You stay so quiet all of the time, it's good to know you talk to someone," Chelsea laughed. She grabbed a man's shirt from a basket by her feet. With a needle and thread, she pecked at the mending. She had her eye on the stew pot over the fire and was satisfied that it was bubbling contentedly.

"Well, I think my aunt in Boston, the 'General', scared my voice right out of me. Honestly, I don't mean to be shy. I am just not sure anymore when it's permissible to speak. She pounded it into me that ladies should be soft-spoken and not speak unless it was important. Whatever I felt was important was shot down. I was sent to my room for my trouble." Corinne gulped a bit emotionally, but then continued. "I was extremely foolish to have gone to Boston instead of with my father. I am making up for that now." Corinne opened up. She started telling the story of Trudie, the white woman who used food, and then a shared interest in plant life and its medicines, to befriend the local Indian women.

"Grandma Trudie learned a crude version of the Cherokee language. If you look through her journal you can see some drawings by a few women she met. They took her up the mountains and showed her places where rare plants grew, and even into caves where the 'healing waters' were. I remember she told me once that the healing water tasted dark. She took a glass jar full of it out of the cave, and said the water was almost pink when she held it up to the sun." Corinne seemed lost in thought for a moment. "She took my mother to that cave once. The next year, Grandma Trudie fell and her knees never gave her mercy after that. Her long mountain trips were finished. A few times a year, a few Indian women came to our ranch and shared herbs and stories with Grandma. My mother tried to earn their trust, but they were there for Trudie. I was ten when Grandma Trudie passed away. The Indian women only came by once after she passed. They brought a young girl with them and she gave me a leather pouch with hundreds of beads sown on it. It is stunning. I still have it. It's carried with my grandmother's journal."

"Did your Grandfather approve of Trudie traveling up the mountains and being with the Indians so much?" Chelsea asked.

"He died before I was born. He was in the militia and was injured. My grandmother was told he died from infection. He always supported her need for knowledge. After that, she always had an earnest desire to cure every infection she came across. She strove so hard to find a cure. In many ways, the knowledge she gained has helped me understand so much about what the world has to offer. If we just keep looking for it and listening to those who have gone before us." Corinne realized she sounded like a professor and was going to laugh at herself when a voice interrupted.

"Is the child boring you all with her stories about plants? She can go on and on," Andrew said, his voice dripping with sarcasm.

Andrew and Reggie walked into the camp. Andrew removed his hat and took a seat on a nearby stool.

"When I sent word to her Father that I would marry her to give her escort, I had no idea what childish prattling I'd have to endure," he laughed again.

Reggie gave Corinne an apologetic look. She lowered her gaze and thought about remaining silent forever. She hoped that she wasn't blushing too hard.

"Actually, Andrew, Corinne was delighting us with her family history about a fascinating woman." Chelsea's face was red from embarrassment for her friend. She now understood Corinne's silence more than she had before.

"Well, dear me, let me not interrupt. I have heard too much of it already. I was hoping for dinner soon. Mrs. Grant the stew smells delightful. I would like to offer dinner at our outfit tomorrow, to give you a rest, after your hard work today." Andrew went from one topic to the next completely unaware of how his words affected people. Russell and Lucas Grant, who sat nearby for the whole story, were astonished at how hard Andrew was being to her. They were coming to the conclusion that Corinne's husband kept a critical tongue for her alone. Albeit, he appeared polite and somewhat charming, just not to Corinne.

Andrew excused himself to go clean up. Chelsea whispered to Corinne.

"I am so sorry dear. I didn't realize that..." Chelsea didn't know what to say. She was very happily married to a man she adored, and who treated her very well. She didn't know what it would do to her, if someone treated her with such disdain. Chelsea's prayers for Corinne started that night. Her desire to protect her did, too.

Corinne just gave them a false smile and stood up. She mumbled an excuse and headed toward the river where the wagons were being assembled. She was embarrassed and humbled but tried to pull herself together. *There is an annulment at the end.* She could make it. It didn't matter what Andrew thought about her. He meant nothing to her beyond this trip. She wanted to cry but refused to allow herself the opportunity. A minute later she ran into Clive at the riverbank.

"Mr. Quackenbush," she called out formally, knowing he preferred to be called Clive. She grinned at him mischievously.

"I do declare Mrs. Temple," he said, with a southern drawl that sounded very authentic. "Yer as perty as a peach pie in der windersill." Clive's different voices nearly had her in stitches.

"Clive, will you be joining us for supper with the Grants?" She was hoping Andrew would behave around Clive. It seemed to Corinne that everyone was on their best behavior when Clive was around. He was well-known and respected for his knowledge of the West, his dealings with Indians, and his business smarts.

"Yes, I will be sharing supper with ya, but I need to discuss something with you. Let's walk a minute..." Corinne gladly took his arm but watched concern wash over his face. He gave her a glance and then looked away when he asked his tough question. "Corinne, has Mr. Temple... well... has he been unkind to you my dear?" Clive hated asking anything that would embarrass her, but he had to know.

"I wouldn't know what you mean, Clive." Corinne's heart hammered in her chest and she searched her mind for a way out of this uncomfortable conversation.

"Well, something Andrew said today bothered me to no end, my dear. I have grown quite fond of you and feel you should know, that he is bragging to everyone here about how quickly he will be rid of you, once we reach Willamette." Clive looked her in the eyes and was surprised by what he saw.

"Yes, I know, Clive." Corinne suddenly felt tired. Andrew's mouth had done enough damage for one day. "He told me as much, the day we wed. This is a marriage of convenience only. He gets me across to my father, and he pays back a favor my father did for him. I can't say I'm surprised. I was hoping he would be more civil to me, but that isn't the case. What I wasn't expecting is his attempts at belittling me in public. Ah well," Corinne sighed. The day was disappointing and she was dreading the response from the other men on the train. Her reputation wasn't being protected much at all at this point. *For all of Andrew's talk about propriety...* She let the thought go.

"I will have a word with the young man. He needs to remember his manners, I think." Clive looked away again. He was so irritated with Mr. Temple. *A college education means nothing without decent human courtesy*, he thought.

"Please don't, Clive. He will end up punishing me or Angela. He has threatened to send her back if I cause trouble or act unbecomingly. I just could not stand that. As it is, we aren't allowed to associate with each other anymore. I think that's why I have grown so quiet. I'm just biding my time until this part of my life is over." Corinne put on a brave face as they walked back toward the river.

The rest of the evening went well. With half the train crossed over the river successfully, the air was alive with excitement. Dinner was delicious. The music started soon after the plates were cleared away.

Chelsea and Angela worked extra hard to cheer up Corinne. She seemed to have crawled back into her shell, since Andrew ridiculed her in public.

The music was lively, and the dancing energetic. Russell, Lucas and Clive all danced with Corinne and kept her smiling. They were her protectors now. Even though her mood was slightly hindered, deep inside she felt honored knowing how much the Grant family and Clive meant to her.

She sat down with a mug of coffee in her hand. Angela winked down at her while sipping from her own mug. Smiling, Chelsea plopped down after having a turn with her husband.

"So, Chelsea, I haven't figured out how you know Clive so well. Is he actually in your outfit, or just knows Russell somehow?" Corinne had pieced together bits from hearsay about Clive and his fur-trading business.

"Well actually, he is my Grandfather. My maiden name is Quackenbush. He is my father's father," Chelsea said with pride. "He goes from the west coast to Michigan every few years. My uncle is in the Willamette Valley and runs the trading post for him. Clive spends a lot of time trapping, map-making or helping others across the trail. He is a real firecracker."

Corinne agreed, as she watched him sweep another woman around in a reel. "That makes sense then. I was curious." Corinne caught Andrew giving her a look she didn't comprehend, and she wiped the smile off her face. That appeased him, and he put his attention back on the group dancing. Several hours passed before anyone went to their beds.

Chapter Twelve
April 19, 1848

Andrew awakened her again, with his early morning routine of thumps and clunks. This was a rest day for the part of the train that had already crossed over. Corinne dressed and joined him at the small fire he had built.

"You are up early again, Mr. Temple." She failed at hiding her annoyance.

"Yes, I'm heading out with the scouts. I have grown fond of traveling along with them and hunting beside them. They know a great deal about the landscape and wildlife. I am eager to learn from them." Andrew seemed happy and Corinne's mood improved knowing he was going to be gone. They both waited in silence for the coffee, and once Andrew downed a mug full, he was gone. Corinne was content with her own company for the next hour before the rest of the world woke up.

The sun came up hot and before noon it felt like a June summer day, even though it was still April. Everyone had their chores to do. Corinne crept down to a secluded edge of the river for her own little treat. On the bank, she found a large rock up against a tree. It was half in and half out of the water. She saw this spot yesterday and knew it would be perfect for her plan.

She had always enjoyed the sun when she lived in Kentucky. By summer's end, she was almost as tan as an Indian. She cared little for the milky complexion popular in society. She loved the warmth of the sun. She had missed it tremendously while living in Boston, the land of parasols, gloves and being locked indoors like a prisoner.

Her favorite feeling was getting sun on her face and feet. It was her guilty pleasure. Glancing in both directions, she waded barefoot into the water. The river, still chilly from the April showers, made her shiver. She plopped down on the rock and leaned against the tree. She grabbed her thin skirts, put them up to her knees, and leaned back. The warm sun was heavenly. Her feet enjoyed the fresh air. Her skin delighted in its freedom from the confines of winter.

The late night and early morning caught up to her quickly and soon she was asleep. The peaceful lapping water was a pleasant lullaby.

"Hello Corinne." The voice was familiar, but her awakening was harsh. The sun's overwhelming whiteness blinded her as she opened her eyes. She heard splashing and a man laughing softly. She scrambled to sit up and see who had interrupted her quiet place. With one hand, she finally blocked out the light. Her other hand desperately pushed at her skirts to make them a more appropriate covering for her legs.

Lucas Grant smiled at her, while also half-heartedly looking away. He had a fishing pole on one shoulder. Once she got settled and she regained focus. She tried to climb down from her perch on the rock.

"Please don't move on my account. I was just heading upstream to see if there are any pockets of fish. I must say, you make a lovely picture in the warm sun." His green eyes were smiling, and Corinne was speechless. "I am a gentleman, but I must admit, when I first came upon you, I did notice that the plant lady has some nice stems." He laughed again. Corinne rewarded him with a serious blush, looking all the redder with her slight sunburn.

"Mr. Grant, honestly! You should have looked away. I realize my spot isn't nearly as secluded as I had hoped." She wanted to be mad, but she could not. "You go on now, before Mr. Temple catches us both here. My lack of propriety is a serious infraction today." Corinne was certain that if her husband had happened upon her, it would have gone so much worse. She instantly frowned and tried to climb down. The water seemed colder, with her dark thoughts hanging over her concerning her husband.

"Mrs. Temple, your secret is safe with me. I will never tell. I owe you too much for what you did for Brody, and for the friendship you have with Chelsea." Lucas saw her face drop. He wanted to ease her mind. It didn't work. He walked over to her and grabbed her arm before she escaped. "Corinne, just so you know. Your husband is a fool." She turned her head and met his glance. Suddenly her world flipped. *What in the world does that look mean?* They both seemed embarrassed and separated quickly, walking away, each in their own direction.

Lucas's eyes had been so intense. 'Your husband is a fool,' he had said.

Of course, he is.

Andrew is also in charge. She had been foolish to sneak off. Her arms were pink already. She pondered what hour it was. How long had she been asleep? Her mind reflected on why she felt so strange suddenly. She thought, perhaps, it was the sun.

———————————

She went back to her wagon. It was well past two p.m. She had spent an hour and a half asleep in the sun. She knew her skin would be a terrific shade of red by the end of the day. In the wagon, she unpacked chamomile and lavender oil. She added several drops to a separate bottle of olive oil. Inside the privacy of her wagon, she applied the mixture liberally, to her face, arms, and legs below the knee. She was hoping the redness would not be too noticeable. Otherwise, a lecture from Andrew was imminent. She should have worn her bonnet less while on horseback. Her skin would have been more used to the sun then. Corinne was putting her bottles away when she heard hoof beats nearby. A voice called for Mrs. Temple. She got out of her wagon and headed behind the wagon where Clover was tied. His saddle sat on the edge of the wagon.

"Your husband has been shot." One of the scouts had ridden hard to get to Corinne. She stared at him in shock. "I think he'll be ok ma'am. It is just a flesh wound in the arm," he gasped.

Corinne wanted to smack him. *Why didn't he start with that instead of scaring me so much?* she thought.

"Where is he?" Corinne finally managed to speak. She had already placed Clover's saddle blanket upon his back. She grabbed the saddle as the young man explained himself.

"They are bringing him here. It was just an accident. One of the scout's weapons misfired. Andrew seems to be handling it ok though. Me, I'd be cussin' up a storm." The young man in front of her started to test her patience.

"Is he bleeding heavily?"

"Not anymore, one of the scouts got to it right away and wrapped it up tightly. He'll be here in a few minutes. I was sent to tell you that you would want to get the bullet out. You will need to get him into his wagon, I'm thinking." The young man's panting was slowing down. Corinne removed the saddle and walked over to

Andrew's wagon. No one was near. Reggie, Cookie, and Angela were off doing some task, away from the outfit. Down at the river, Jimmy and Joe were on shift, working as extra hands with the animal crossing. Corinne peeked into Andrew's wagon and realized no one slept in it. It was for storage only. Blast!

Corinne quickly ran over to Chelsea's wagon and requested aid. "My husband has been wounded. He is out of danger, but I need a space to remove the bullet. His wagon is a mess. I need some strong arms to help me and my crew seems to have vanished today." Corinne watched Chelsea go into her own serious mode. It's that thing women did when something went wrong. They got the bleeding stopped, the fever down, the animal calmed, and the mess cleaned up. They were only allowed to fall apart afterward.

"I will go fetch Lucas. Then, I'll go down river to see if Clive or one of your boys is available. Russell is out with Brody getting firewood. Otherwise, I would find them too." Chelsea took off down to the river, hollering for Lucas. Corinne headed back to her own wagon. She grabbed her bag of bottled oils and her first aid bag. Inside her case there were a few doctor tools she had inherited from her mother, and some cloth for bandages. She grabbed a worn-out petticoat just in case she needed more bandages.

Andrew's wagon was still a mess, five minutes later when Lucas arrived and climbed in. "I heard Andrew is hurt. I'm here to help." She explained the situation. With Lucas's help, they cleared a decent space. Corinne jumped out to look for Andrew's bedding in his tent. She could not tell whose bedding was who's in the tent. She grabbed one set, carrying the bulky bundle to the wagon. Wordlessly, Lucas and Corinne put the area together. She gathered several lanterns, keeping them close. It was still early in the day, but from experience, she knew it might be a long night. When removing a bullet, a gunshot wound could grow dangerous.

Though Corinne wasn't a doctor, on many occasions, she witnessed her mother remove bullets. For several years, her mother was the closest thing to a doctor in their town. The nearest doctor had been a hundred miles away, after the local one had passed away. Corinne learned a lot from watching her. Though her mother loved the medicinal plants and how they healed, Corinne knew her mother thrilled at the deeper side of medicine. She thrived on keeping people alive.

Corinne heard horses outside. She jumped out of the wagon and saw her husband riding behind one of the scouts. His horse was following slowly behind them. Andrew looked slightly pale and agitated. Someone helped him off his horse. He started shouting orders for someone to take care of his mount.

"This way, boys. Can you put him in the wagon? I've got it prepared," Corinne stated matter-of factly, to the men carrying Andrew by his underarms. He protested weakly, tried to walk on his own and failed. He allowed them to aid him in getting to the wagon.

He heard Corinne rattling off instructions and was mildly impressed. Andrew was surprised that she took charge, but he lost focus when the men at his side manhandled his arm. He walked along with them but seemed a bit wobbly on his feet.

Andrew was comfortably lying down within a few minutes. Corinne thanked the men for taking good care of him. They explained how the incident happened.

"It was a misfire ma'am. I will never know how Charlie Baker's gun went off. No one was touching it. Charlie swears it's never misfired before." The older scout was sincere. Corinne sent him off, gently assuring him that she knew it wasn't intentional.

As Corinne watched them leave, she built up her courage.

Chapter Thirteen
April 19, 1848

Andrew was enraged. He hid it well in front of the scouts but now he wanted to spit nails. He was laying in the wagon, his arm throbbing and burning, like nothing he had ever felt before. The moment the bullet entered his arm, he didn't feel a thing. He had an adrenal reaction, a hot flash of sorts, flowed through his body. It was a warning and he glanced at his arm in disbelief. A growing hot sensation spread in his arm. Not really a pain, just warmth. But when Joe Worthington tightly wrapped it with a long strip of clean cloth, the pain got intense. Blinding hot pain. He went to vet school, so he knew what was about to happen. He was preparing himself for it. Deep breaths and steel courage. It was not going to be pleasant.

Corinne joined him in the wagon, greeting him with soothing and kind words. She seemed like a different person, older, perhaps. She was in charge and confident. He ventured this is what the Grants saw. *I guess everyone has their own talent. Maybe she has one, after all,* he thought.

She laid out her tools. Inwardly, Andrew was cringing. The tools would be probing inside his arm shortly. Outside the wagon, he heard voices, probably Reggie and the Grants. Within a minute, someone climbed in. The jostling annoyed him further. He tried to move his arm in a protective gesture but fresh pain welcomed him back to reality.

"I'm here to help, Andrew. I brought an old friend with me. He helps a lot in these kinds of situations." Clive was a cool head. Andrew was glad to see him. Clive had a mug in one hand and a bottle of whiskey in the other.

Clive poured, and Andrew drank. Its harsh, woodsy taste burned its way down Andrew's throat. Half of it spilled down his chin. Clive lifted Andrew's shoulders up a little and he drank some more. Clive brought some clean rags with him. Corinne and Clive discussed a few things. Andrew tuned them out. He didn't want to hear the details. The array of tools next to Corinne was mocking his nerves. He worked hard at ignoring them, too. This was not a good day.

The alcohol was making him feel warm. He wasn't a big drinker and his empty stomach made him an easy target for the alcohol.

"You will need to hold still. I will do my best to do this as quickly as I can. Clive, can you ask Lucas or Russell to come in. We may need extra hands." Corinne's voice was calm and controlled.

Corinne unwrapped the arm and soon got to the bloodiest part of the wound. The fabric was stuck to the skin. She poured a little water on the stuck fabric. Using sharp scissors, she cut the fabric off around the wound. She gently pulled. After a minute, the fabric gave up its grip.

Andrew felt the wagon move again but didn't care as much. Clive lifted him up once more and offered another mug of whiskey. Andrew saw the bottle sitting there. On its label, there was a man in a top hat, and a woman with a rose in her hand. He wanted to laugh. *Do all girls pick flowers?* he wondered.

<hr/>

Corinne started washing the wound. The musket ball must have been half an inch or bigger to have created a hole this size in his arm. The washing made it bleed again. She used a clean rag, dipping it into the basin of fresh water by her side. She squeezed water over the wound and pressed it firmly with a dry cloth. She gave Clive and Lucas a look that said "be ready."

"Ok, Andrew, just try to focus on something else." Corinne washed her hands once more, for good measure. She then took her index finger and began to reach into the bullet wound.

Andrew felt the blur from the whiskey, until that moment. His legs and arms started squirming involuntarily. Lucas and Clive successfully held him down, while Corinne searched for the bullet. The bullet cut a deep hole. Before she found the metal bullet, she felt blood and torn muscle. She kept blotting as more blood poured out of the wound. Andrew was handling the pain by grunting and breathing heavily .

Corinne felt something foreign. She grabbed a pair of thin pliers. She kept her finger on the object and used her other hand to guide the pliers. Andrew lost his nerve momentarily, and a louder grunt escaped. He squirmed a bit more. After a few attempts,

Corinne clasped the foreign object in the jaws of the pliers. She pulled the object out slowly. She at once saw what it was.

"Looks like cloth. Part of his shirt?" Clive asked, fascinated by this young woman's skill. She nodded, trying to wipe her forehead while leaving her hands in place. Lucas used his free hand to dry her forehead with a towel.

She poured a little more water on the wound and patted it dry again. She dreaded digging deeper, but knew she had to remove the bullet. She pushed further into the wound, ignoring her husband's squirming. Her fingertip hit upon a hard edge deep within the muscle. The blood flow was too heavy to see into the wound, so she moved the hard object around, making sure it wasn't bone or a tendon. She realized she had found what she was looking for. The round shape was now unmistakable. She grabbed the pliers again. Using her finger as a guide, she found the bullet. This was the tricky part, grabbing the bullet without pushing it further into the damaged tissue. She opened the pliers and on the first try, she gripped the offensive bullet. With a tug, it was out. Everyone, including Andrew, gave a sigh of relief. Following a ritual from her Grandmother Trudie, Corinne flushed out the wound using a clean cloth containing a few drops of lavender and a new oil from Australia.

"What are you using on me?" Andrew was so much happier now that she was no longer inside the wound. But, he was still a bit apprehensive about her plant extracts.

"My grandmother passed along the information about the oil of lavender, and the tea tree plant from Australia. She loved reading the medical journals. She came across a story about Aborigines who used the leaves to stop infection in cuts and wounds." Corinne washed her hands, grabbed a thin sewing needle, and began to thread it with strong black thread. She kept talking to keep everyone calm, while she stitched the wound back together. A few grunts escaped Andrew, though she handled his tender wound as gently as she could.

"The Aborigines would cut up the leaves. They would use mud to hold it on a wound. Word spread from a British navy captain who met these Aborigines, and the medical community started taking notice. If you distill the leaves, it creates an oil that has many wonderful applications. It is difficult to purchase, but I do have a small supply that I procured in Boston. I save it for emergencies. We don't want this to get infected." Corinne tied off the last stitch and was satisfied. She applied another dose of oil around the stitched area and then bandaged the wound.

"Andrew, it's done. I trust that as a veterinarian, you know how to treat a wound. You stay still for at least a day. I want your word. Infection out here is a killer." Corinne watched him nod like a child. He was still a little worn out from the procedure and the alcohol.

"You rest," Corinne ordered.

Clive and Lucas silently helped her cleanup the area and they slipped out the back of the wagon.

As Corinne exited the wagon, all her nerves hit at once. She was overwhelmed and needed to sit.

"Rest here, my dear." Clive pulled up a stool and helped her to sit.

Corinne laughed nervously, "I always get nervous afterward. I can handle the pressure during, but it nearly knocks me over when I'm done. I will be fine in a minute." Corinne's heart melted a little to see both Clive and Lucas so concerned for her. "I used to help my mother all the time. There were always skirmishes in the Kentucky hills. Indians, farmers, and wildlife often collided. My grandma would say that men had to be wild to prove they were men." Corinne knew she was nervously prattling.

"I think she was right," Clive chuckled and nodded. "Your mother would be proud, my dear. You handled yourself magnificently." He patted Corinne's shoulder affectionately.

"I can't believe what you just did. Corinne, you are amazing!" Lucas said, with obvious sincerity. She felt a little jump in her stomach.

"I have never seen a young lady that calm under pressure. I am so proud of you, my girl." Clive gave her shoulders a squeeze.

The night went smoothly. Andrew tried to get up only a few times, for reasons outside necessity. His patience for being still, however, was going to be an issue. Corinne could see that.

The wagon boss, Mr. Walters, came by to check the status of Andrew's wound. He was pleasantly surprised. Seeing a good man taken down by accidental misfire was a terrible shame. Watching him die from it would have been a tragedy.

"The day has gone well," he said. "The river crossing was nearly perfect, but there were two accidents and the wagons are going to need repairs." Mr. Walter's voice was a little hoarse from yelling all day. "No one was hurt but a horse got spooked and ran off. The scouts are out trying to find it." Mr. Walters enjoyed a cup of coffee at their campsite, before heading off to talk to the other groups. He shared the good news. They would be resting for a day, to allow the wagons to be repaired and Andrew to recuperate.

That night Corinne broke the rules and helped Angela with the laundry down at the creek. They talked and laughed like friends again. It made Corinne forget about the grueling day. Before dinner, Clive came by the campfire. He carried a pair of scissors and had a soft cloth around his neck.

"I do believe you promised me a haircut. I figure if you can pluck a bullet from a man's arm, a haircut is not beyond ya." His mood was jovial, and it spread around the Temple outfit like a calming breeze. Corinne trimmed his hair. Angela heated a towel with hot water and gave him a barber style shave. All the men begged for their grooming services for the next day. Flattered, the girls agreed.

The meal around the fire was very relaxed. Cookie shocked everyone with a story about his younger days as the second son of a fisherman.

"I never found my sea legs," he stated, with his gruff voice and a smile in his eye. "It was a terrible disappointment to my family who had been seafarers for more than ten generations. The years I spent aboard my father's fishing vessel were torture for everyone. Especially me." He held his mouth and shook his head, remembering the never relenting rocking of the boat.

"I learned so much about the sea from my family but never gained the ability to live aboard a rocking boat. I used my knowledge to open a seaside restaurant on the New Jersey shore when I was nineteen. I got fresh fish from my family's boats and started getting a loyal following of customers. A few years of serving affordable fish and chips, my business grew. Then suddenly everything went sour. Competition came in and things got ugly. They had supporters that wanted me to leave town. They were the kind of people you didn't say 'no' to. I felt my life was better served being alive than owning a small restaurant. The threats worked on me and I closed my place."

Angela and Corinne both sighed after hearing his story and felt badly for his loss.

"No worries my ladies. I found jobs working in other restaurants, and in a few hotels. I may not look it, but I am a well-known chef in New Jersey now." Cookie straightened his shoulders and looked younger for a moment.

"I hear California is the place to start over. I plan on rebuilding my restaurant on the coast." The girls all cheered and declared they would visit his restaurant someday.

The warm night and the starry heavens created a pleasant mood for all. Corinne visited Andrew's wagon before she headed off to bed. The bandage was clean and the area outside the wound was cool, no sign of infection. Corinne was relieved. Andrew asked for more water and after she retrieved it, she was dismissed. He had yet to thank her.

Chapter Fourteen
April 26, 1848

Another week of fair weather traveling got them 130 miles further on their journey. Corinne continued with her 'plant lady' duties and not much more. Andrew had successfully avoided contact with Corinne as much as possible. He endured her prodding about his gunshot wound until the fear of infection was no longer a worry.

Clive rode next to Corinne a few mornings a week when he was nearby. He was only on-call if needed, for scouting duties on this trip. He wasn't hired as a scout, but he was a very experienced one. He was traveling along with Chelsea and her family to help them. Clive and Chelsea had sort of adopted Corinne. They wanted her to be safe and cared for like a family member. Corinne felt the same about them, too.

The wagon train was full of hardy families, and some single young men hired on for a multitude of tasks: wagon handlers, scouts, animal caretakers, and more than one cook. There were a few women who were outspoken about their dislike of the journey. The other wives either agreed with their men's needs to go west or knew enough to be quiet about their dislike.

Besides the young infant who died under a wagon wheel, there had been total of five deaths so far on this journey. One man drowned during a river crossing. He got impatient and tried to cross in an untested area. His horse got caught in quicksand, spooked, and tried to get out. The man fell off his horse and hit his head on an underwater rock. Men tried to fish him out but a minute later he was gone. Another was an elderly woman who started the journey sickly and could not handle the jostling of the wagon or the walking. She had died in her sleep a few nights passed. Two children, under the age of five, died of a strange fever. That scared everyone. They weren't in the same family. Everyone was holding their breath lest there be an outbreak that spread. The boy and girl were the only ones that got the high fever. They had died last night. Corinne brought each family feverfew tea and some white willow bark, but the fever was fast and unmerciful. The children were quickly buried, and the train moved along. Two weeks didn't seem such a long time normally, but it felt like this traveling group was somehow becoming a large family. Sharing in each other's burdens. Burying their dead together.

Corinne tried to harden her heart to the reality of death on the trail, but she had failed so far. She had cried over the many grave markers they passed, more than a few times a day. When she got too overwhelmed, she would go walking with Chelsea and Brody. Chelsea had such a healthy way of looking at life and it usually rubbed off on Corinne quickly.

The train was buzzing about getting to Fort Kearney within the week. Corinne wasn't sure about the food supply for the Temple outfit. She heard several women complaining about how quickly they were going through their own supplies. There was a pony express station at Fort Kearney. For money, you could send word off to family.

Corinne had written a letter to her aunt about the journey so far. She kept Andrew out of it though. No need to upset the applecart. Just the night before, Corinne and Andrew finally had a battle of words. It had been brewing under the surface. Corinne asked politely for him to lift the ban on her being able to help with the chores. He responded by ignoring her. He gave her a glance, but Corinne was tired of taking orders from him.

"You don't understand Andrew. I am a woman, not a doll. You are learning new things by going off with the scouts. I wish to contribute, too. I am a grown woman and want to do my share." Her voice was raised, and her face was turning pink from embarrassment and anger.

"I thought I made my instructions simple, dear girl. If you want to raise a racket, feel free to do so. But remember the consequences." He looked over at Angela who was helping Cookie prepare dinner.

"You are the most insufferable man. You take delight in having power over people, don't you?" Corinne was more than a little pink now. She heard a snicker beyond the wagon outfit. She realized they had an audience.

"Well I can be happy, knowing I was right about you Corinne. You are a spoiled child who huffs and puffs to get her way. No wonder your father left you behind. I feel sorry he will have to put up with you when I'm done with you." Andrew was so flippant with his insults. He went back to his mug of coffee and barely noticed his young wife's stunned tears.

Corinne knew she had lost. She tried to reason with him and not only failed but was knocked down a few more pegs for her trouble. She would do as told and behave as the lady he commanded her to be.

The Grant family, who was always nearby, spent days with Corinne, trying to cheer her spirits. Clive was the best at it. He would have her almost smiling, but they noticed the smile never reached her eyes.

After four days of rainy travel, everyone's spirits were low. More than a few families were sharing sniffles and colds. Corinne herself was fighting off a small fever. She kept that information to herself. She wanted to stay out of Andrew's attention. Being sick was miserable enough without his words cutting her down to size. Corinne rode Clover during the day and stayed quiet at night. She had a routine and was sticking with it.

Chapter Fifteen
May 1, 1848

Angela stooped down to gather twigs and anything that would work as kindling. Firewood materials were starting to get sparse in the area . The next step was to look for buffalo chips to burn. The rain had been off and on for days, so finding anything dry was difficult. Angela kept her mind on task and focused on her search. After more than an hour, she was certain she had enough to satisfy Andrew.

There was a full firewood box in each wagon, but he insisted on her going for kindling daily, even in places where it was sparse. *Ah well. He was the boss*, she thought.

She missed her friendship with Corinne. The days were filled with work and silence. The other women enjoyed camaraderie and the chatter of womanly friendship. She was watched carefully. Whenever she attempted to chat with Chelsea while they were doing wash together at the creek, Andrew threatened her. He took Angela by the arm and gave her the 'you are the hired help' speech. Chelsea gave Andrew a glare. She lectured him after he returned Angela. She told Andrew that Angela was pleasant company and he should stop being such a bulldog.

Angela walked back into camp carrying her sticks, kindling and a small bag of buffalo chips. Dinner was nearly ready, and Angela's stomach growled in appreciation of the smells coming from the fire. *Looks like someone had a successful fishing adventure.*

Reggie gathered her items and added them to the wood box for Andrew's wagon. Andrew strolled over purposefully and examined Angela's offering.

"Angela, this is not what I expected from you. I wanted a full bag. There are barely ten chips in there. There are certainly more to be had." He paused for a moment, reflecting on the look of disappointment on her face. "My father used to say to his servants who had been lazy, "If you don't want to work, you don't want to eat.'" Andrew nodded and handed the bag back to her, pointing to the open field.

"Andrew the sun is going down. There is no moon tonight. It is too dangerous for her alone out there," Reggie protested gently. Corinne stomped over and made her presence known as well.

With bag in hand, Angela swallowed her pride and stepped away. *Andrew was always right,* she chanted, to make it seem better. They continued to argue but she still had to do the work. Andrew had taken a dislike to her when they first met. She would bear it until he was no longer her charge. She heard Reggie volunteer to go with her. Corinne's voice got louder as she argued with Andrew about her friend's safety. Angela was determined to fill the bag as quickly as she could, in the failing light of dusk. Within ten minutes of heading away from the wagon outfit, Reggie brought her a lantern. He apologized. She just nodded and kept silent. No need to make a fuss.

The area had been picked over. She knew it would be a long walk to find any chips or firewood.

She passed the time as usual, thinking about her brother, Sean. She wondered what he was doing with his life. The work orphanage in Boston had not been pleasant for him. He was three years older than her. She knew the boys there had been a rough lot. He'd had a black eye by the end of the first day. Their mother had always told them that fighting was a last resort. Patience and kindness were the first things to do. That didn't work well for him. He ran away five years later. Thirteen and on the run. She received a letter from him a few months later. He was working as a farm hand in Vermont. A nice family had taken him in. He liked it there better than the orphanage, but the work was hard. Angela had always wondered the *what if* questions about Sean the most. He had been so smart in school. Math and science were his specialty. She could've seen him in a bank or as a scientist working with doctors. What if her mother had lived on, would Mr. Lankarski have happily kept them all? Mother had only been married to Stan Lankarski for a year when she passed away. Eight months pregnant, she died carrying a full washtub down a flight of stairs. She missed a step, the tub flipped and her momentum carried her in a deadfall to the bottom. Angela had been the one to yell for the neighbors to get help.

They had shared a pretty, two-story home in a nice neighborhood. Stan owned a thriving lumberyard business, and everyone enjoyed each other. Three weeks after the death, Stan called Angela and Sean to the dining table. They had not seen him in several days and had been left with the housekeeper. "Children, I am getting remarried. Her name is Alice. She will be coming here to live with me. I have found a great place for you to live where you'll have lots of friends your own age." With his sweet smile and charm, Stan had them so excited.

For two days Angela barely slept, thinking they were moving to a wonderland. They had no idea that their new home was a workhouse. Fifty children under sixteen years of age. Angela met Alice the day they left. Alice was well along in pregnancy just like her own mother had been. It took Angela a few years to put all the pieces together about her stepfather, Stan. Her mother had picked a second husband poorly.

Angela pushed those memories aside as she found some decent firewood selections behind a briar bush. She used her elbow to hold the thorny branches aside. She knelt to reach her find. After she pulled it, she tried to release the thorns. It didn't work as easily as she hoped. She left some skin behind and part of her shirt. Her arm was now itchy and bleeding a little bit. She laughed at her foolishness and kept marching. She looked behind her occasionally, to keep her sense of direction intact. She didn't want to get lost in the middle of the untamed wilderness. Indians, wolves and insects would take advantage. She laughed at the image of insects carrying her away. The swarms she pictured were large, but she had never seen them carry a person away. Her smile lasted a few minutes while she kept on searching.

An hour passed and then another. Angela gasped at her half-full bag. As she started to worry about how she was going to explain her poor performance to Andrew, she heard a low growl. She held up her lantern and looked around. Seeing nothing, she cautiously looked back toward the wagon train. It was out of sight. There were a few dots of light that were certainly fires from wagon outfits, but the night was a dark one. A screech startled Angela for a moment. She realized she needed to head back to camp. A raccoon made a high chick-chick noise then a screech. Another growl joined in and the raccoon started a wail that chilled Angela's blood. A fight was starting. She wasn't sure what it was about but she wasn't going to join in. The raccoon made the sound again. The growls turned into a muffled scuffling noise. Angela turned and headed away quickly from the noise. She envisioned a scenario in her head about a wolf and an unlucky trapped raccoon. She walked quickly and soon was on a small rocky incline. She could see lights ahead of her, but in the darkness, she felt she was facing the wrong direction. She tripped over a large rock protruding from the ground. She landed badly. A small yelp escaped her as pain shot up her arm. Her bag had flown a short distance out of sight. Angela sat a moment as she realized the desperate situation she was in. She thought about calling for help but changed her mind. She used her good arm to push herself up, then grabbed the lantern. Her left arm was hurting but she could move her fingers slightly. She glanced around for the buffalo chips bag and headed to a big rock to see if she could find it. The raccoon-wolf fight was still going on behind her. She cringed at the intensity of it. She wanted to leave this place and go somewhere safe.

She found the bag a few minutes later. She headed toward the direction she thought the wagons were located. Her lantern flickered. Her heart nearly stopped as she watched it flicker again. *Had Reggie filled the lantern with more oil since yesterday?* She gently shook it and heard no fluid. It was going to be very dark, very soon.

Her heart played its own little fearful jig and she began to run. The small flame gave her very little light in front of her. Within two long minutes she tripped twice. Her second landing caused the flame to go out completely.

Alone in the dark, Angela took a moment to do what any healthy young girl would do at this moment... cry.

She sniffled a minute later and looked at the sky. No moon was visible. Even the stars seemed to be hiding behind some night clouds. She knew any night vision would be of little use to her because of the rocky and sparse terrain. She realized she was in trouble. She stood up slowly and spread her arms out wide in front of her. Her left arm was protesting but she tried to ignore it. She moved a few small steps forward, reminding herself to take slow, easy breaths. She had to think about where she was walking and not be distracted by the animal noises she heard. The buzzing of the insects around her was also distracting but she plodded on. She reached an edge, possibly a large boulder. She squinted to see if she could tell where to go next. She moved to the right and found a large briar bush. She backed away as if it was hot. She didn't want to get stuck in that all night. She turned to her left and used the large rock for guidance. Her feet stumbled on some ground clutter. Tree roots or rocks, Angela couldn't tell. A hissing sound broke her concentration. It was nearby. It could be anything, a snake or a rodent. She forced herself not to panic. She took two more uneasy steps. Her ankle wobbled on another sharp-edged rock. This was terrible terrain to be stumbling around in the dark. The hiss came again. This time it was closer. She jumped slightly and her right arm lost hold of the boulder. As she swung her right arm wide to find it again, she lost her balance. She lunged forward about four steps, then Angela's world turned over. Her left foot stepped out, but found nothing to land on. Her right ankle rolled on the uneven surface and her body lost all control. Within a split second, she was moving fast. Down, down, down. Something sharp pierced her shoulder. She held her arms over her head, but they were knocked askew as she bounded downhill. Her right leg hit a rock. Pain like she had never known before, forced her to yell out. Within a moment her body caught the edge of something. She slowed to a stop. She cried out for help, her body a ball of pain and helpless to move.

Chapter Sixteen
May 2, 1848

Corinne sat at the fire tapping her foot. She glanced at her watch. It was one a.m. No sign of Angela. When Andrew sent her friend away, she talked to him until her throat was hoarse. Corinne was still fighting off a cold from the rainy week. She needed her rest, but Angela out in the dark was too much for Corinne. Her emotions were out of control. She had no say, no opinion that mattered. It was difficult to be around someone who believed you had no worth. In a way, she and Angela were the same in his eyes. Worthless females bent on making his life difficult, is what he would say. Andrew was in his tent sleeping peacefully.

Reggie tried a few times to fall asleep but ended up next to Corinne at the fire. Looking into the darkness, he paced around the edge of the wagons. Reggie felt guilty for not going with her. He tried to get Andrew to allow it, but all he got was a lantern to hand to her. Before leaving, he went to fill it with oil. Andrew stopped him.

"It still has enough oil. Take it as is." Andrew's word was final. Hours later his fear for Angela's situation grew into a ball of dread in his stomach. *Where was she?*

A dog barked nearby. Corinne and Reggie jumped. The night was quiet but for the crackling fires. Corinne heard someone stirring on the far edge of camp, muffled voices and a few more barking dogs. Corinne held her breath a minute to listen closer. Some men on horseback were riding by. They stopped when they saw Reggie and Corinne were still up. The three men on horseback looked anxious.

"There is a female yelling in the distance. Is there anyone missing from your camp?" the man asked.

"Ye-es..." Corinne faltered. Her heart was pounding so hard she could barely breathe. "Angela Fahey was sent out hours ago. We don't know why she hasn't returned." Corinne looked over at Reggie and saw him holding his hands over his face.

The noise woke the camp. Andrew joined the men on horseback. They were discussing strategy. Jimmy and Joe were up. The Grants headed over as well. Corinne sat on her stool and sobbed. Her mind played a terrible game of "what-kind-of-catastrophe has happened to her friend."

Chelsea was at Corinne's side, stroking her back and trying to calm her. After a few minutes, Corinne was calm but wore her grief on her face. She overheard one of the men asking, 'What would make a young girl go out on such a dark, moonless night?' Corinne turned to see all the men looking to Andrew for answers.

He smiled, and said, "Girls do many silly things, don't they?"

Blood pounded in Corinne's ears. She reacted like a cat and was in his face within moments. She tried to smack him, but he had that gift that all boys have of holding a girl's hands prisoner.

"You sent her out to kill her! You sent her!" Corinne yelled and sobbed. "You don't care for anyone! You don't care if SHE DIES!" Chelsea and her husband were standing behind Corinne trying to calm her. She continued to rail at Andrew.

"I begged you, Andrew! I said it was dark. Reggie begged you!" Corinne got her hand free. She smacked Andrew across the cheek. He responded quickly by pulling back a free hand of his own. It never found its mark. Clive was there and had a firm hold, stopping any violence or abuse. Russell and Lucas pulled Corinne away as she was muttering.

"She is just a sweet girl and you hated her. *Just like you hate me, too.*" Corinne cried again as Russell carried her away. Chelsea followed behind.

Chelsea glanced back at Andrew and made eye contact. Andrew's look was smug. He still thought he had won. Chelsea realized how dangerous that man could be.

Lucas and Clive packed lanterns and extra blankets and got on their mounts. They joined the party of men that was quickly forming. A plan formed, they rode out a few minutes later.

It was two hours of waiting. Corinne sat with Chelsea and sipped some tea. It helped to stop her from crying, but fear was still hanging over her. She knew in her heart it was bad. Her thoughts were choppy and cut short. She didn't even have words for prayer. Angela was like a sister to her. Now she was in danger. Corinne focused on breathing slowly and keeping her mind quiet. It was all she could do.

In the distance, there were gunshots. Corinne perked up at the sound, but without knowing the reason for them she had to calm her heart. It was an eternity later when she heard horses coming closer. The whole search group was there. One of the scouts was carrying a large lump covered in a blanket. Lucas rode up to Corinne to prepare her.

"She is hurt pretty bad, Cori," Lucas said, using the nickname he had heard Chelsea use. Corinne felt lost for a moment, then gathered herself together. She started telling people what she needed. They pulled out a sleeping mat near the fire. They laid her out gently. Her eyes were closed and she moaned when she was moved. Corinne removed the blanket and saw the damage.

Angela's face was covered with dirt and blood. She held her left arm close against her chest. Her torn dress revealed a deep gash, several inches long, from Angela's arm connecting up to her shoulder. Corinne peeked at the rest of her. Angela's ankle was swollen three times its normal size and she was missing a shoe on the other foot. Nearly every part of her was scratched and bruised. Chelsea and Corinne chased the men away. They began to painstakingly undress and wash Angela's wounds. Angela was awake through the entire process but didn't respond well to questions. It was as if she had gone into a safe, quiet place within herself and only came out when the pain forced her to. Chelsea pointed out a terrible bruise forming on Angela's left thigh. Corinne assumed she had fallen and a rock was the culprit. Corinne washed and bandaged the gaping wound on Angela's shoulder with Grandma Trudie's recipe to fight infection. Chelsea and Corinne prayed and cried as they went about their work. After all the wounds were bandaged, Angela got dressed in a very loose gown. Corinne got her own brush and began to brush Angela's hair. That simple gesture brought Angela out of her stupor. She began to weep. Chelsea and Corinne held her lovingly and they all shared some tears. Words weren't necessary.

Chapter Seventeen
May 3, 1848

After one day of rest, the train moved forward. Corinne rode with Angela and cared for her tenderly.

Andrew tried to talk to Corinne about the inappropriateness of the situation, but the glare he received from Corinne silenced him, for once. For the majority of the day, he and the scouts stayed away from the wagon outfit. No one respected him after the incident. His crew still obeyed his orders, but the glances from his men spoke volumes about how lacking they found his leadership abilities.

Angela was miserable. Every jostle of the wagon, every necessary move she made, was pure agony. After careful examination, Corinne was certain Angela's arm was broken, ankle severely sprained or broken, and leg had a deep tissue bruise. The gash on her shoulder was red and raw around the edges. Corinne seriously feared that infection was setting in. Chelsea and Corinne made the painful decision that the wound would have to be cleaned out again thoroughly. After fifteen miles bouncing around in a wagon box, Angela mentally prepared herself for a wound bath.

Clive brought a bottle of whiskey. With her permission, Clive joined the women for the scrubbing procedure. After a medicinal dose of whiskey, Angela shed a few tears. Then she gave them the sign to move ahead. Angela laid on her stomach. She held Clive's hand for the next twenty minutes. The soaking and scrubbing revealed a few thorns and dirt pieces were still present in the wound. Clive proclaimed over and over how brave she was. Angela concentrated hard, trying not to scream. She held her breath a little too long and got dizzy, nearly passing out a few times.

Corinne and Chelsea worked well together and kept their composure most of the time. At one point, Corinne silently sobbed, holding her mouth, to keep Angela from hearing her. She knew what she had to do but hated doing it. Corinne recalled her own mother being worn out from taking care of someone. Corinne overwhelmingly longed for her mother's presence. She didn't want to be this person, causing her friend such horrific pain. Yet she knew she had to be strong. She had the ability. She would get it over with, to help Angela survive.

Corinne applied a clean bandage and tied Angela's nightgown back into place. She looked pale and worn out. Corinne forced her to drink some water. She tucked Angela into her own bed. The worn-out women joined Clive outside the tent.

"I never want to do that again in my life," Clive said, seriously. Corinne smiled at him weakly. Next to her, Chelsea lost composure and began to weep uncontrollably. Corinne was crying too, but suddenly the emotional toll overwhelmed her. She ran to the nearest bush and gave up her dinner. It wasn't about the blood or touching the wound, but simply the pain she had caused someone. It was brutal, but necessary. With every part of her being, Corinne wished there was a way to numb the pain.

Cookie created a hearty dinner for everyone of fried fish and potatoes. Corinne pushed her food around for a while, then hunger kicked in and she ate her meal. Russell and Lucas kept the conversation light. That suited everyone. Lucas was a good storyteller when he wanted to be. Brody sat on the ground and played a made-up game with rocks in the dirt. His little comments he made to no one at all, greatly amused everyone.

The wagon boss came by to remind them that tomorrow they would reach the fort. "Have your supply lists ready tonight, if possible." Since Andrew was gone with the scouts, Cookie gave his list to Corinne.

Angela woke up an hour after they had eaten and needed help. Her body was getting weak from the struggle. She took care of her body's basic needs and then gratefully went back to sleep.

Everyone was very excited the next morning. The rains and the mud did little to dampen their spirits. Fort Kearney was near, and despite the mud, they quickly traveled the few miles . Andrew got the list from Corinne, and with the other men, headed toward the buildings. The women took this opportunity to clean out the wagons, and then socialize. Corinne stayed with Angela and read her a book from out of her trunk. Angela's fever was low, but her bruises and broken bones etched pain across her face. Corinne was at a loss as how to help her.

◆•◦•◆◦▬▬◆▬▬◦◆•◦•◆

Andrew and his crew came back with provisions and instructions. "Corinne, I need you to gather Angela's things. We are going to be moving out in the morning. We need Angela to be ready tonight." Andrew tapped on the side of the wagon as his cue to hurry up.

Corinne jumped out and instantly lashed out at him. "Just what are you talking about? Why do I need to pack for Angie?" Fear of his next statement showed on her face. She knew the words he was about to say, even before he spoke.

"We are leaving her here. Before you get yourself all tied up in knots and hit me again, I have found someone here to care for her. Angela is too injured to continue. We would take her with us if there were no other choice, but there is. The Captain's wife is more than willing to help Angela recover. I have paid her handsomely to care for Angela. They have a comfortable home with an extra room for her. Does that satisfy you, **wife**?" He said everything nicely except *wife*. He was still harboring mixed feelings about their relationship since Angela got hurt because his unwise decision.

Corinne knew he was right about Angela's chances on the trail though. Injury on the trail was very dangerous. Unclean conditions and the jostling of the wagon could finish a person if they weren't cautious. "I will make sure she is ready to go. I hope you understand I will have to assume some of her duties, unless of course *you* want to do the laundry scrubbing?" Corinne knew she shouldn't talk to him like that, but she felt a little bold just then. She was losing her dearest friend. He was likely going to gloat for days.

"I will back down on my rules for now. Just don't take advantage, child. I am not the monster you think I am. Maybe I just know best about how to behave." Andrew turned away and left. How did he always manage to say the thing that would infuriate her the most? She peeked in on Angela. She rewarded Corinne with a weak smile.

"I will recover my dear Cori. I will stay here to heal and will see you next year, in the fall." Angela was earnestly looking forward to a bed that didn't shake, and a comfortable roof over her head. If Angela could accept this fate, then Corinne knew that she should, too. Her heart was so very broken though. Her inner most deep part knew that God had found a way to save Angela's life. He was watching out for her. They packed up all of Angela's things. Corinne and Angela took turns wiping away tears, as the minutes ticked by.

Reggie, Jimmy, and Joe made a makeshift bed for Angela, then began the trip to town. The rain stopped. That made the trip quick and comfortable. They were so very careful with her. Corinne thanked them so many times.

Andrew was right about the Captain's wife. Her name was Edith and she was a pleasant soul. Corinne was taken with her instantly and this mothering creature embraced her several times that night. Corinne enjoyed the mothering more than a little. Edith and Corinne tucked Angela into a soft bed. She had all the amenities of a lovely home on the prairie. Captain Henry Sparks was a fun-loving guy, with a gigantic mustache and smile to match. Corinne stayed the evening, enjoying the stories and practical jokes. Angela would have a pleasant stay. Corinne made sure they had enough money for a year's worth of room and board, for her dear friend. Edith pushed away any attempts Corinne made to offer more money. She did accept a bottle of lavender oil, for she knew its benefits. Edith declared she would treasure it. Corinne made a mental note to write down Edith's name in her journal. Someday she would send more lavender to her. Corinne fussed and patted Angela, eventually saying her tearful goodbyes. Angela shed a few tears of her own. She promised to write letters and send them by the pony express that had just come to the fort.

As Corinne was leaving, Clive and Chelsea came by with presents for Angela. Reggie, Cookie, and the Blake boys left parting gifts for her, too. Corinne walked back to the wagon alone to deal with her emotions. So much had changed since the day she left Boston. She had learned so much.

She wondered how much further they had to go. This was just the beginning. The Great Plains were ahead. Many miles, many dangers. She spent some time that night praying for strength for herself and healing for her friend.

Chapter Eighteen
May 10, 1848

For several days, the wagon train traveled alongside the Platte River. Fort Kearney gave everyone a second wind. The warm weather spread the scent of spring. The fresh growth was inspirational. The beginnings of spring flowers popped up their heads through the landscape. A few rain showers made the land green with tall grass. Clumps of trees displayed buds and young leaves. Several times a day, the wagons stopped to clear rocks or saplings out of the way. Mostly, the wagons rolled along, spread out across the wide flat expanse that was in front of them.

The routine of the trail had become second nature to the travelers. Early mornings, they packed up quickly, then on they rolled. They stopped for a biscuit and some cheese for lunch, then moved out again. Evenings were the only time to get things done. Washing, cleaning and a large dinner. Animals tended to and chores finished. People bathed in nearby creeks when one was available. They enjoyed being clean, for the brief time it lasted.

Corinne was quiet for a few days after Fort Kearney, but then started coming out of her shell again. She enjoyed helping Cookie with meals, and doing the laundry with Chelsea at the creek. They had just completed an easy river crossing. The evening was perfect. The sky was pink, and Chelsea and Corinne enjoyed the view while planning the future.

"So, Corinne, I know you aren't happily married," Chelsea said uneasily. She made a grimace then continued. "So, what do you want to do once you reach Oregon? I know you love plants. Will you start your own farm?" Corinne laughed at her friend's comedic way of making her marriage seem less tragic.

"I hope so. I know my Father bought some farmland for his ranch. I don't know what will happen when we arrive, and I get an annulment. Andrew seems pretty eager. He may beat me to it!" She laughed, imagining the foot race to town.

"Well, I can see your love for plants and medicine. I picture you doing amazing things, my friend." Chelsea's warm smile was very sincere.

"I do have a dream of making my own medicinal oils. I hope to start with lavender." Her eyes went a little far away. She blushed and grew silent for a moment. "I am not sure if I will ever be brave enough to tell my father or any other man about it, though. What man would understand a business plan based on flowers? There are few men in the world that truly would even comprehend what I want to do." Corinne continued to scrub the clothes, embarrassed a little for sharing a glimpse of her dream.

"Well, the right man will come along. He will see your dream and help you to fulfill it," Chelsea said thoughtfully.

"From your lips to God's ears." Corinne grinned but realized, seriously, that those kinds of men were rare. Corinne wasn't sure if she had Chelsea's luck for finding and keeping one of the good ones.

"Chelsea..." Corinne decided to get bold after a few minutes of silence. "Will you pray for me?" Corinne felt a tear slip out, as she grew silent. Suddenly, she was overwhelmed with her situation.

"Oh, sweet Corinne. God and I have talks about you every day." Chelsea gave her a squeeze. They returned to their work, grinning that bittersweet way women did, when the heart was left a bit raw.

Corinne felt lucky for their growing friendship. They continued their duties and got back to scrubbing shirts. Lucas and Russell came by after their chores and brought stools. The men were worn out but wanted the company of the ladies. Russell kissed his wife so soundly when he sat next to her, Corinne blushed and turned away. Unfortunately, she met Lucas's gaze with her own, and felt even more embarrassed. They both laughed nervously, and awkwardly searched for something else to do.

"Sorry Corinne, I guess my husband missed me," Chelsea chuckled warmly. Corinne rolled her eyes dramatically.

"Well, Andrew and I will be sure to shock you later with our own affection." Corinne enjoyed everyone's laughter. They all had trouble imagining Corinne and Andrew in anything but a wrestling match. Corinne felt like herself around the Grant family, magically wishing to be a part of it. Chelsea would be a great sister. Corinne tried to distract herself from her own wishes by trying to focus on others.

"Lucas… is your fiancé, Sarah Ballentine, coming next year to meet you? I am quite surprised you didn't marry her first and drag her along. A wagon train honeymoon has been wonderful for me." Corinne smiled and watched a strange play of emotions cross his face. Lucas and Russell were both dark haired, tall, and practically identical, but Lucas was usually always smiling. It was strange to see him otherwise.

"Well, to be honest, I had asked her to marry me two years ago. She knew our plans for coming west but continued to put off the date. She eventually promised she would join me after I got settled in Oregon." Lucas tried to make light of the fact that she was delaying the marriage, but they could all feel his thoughts. He was starting to doubt. "I have had lots of time to think. I don't think I'll ever see her again. Somehow, I expect to hear she's too afraid of the unknown west." Lucas grinned again, in a sad lopsided way. He shrugged, "I'm just a farmer after all. Her father is a rich man with land and lots of horses. I can't expect any girl to give that up for a small house and a few acres of farm land."

Corinne kept her hands busy as she listened to Lucas. She knew the kind of girl that Sarah Ballentine was. Corinne had been just like her before her father left for the west three years ago. Corinne was fourteen and spoiled, wanting to be a child for just a while longer. Her father was lonely and desperate for a change after his wife died. He was still young and wanted to be just like Lucas was now, free, and on his own life path. Corinne could see how her father had been so disappointed. To share your dream with someone was difficult. Then to have it spit back at you in disgust must have been heart breaking.

Corinne said her goodbyes. She grabbed her tub full of clean laundry and headed back. Lucas volunteered to bring back her washboard and water bucket, so she didn't have to make a second trip. She nodded and quickly walked away. There was something about Lucas lately that made her very happy. And uncomfortable at the same time.

Later that evening, the Grants invited the Temple crew to dine with them again. Cookie was happy to get time off. He used this free time to clean out his small stove. It was always giving him fits when ash clogged in there.

Andrew sent word that he was going to be gone for several days on a scouting trip. Everyone breathed a little easier. Corinne walked into the Grant camp. She smiled at the scent of pipe tobacco drifting toward her. Its warm woodsy aroma made her feel welcome and homey. Leaning against a tall sapling, Clive watched little Brody play with a small-carved horse. Clive leisurely puffed on the pipe and seemed quite pleased with himself.

"That smell is heavenly, Clive. I didn't know you smoked." Corinne had a bit of a bounce in her step today. She joined him next to the sapling, after saying a quick hello to Chelsea and Russell.

"Well, I don't actually smoke verra often, but every third full moon or so I get a hankerin.' I don't like thinking I have to have it, but I do like the warm way it settles me." He smiled and took another puff.

Corinne laughed. She sat with Clive for a few minutes until she felt the urge to get up and stretch the tightness out of her arms. She was still getting accustomed to doing chores. She knew her arms and hands would take a while to adjust to the increased labor. She welcomed it. It was her proof of serving. She was no longer a child and was now sharing in the burden.

<hr>

Dinner that evening was hearty, and the company was excellent. Outside the camp there were some hoots and hollers. They soon discovered they had company. Some native women and children arrived outside the wagon train. They had brought wares to trade. Several groups came near the Grant camp and everyone made them feel welcome. Clive jumped up, used some simple hand gestures and a few words that Corinne didn't understand. He told Chelsea to serve up some extra dishes.

Corinne told Cookie to go get some leftover biscuits and a small pouch of coffee beans for trading. She had a few flannel shirts she bought, just for this type of moment. She went to her wagon quickly and got a small bottle of lavender to amaze the native women. As she got back to the Grant camp, the women were eating happily. A lively trading session was taking place. Clive was the interpreter. He was doing an excellent job of keeping the situation upbeat and fun. Corinne got a few beaded necklaces in trade for the two shirts she brought. They traded a few fresh fish for the biscuits and cheese. The biggest thrill was when Corinne approached the women with her lavender oil. She opened the vial and lifted it to her own nose, then put it closer to them. They all sniffed, smiled, and began talking fast in their own language. Corinne took put a dot of oil on her own finger then touched it to the side of her neck. She then put another dot on her finger and held it out for one of them. The youngest girl came first and got the sweet floral scent put on her neck. After that, the girl giggled and showed off her new scent to her friends. Many of the women and children requested to be 'perfumed' by Corinne. The trading and visiting had gone delightfully well. The native visitors left with many good trades and full bellies.

Everyone in the wagon train felt charged up and a gathering was inevitable. A few musicians got their instruments out and began warming up. Jimmy and Joe announced they wanted to sing, and with a flourish, they started singing a spiritual hymn. That made everyone feel grand. The Temple's ox handlers had a way of singing that put everyone in a happy mood. A few more camps moved in and the music got lively. Corinne went to her bed that night having lived a grand day.

Corinne woke up with a start. For a moment, the sky was bright. Then a crack of thunder shook the earth. She drew a shaky breath and tried to clear the cobwebs out of her sleeping brain. It was obvious, there was a storm coming. So far, they had avoided any storms nearby. The wagon canopy again lit up as bright as morning. Within two-seconds, the boom of thunder nearly shook Corinne out of her skin. Thirty-seconds later the rain started its torrent. She could hear it hitting the semi-dry ground with slapping sounds. She crawled back to the flap and peeked her head through. Lightning lit up the sky. Corinne could see the fat raindrops coming at a slant, driving into the ground with determination. The wind was picking up speed. For a brief moment, Corinne wanted to cry out, but another boom of thunder shook her powerfully. She lit her nearby lantern and decided to put on a comfortable dress. If the wind got any stronger she might have to retreat under the wagon.

The storm raged on through the night. Corinne had time to consider that this could happen every day. The cold, driving rain and the unmerciful lightning had its own life and agenda. She felt like such a tiny speck, alone in the middle of the wilderness. She started believing that they were at the mercy of the elements. She kept calm as the hours crept by. She leaned on a trunk and blew out the lantern. She fell back to sleep several times during that long miserable night, but the thunder always had a way of getting her attention.

The camp was up early. Along with everyone else, Corinne dragged up her weary self. The rain had turned their camp into mud. The creek nearby was swollen and appeared larger than it had been earlier. The area was pretty flat, and the water had few places to go. It formed puddles everywhere. By the time she finished her breakfast and took the necessary walk with her women friends, Corinne's boots were wet and cold throughout. The rain had stopped, but the clouds were a dreary gray that blocked out nearly all sunlight. By eight a.m., the wagons started rolling, but several had major problems immediately. At the front, there were two wagons with one or more wheels stuck in the mud. A few oxen were having trouble pulling the wagons through the muck and rocky terrain. The day was not starting well.

Corinne was riding Clover when she heard a loud crack nearby, followed by Jimmy Blake shouting . Corinne rode over and saw that her wagon was leaning haphazardly to the left. She saw the culprit a minute later. A broken wagon wheel was on the ground. The remaining front wheel looked like it was hanging on to nothing. Jimmy and Joe unhitched the animals, getting them safely out of the way of other traveling wagons. Then, they used all their strength and muscle, along with the help of a few wagon jacks, and put the wagon back to its proper angle. Andrew's wagon had the spare wagon parts. After a short while of jostling things around, they found the tools and parts needed to make the necessary repairs. Corinne rode ahead slowly through the muddy path to find the Grants and warn them that they would be behind today. She found them having their own set of mud caused troubles. Russell explained that the terrain didn't handle the water very well. It waterlogged quickly when the rain came, so much so fast. Corinne observed that the area was getting sparse of trees, so there was no way of using the ropes and pulley systems for getting out of the mud. Just men and brute strength. She appreciated how resourceful all these men were.

For several hours, the Temple outfit grunted in the mud, wrestled with the wheels and finally hooked the oxen team back up. The movement was slow and labored. The fear of getting stuck in ruts made by other wagons, was a real one. The land laid out pretty flat, and reached far in both directions. The ground was a mess of mud pits and animal's tracks. Corinne felt bad for the mess they were leaving in their wake. The Temple outfit rolled up, joining the other wagons around eight o' clock that night. Everyone was exhausted and did their duties quickly. Cookie made coffee and biscuits. Everyone ate silently and crept into their beds.

The next day, when the whole train were drinking their coffees and sitting around their fires, the dogs started making a racket. Everyone's gaze was soon drawn to the South where twenty natives were outside the camp on horseback. Their faces were impassive. They seemed calm, but the outlandish stories newspapers back home painted about Indian scalping parties, made the wagon train occupants a bit wary of surprise visits from the native men. Clive quickly mounted up and headed over in a peaceful zigzag fashion. Everyone watched excitedly to see what would happen next. There were several gestures. If Corinne focused hard, she could hear them grunting in their own way of communicating. Clive rode back with three of the men. Corinne watched in startled fascination as they headed closer to her outfit. She nearly gagged on a sip of coffee as it registered that they really were heading for her! She bolted up from her stool and with eyes as big as her coffee mug, she gazed up at Clive.

"They came to talk to the medicine woman." He had such a proud grin, his face would surely crack open.

"Medicine woman? That is funny Clive! What can they want with me?" Corinne wondered if her bit of fun with the native women had offended anyone. Her heart was pounding a quick step in her chest.

"They want to trade you many goods for the bottle of medicine you showed the women." Clive gestured to the men and they all dismounted. Corinne was very embarrassed at their near naked state. Clothed only in their simple loincloths, the warm weather was certainly no problem for them. They pulled goods down from their horses and began displaying what they had to offer her. Corinne blinked and explained to Clive she would be a moment. She walked over to her wagon and grabbed her small pouch hanging just inside. In it was the bottle she used the other day, to show the women her lavender oil,

She had many bottles packed in her things and would not miss just one, though the oil was expensive and precious. She made this batch while volunteering at the Boston Greenhouse. The small lab there taught her everything she needed to know. It had been thrilling to learn. The fact that these native men were excited about something she helped create, was even more thrilling. Her goal was to make more oil, if she could convince her father of her plan. She ran back to the group that had gathered, her heart thumping happily within her. Being appreciated was a boon to her wounded ego.

She showed the native men the bottle. She then opened the stopper and they all sniffed noisily, excited to see it. She closed the bottle and handed it to Clive. She nodded to him then to the men. They communicated happily with Clive. She trusted him entirely to do a 'good trade' as she had heard a few Indians say in a stunted accent. The leader of the pack settled on some sort of agreement and Clive handed the bottle over to him. The man spoke directly to Corinne, looking into her eyes with his own dark ones. He clasped his hand over the bottle and gestured over his heart then to his head. He glanced back to the man behind him. With a necklace held forward, the second native approached Corinne. She responded by leaning forward as he placed it around her neck. She smiled and admired at the artistry of the necklace.

It appeared to be bear and wolf claws surrounded by beads, and a few dark blue stones. She looked up to see the first native carrying fur to her. She opened her arms and they deposited a heavy pile of fur. She knew the worth of fur and wanted to protest. She looked to Clive. He told her to accept them. A minute later, Lucas was behind her taking them off her hands, as they came forward with other gifts. They presented a small bead covered pouch which had a long leather handle on it. They placed it over her shoulder. The beadwork was so elegant. It nearly made her cry. They also held the last gift tenderly. It was a hollow leather bag with no ornamentation. She knew they used empty bladders as canteens. They opened it and inside was a white paste. They spoke to her again and Clive translated.

"They said you make good medicine for the heart and the head. They say you gathered the flower of many good medicines in that bottle. They respect what you offer and give you a token of that respect. This necklace proves you have found great honor in their sight. The pelts are to pay you. The beaded bag is for you to gather more. The last is their own medicine to share with you. They say it will drive the stomach demons away." Clive chuckled as he finished, greatly amused by the gasps of the wagon train population behind them.

Corinne accepted the lavish praise by blushing and bowing to them out of respect. They mounted up and left a minute later. The 'good trade' was over.

Within a moment, she had a crowd around her. Chelsea reached through to give her a big hug and get the first look at the necklace and gathering pouch. The crowd was amazed. It seemed like breakfast had been forgotten, because of the medicine woman in their midst. Corinne said 'it's silly' whenever anyone called her that. She was secretly thrilled though, her Grandmother Trudie would have been so proud.

The Grant family joined her by her wagon. She wanted to get a closer look at the pile of fur that Lucas held for her. They were astounded to first see a large wolf pelt, then a stunning shining black mink, and wrapped inside were five snowy white rabbit pelts. The women gushed over the softness. The men commented on the quality and worth of such handsome specimens.

"I have a few things I can do with those rabbit pelts for you my dear girl. If you trust, me I think I can make you something of a keepsake." She handed them over gladly, slightly excited and curious to see what her dear Clive would come up with. Lucas and Clive then procured a rubber tarp. Then with some thin rope, they secured the furs within the tarp. And, did it in a way they said would be nearly catastrophe proof.

She grinned at Chelsea, who felt like her, about the men's need to tie things up, and then explain to the women why they did it. Men were just as silly as women sometimes. She gave Clive a kiss on the cheek and thanked Lucas warmly for the help. They both seemed to gush over her praise. Chelsea and Corinne both wondered out loud, about the strange way the men reacted to the Indians' gifts to Corinne. The men were treating Corinne with such awe. It nearly made them giggle. "Well, that was an interesting way to start the morning," mused Chelsea. They both laughed.

Getting the respect of men was a hard-earned battle for any woman. They figured the respect would fade quickly as new adventures unfolded.

Chapter Nineteen
May 25, 1848

The muddy plains became the dry plains as they traveled near the Platte River. The river would soon branch off and a hard crossing was due in a few days. After a week with no rain everyone tired of the dry weather. They were longing for some fresh water.

For days, Corinne had seen the bottom of their water barrel. The water they got from the nearby Platte was muddy and had to be strained. She used a handkerchief to strain the water, over and over. Still, it had that strange metallic taste. She often had Cookie boil it. Sometimes, its sour taste turned everyone's stomach.

The land stretched out. The wagons had little trouble getting fifteen to twenty miles per day but caring for the animals was becoming harder and harder. The heat and lack of water was starting to get to them. Animals were dying nearly every day.

The scouts came back after a week of travel, exclaiming the good news of the Southern Platte crossing. There was a rumor that fresh water was on the other side. With the scouts came Andrew looking pale and grumpy.

Corinne hadn't seen her husband in a week. She tried to be polite when he strolled into camp looking filthy and grumpy. He was covered in trail dust and his pallor had taken on a sick yellowish tone.

"Andrew, you look worn out. Have a seat. I'll get you something to eat." She watched him slowly walk over to the stool, then slumped his body down to a sitting position.

"Thanks Corinne," he said softly and politely. Corinne and Cookie gave each other a shared look of shock. Had he ever spoken politely or called Corinne by her name? Corinne thought for a moment, admitting she was pretty certain he never had.

She grabbed a rag and dipped it in the bucket of brackish gray water used for washing dishes. She walked over and without a single pause, wiped the trail dust off her husband's face. He didn't 'shoo' her away, so she took a chance and felt his forehead with the back of her hand. He was warm, but not terribly so. Perhaps, he was just overheated.

The evening meal was fried fish and boiled peas. The peas didn't taste very good after being boiled in the questionable water, but they had to be eaten. Andrew pushed the food around his plate, only eating when prompted. Corinne was certain he needed a good sleep and would be feeling better by morning. She knew how men could get on the trail. The scouts often skimped out on sleep.

Within an hour, Andrew was retching behind the wagon. He had gone to lie down, but was up and pacing within minutes. Corinne had a small supply of drinkable water. She filled a canteen and let him drink from it, after he finished being sick. Andrew was sitting on the ground by the fire when he began to vomit again. After he finished, Corinne felt his forehead again. He was now hot to the touch. Within a brief moment, what had started as a slight concern in Corinne's mind, jumped straight to fear. She would not say it or even think it out loud yet. It could not be...

"I need to get out of these clothes. Please help me." Andrew's ragged voice sounded feeble. He moaned as he walked. His one hand gripped over his torso, in a universal gesture of stomach cramps. Corinne helped Reggie get Andrew into the tent. Corinne left them to go get a few things from her wagon. Clive was waiting there for her. The look on his face was grave. She knew before he even spoke. The worst of their secret fears was coming true.

"The scouts are all sick, my dear girl. We can hear Andrew being sick, so I rode around to see if any of the rest of them are feelin' poorly. It's not good." Clive took off his leather hat and ran his fingers through his thick hair. It was peppered with a few stubborn dark strands that were clinging to their color. "Ralph Hammond said they all drank together from a small divot they found yesterday. It wasn't very fresh tasting and they all woke up this morning with stomach cramps. They didn't think anything of it then." Clive looked her in the eye and said what he really meant to say this whole time. "Girl, I think you know what to do. If he can't hold down water or food by tomorrow, you need to get rid of everything he touches. Burn it, bury it, whatever needs to be done. I've seen what happens, child. I will pray with the last of my breath that this isn't what I'm thinkin' it is."

Corinne nodded, reached out and squeezed his hand. She had no words. She just wanted to care for Andrew, watch him improve by morning, and be his grumpy self again.

Clive headed over to Andrew's tent to help in whatever way he could. Corinne saw Reggie and Clive holding up Andrew. They were walking toward the shallow Platte River nearby.

"Perhaps just cooling him off will give him some relief," someone said. Corinne recruited Cookie to get two shovels from Andrew's wagon while she threw the dishwater into a large empty pot to boil. His dishes would need to be boiled clean. Corinne put the pot over the fire and then joined Cookie behind the wagon. They dug through the dry earth to clean and cover up where Andrew had taken ill. They did the same by the fire. As they worked, Cookie wore the same look of fear on his face. Cookie's fear was worse though. His fear was one of experience. He had seen this before. The rice-like chunks he just shoveled over, was the final clue. Cholera was in their midst.

Andrew returned with the help of Reggie and Clive. Corinne was waiting, with a fresh mug of peppermint tea in hand. Sitting on a stool by his tent, about twenty feet away from the wagons, Andrew started sipping his tea. He was bare-chested, and his hair and skin were still wet. After a few minutes of sipping, he declared the tea to be good.

"You all can go about your business and stop your staring." Andrew smiled weakly and sent them all away. Corinne silently communicated a concerned look to Reggie. He understood and nodded. He would not be far from Andrew's side, not even for a minute.

That night, they all went to sleep reluctantly. Andrew kept the tent for himself. Reggie pitched a spare tent nearby. They were all awake within a few hours, as Andrews's illness grew worse. Corinne heard mumbling, gasps, and cries throughout the wagon train that night, but she barely acknowledged them. The Temple outfit was having its own tragedy as Andrew became more ill.

At one point, past one a.m., everyone was in fear and desperation to keep Andrew from vomiting up any more water. Corinne dug through her 'medicine' bag and found the mysterious Indian pouch. They claimed it chased away stomach demons. She could not think of anything more demonic than what she had seen that night. Andrew was barely recognizable and weaker than a newborn. Corinne dipped her finger into the white paste and brought it up to her nose. She flinched at the horrible stench of it. It reeked like rancid animal fat and something oddly sweet. Maybe licorice root or something like it. She tasted it and realized it wasn't as bad as she had thought. She got a spoon from the chuck wagon and headed over to Andrew.

He looked gray and was almost unconscious. He had been in and out for nearly an hour but seemed to stay awake a little more. Corinne got a spoonful of the paste and told him to eat it. He pushed it away and refused.

"Andrew, I will not sit by and watch you waste away without trying everything." Corinne tried to shove down her fear, but it came out in her ragged voice. She glanced at Reggie and Cookie who nodded with her as they held him. She shoved the spoon into his mouth as he fought half-heartedly. She watched him swallow and gag, but he kept it down.

"I tried it myself Andrew, it is from the Indians. Maybe it will chase away your stomach demons." Corinne's voice had a desperate tone in it. Who could blame her? She had tried to sound cheerful, but it didn't work. As the night wore on, she realized the paste had done very little. Andrew's cries of agony grew louder. The smell of the horrible things the illness was doing to him escaped out the tent and surrounded the camp. Similar problems were unfolding that night in other camps. An ominous plague had crept its way through the waterholes and into the few unlucky souls that had had a thirst for something deadly.

———◆•◉•◆———◆•◉•◆———

The fire burned hot against Corinne's face. It was midday, but the bright blue sky hadn't reached into Corinne's heart. She watched the last remnants of Andrew Temple's clothes burn. Anything he wore just recently. Corinne went through the motions and seemed to know what to do. They all did. Cookie had made brackish coffee. Reggie had cleaned the mess that had been Andrew's tent. They all had bathed heavily down at the Platte River.

They were going to bury Andrew as soon as Russell and Lucas came back from digging the graves. In total, there were four dead this morning. One of the scouts lived but was barely holding on.

Reggie had haunting dark circles around his eyes. He had thrown up this morning, and for about an hour, they all feared the worst. But Corinne was now certain, Reggie had done some nasty cleanup that caused his stomach to turn. Corinne was truly surprised all of them hadn't taken ill. Corinne had seen so many horrifying things just last night. She watched a man go from healthy to dead, in one night. She had heard stories about the unmerciful horror that Cholera brought on its victims, but she never expected it to be so violent and terrifying. At one point in the night, Andrew looked so wretched that Corinne wept as she held his hand.

His words made her cry all the harder."You are a good girl Corinne. No matter what I said. You are a good girl."

He then curled into a ball of pain and moaned for nearly an hour. Corinne was certain he would die soon but he lingered, rallying as they got him to drink. Only to watch in sadness, as it escaped him. He lived on the chamber pot for most of the night. His face and skin so pale, his body would collapse. They would cool him down and clean him up, like a sick child. He was not embarrassed by his nakedness or that others were cleaning him. They all knew it would be over soon. The morning came, and Andrew was gasping for air. They sat with him as he faded slowly. After a while, he was gone.

The cleanup was just about done. All that remained were the ashes in the fire. Andrew and the other men's bodies were wrapped tightly and brought to the outskirts of the camp, where the Grant men and a few others were digging graves.

The burial was quick but meaningful. The wagon boss spoke a few bible verses and the Blake brothers sang a hymn. Corinne and her tired crew gathered around the graves for a few minutes, after the crowds dispersed. The wagon boss asked them if they would be okay to move out in a bit. Corinne nodded and said what they all are thinking.

"Let's leave this place," Corinne said flatly, and turned to walk away. They followed her silently.

Part Two:

Chapter Twenty
May 26, 1848

They all used what reserve strength they had to prepare the wagons and douse the fire. The wagon train as a group had decided to continue until they reached the crossing. They all would be traveling through the night.

"If you need to rest Corinne, just climb in your wagon, no one will think badly of ya for it." Clive joined her after the train started rolling. His eyes held concern, but he saw her inner strength when she looked straight at him.

In his mind, he relived the recent events. He never liked Andrew, but no one should die like that. Clive had been there for part of the night, getting them what they needed. Watching the life drain out of a man left a mark on anyone who saw it.

Corinne didn't have the energy or mood to smile at Clive, but she nodded that she heard him. Her body felt tired but energized, a strange unreal strength. She was certain it would wear off eventually, but in the meantime, she would have to suffer through it. Her mind was swirling because of everything it had seen and the new reality she faced. She was a widow!

She faced a long road with only herself to take charge. She felt lucky to have her friendship with the Grants, but she knew she didn't want to lean too heavily upon them. They had their own journey to make. She knew she had much to learn, but somewhere inside her a determination was growing. She would face what lay ahead, with something her Grandmother used to preach about. Grit.

"As a woman, you have to face what the world throws at you. A little grit is just your willingness to do what's hard and get through." Grandma Trudie's words had stuck with Corinne. She looked at her crew. It was a hardy group of men. Jimmy, who walked alongside the oxen directing them, led her wagon. Joe was in the seat, holding the reins lightly, but was there watching for obstacles ahead, and braking when needed. The other wagon was shorter, and the chuck wagon was attached to it. Reggie and Cookie were the ox handlers. Then there was Corinne.

What was her role now? Corinne realized she had to stop her mind, she was over thinking everything. She needed to relax and just breathe for a while. Clive reached over and gave her arm a squeeze. She had an urge to get off her horse, hold up her arms like a child, and see if Clive would hug her like a father would. She knew in a heartbeat he would. That thought gave her comfort, but now was not the time for sympathy. There was a river crossing and fresh water ahead. They would rest when they reached water. She would sleep and if necessary, weep then.

But not now.

The southern split of the Platte River was shallow and easy to cross. It was roughly a mile wide, but the water was no burden to the animals and wagons. The group plowed through the murky waters. They faced a difficult obstacle just within sight of their goal. They had traveled nearly twenty-four hours straight, stopping only for a couple of minutes every few hours, to let the animals rest. They would give the animals water and then charge ahead. There was a valley ahead called 'Ash Hollow.' That was their haven: fresh water, cold bubbling springs, lush green grass, and shade trees. They had not seen a substantial tree in a few hundred miles. It lay before them like a well-earned treat, but they just had one more obstacle to learn from.

The steep hill down into the hollow was one that made them all take notice. The land had been so flat and colorless that the sight of green made them want to be foolish, but they consulted the wagon boss and measures were taken. They gathered ropes and hook-up chains. One by one, the wagons went over the crest of the hill. Fifty men held the ropes as human brakes. The oxen and mule in front of the wagon were skittish and somewhat unwilling. The ox handlers kept the whips flying and yelled until their voices were hoarse, to keep the oxen moving. The third wagon was crossing smoothly when, at the steepest point of the hill, a mule turned sideways. Twisting the harnesses with a fatal jerk, and the mule began to run. No one could be certain where the mule was headed, but the damage was done. Within moments, the human brakes were powerless, and the chains broke. There were rough sounds of wheels grinding on the dry dirt. The crunch of wood, as pieces splintered away. Animals flipped end-over-end toward a messy death at the bottom. All the animals and the driver were lost. The family watched in despair as their father perished, in a horrific drama that slowly unfolded. Weary men dragged up the ropes and chains, while others performed a hasty burial. The next wagon had to roll out. Corinne watched in silence until her nerves could not bear any more. Her body was shutting down.

Corinne had been standing next to Chelsea and her family near the edge of the hill. She gave Chelsea's arm a tug to tell her she was heading to her wagon for a rest. Suddenly, her vision went fuzzy and everything started sounding far away. She saw Lucas saying something to her, but it wasn't connecting. Her world went dark a moment later.

She awakened to a cool sensation on her face. There was water on her lips and she eagerly tried to drink it. A few drops made it to her scorched throat. It was cool fresh water. Her body responded, and her eyes forced themselves open. Lucas was holding the canteen and Chelsea was sponging her face with a cloth. Corinne drank a few more mouthfuls.

"Did I faint?" Corinne felt stupid for asking. *Of course I had fainted.* She did a mental examination of her limbs. She was not in pain, at least.

"I mean, where am I? Am I down the hill? Is everyone well? No one is hurt?" She sipped more water, feeling a bit woozy again. She tried to sit up, but Lucas gently pushed her back down. He shook his head and smiled that said he was in charge. She closed her eyes for a moment again and then fell asleep.

Corinne awoke a few hours later feeling refreshed. She escaped her wagon to see everyone smiling and enjoying themselves. The men had wet hair and shaved faces. The trail dust had been cleaned away. Chelsea walked over and gave Corinne a warm hug.

"Cori, I do believe you were worn out completely. You got color to your cheeks now. I think you needed the rest." Chelsea pointed to a stool and handed her a plate. The stew and biscuits tasted so good. Corinne helped herself to a second plate. It was heartwarming to hear Chelsea call her 'Cori'. Both her parents called her that, and Angela... She wished so much for her young friend to be there.

"I'm heading out for a walk. I need to stretch my legs and enjoy the green valley we have found." Corinne stood, stretched, and put her plate in the wash water. She found she had a few people shadowing her movements and she smiled. They were going to keep a close eye on her for a while, she supposed.

"The air is so fragrant. There are roses nearby," Corinne said absently. She was thinking about something that gave her immense pleasure.

"Yes, actually many roses and other blooms as well," Chelsea chimed in. She spent the morning enjoying the view. The landscape was surely heaven inspired.

"Oh!" Corinne gasped, as the beauty of the fertile valley also took her aback. No landscaper or gardener could ever plan a more thrilling garden. Its wild tangle was calling to Corinne. If she hadn't had company nearby, she would have certainly lost her composure and shown her excitement like a child. Her face gave away all the joy she felt, and more than one observer saw the natural unhindered passion she felt. It was a very charming and attractive look for her.

"I do hope we stay for a few days. I do want to collect some samples. There is so much to discover." Corinne looked to Clive who stood nearby. He was distracted but answered her look.

"Umm, yes we will be ...will be staying." Clive knew what she wanted and would gladly oblige her. He also saw some men nearby with other intentions. Her girlish exuberance was charming and attractive, but she was alone now, her husband and protector gone.

Andrew had advertised his dislike for the marriage state and the un-kissed state of their union. There were about thirty men on this train that were unmarried. And now, there was one eligible, attractive female who was innocent, talented, and wealthy. Clive felt his hackles raise, when he saw some looks that were directed at his young friend. He was beginning to feel like a protective father again. He had done this with his own daughters, decades ago, and gotten them safely married with no mishaps. He would do it again.

The wagon train spent three days at Ash Hollow. The time was spent repairing wagons, mending clothes, and socializing. Corinne received bags of plants from her young friends and she gathered two bushels of jasmine seedpods for planting. She was determined to find a way to make her own oils and have her own farm somehow. Her daydreams were of lavender and jasmine fields, a grove of sweet almonds, tall pines, and maybe olives, if the climate was pleasant. Somehow, she would find a way.

Corinne enjoyed the freedom of her days as she got her work done and went visiting. The Grants were her favorite friends but soon others were getting to know her. Because of her 'good medicine' with the Indians, her fame throughout the train had made an impression on everyone. She enjoyed talking with people about what she loved. It was good for everyone to know the benefits of plants and their healing properties, even if she shared just a little.

A small wagon train joined up with theirs, on the second day in Ash Hollow. It was a small group consisting of six wagons. They had some bad luck, a fever wiping out more than half the number of their train. The hardy folks left looked as haunted and drained as Corinne was from her ordeal. Her empathy made her bold and Corinne was one of the first to invite a family to her camp for supper. The Grants wanted to help. It became a large affair with makeshift tables of food, and music fit for a barn dance. It reminded Corinne of her church picnic childhood days, where the townsfolk would bring out the best pies, cakes, and fried chicken.

The family that joined them wasn't shy at all. There was a tall woman who seemed to run the outfit. She dressed well that evening in a fine traveling suit. It had enormous puffed sleeves and was a dark ruby color. Corinne thought to herself that the woman looked a milder version of Aunt Rose but was proven wrong when the lady spoke.

"Just call me Ellie Prince. This here is my son, Sidney. My daughter passed away a few years ago, of the scarlet fever." She elbowed her son to get closer. He was tall and had a mild-mannered look to him. "My husband came up thissa ways just two years ago.

He has a successful lumber outfit on tha' Willamette." Ellie Prince spoke boldly.

Corinne and everyone shook Ellie's hand. Sidney shyly approached Corinne for a handshake, too. He had a small sincere smile, and he looked her in the eye. *He seemed to be a nice boy*, Corinne thought.

They got plates full of food for themselves and were enjoying the company of this interesting family. Ellie was bold and a little loud but entertaining, as she shared her history with everyone.

"We recently settled in Michigan." She gave a low whistle. "The tree business there was hopping but the Indian wars were getting fierce. I don't agree with treatin' them as bad as they did there. Them reds there were a peaceful lot that never hurt a fly. They jist got tired of being bumped around by da gov'ment. Go here-go dare. They may has stole a few muskets and made a big show but I fear the militia gonna push 'em all out."

Corinne could not help but agree with Ellie. Ellie had a coarse, no nonsense way of speaking that put Corinne at ease. She was 'good folks', as her Grandma Trudie would say.

"I am anxious to see my man again. After all, it's been two years… I think he will have shacked himself up with a new woman. But for his own safety he better not 'uv. I may have given him two children and may not be the beautiful young thing anymo' but I got some good years left and he better be ready for enjoying the rest of 'em." Ellie's face was animated as she spoke.

Everyone listening laughed at Ellie's stories and felt an instant connection to her. Later they enjoyed music and dancing together. They were all shocked by the clear alto voice she produced, as she sang along with the folk songs. She seemed to be full of surprises.

The next morning the ox handler was sent over from Ellie Prince to see if they could ride near the Temple Party. Corinne gladly agreed and sent the ox handler back with an invitation for them to camp nearby at night. The ride out was a pleasant one through the fertile valley. It pleased Corinne to have so many new friends. The Grants and the Prince's would be living nearby when she reached her new home. She freely breathed the fragrant air and had sweet daydreams of an easy future, surrounded by friends and loved ones.

Chapter Twenty-One
June 4, 1848

"Chelsea, I have heard mention of something lately and want to hear your thoughts on it." Corinne rode Clover and dismounted as she spoke. "Have you heard anything about a nickname 'the Virgin' being passed around?" Corinne felt herself blushing just thinking about it. They had been traveling four days since Ash Hollow. Several times, when Corinne headed to the spring to haul water at night, or when meeting other women to do 'necessary' things, she heard the men whisper things. She understood one phrase said yesterday, 'Virgin Widow.' Though it rang true, Corinne realized the indelicacy of it as a topic of conversation. Especially from strangers, and even worse, because they were males.

"Yes, my dear Cori, I have heard. So has Clive, and he has warned all of us to keep a close watch on you. Lucas punched a cowpoke in the face yesterday for a comment that was made about you." Chelsea looked sad for a moment. "I have prayed about whether or not to tell you or to shield you from this, but honestly, a woman out here needs to be aware of the dangers, *all* of them."

Chelsea walked along, carrying Brody, but he began to fuss. His eyes were red rimmed and droopy. Chelsea took him to the nearby wagon and set him in it. Corinne made sure that Clover was tied securely behind the wagon.

"I do not wish to speak ill of the dead, but your husband did you very few favors to protect you. He had been heard during a few · raucous conversations where he should have remained silent, often speaking of his wish to be free of marriage in general. He talked about how he never touched you, claiming that you would certainly never have agreed to the annulment after you had 'sampled his charms'. There are many single men on this wagon train and you are the only single woman. There will always be men who will be crude about females. I do not understand it but accept it as truth." Chelsea watched Corinne's face go from embarrassment to anger as she listened to Chelsea speak. Chelsea understood Corinne's abhorrence to male crudeness but was at a loss how to help.

"I remember a talk I had with my mother before she died. I was starting to develop, and I had started my monthly flow. She had said something that I never understood until now. She said 'sometimes men are like eager hound dogs on a scent. They act all crazed until they find what they are hunting.' She warned me to be careful how I act around men and not to stir them up. In Boston, I had seen several girls that were daring with their clothes and actions and had gotten themselves into trouble. I do understand what sex is. I was raised on a horse ranch." Corinne made a face and Chelsea could not help but chuckle. "I am not sure if men don't put such a significant importance on the act, that they forget that there is a person they are exposing. I have heard that relations between a man and wife can be amazing and special. My question is, how can talking about a young widow mean anything to these men who, to me, are strangers?" Corinne was wringing her hands as they walked along. "Do I need to be afraid to walk alone?" Corinne suddenly felt very exposed and vulnerable.

"You should be aware of your surroundings. The wagon boss was informed of some of the comments that have been made about your single status. He will talk to the men and make sure it's understood that everyone is to act like gentlemen. Any comments in the future or misconduct will result in swift judgment."

"I am not sure how comfortable I am with all this, but at least, I am surrounded by a few people who care about my safety. Be sure to thank the men for me, if ya think of it. I may be too embarrassed to mention it."

Corinne and Chelsea fell into a companionable silence, as many did on the long trail. Sometimes they would think of something to say, then fall silent again. Corinne was certain she had never had so much time to think and pray in her life.

⸻◆•◉•◆—◆•◉•◆⸻

The buzzing in Corinne's tent was going to test her sanity. She had lavender and lime oil on her person and had hung a rag with the natural bug repellent spotted on it. Still, the buzzing could be heard. Overnight, the bugs had created a cloud that clung to the weary travelers. Despite her attempts, the bugs made it past her repellent. She had a few welts on her ankle where the pests had chewed. Corinne ignored the itchiness, but the sound was her undoing. She finally resorted to placing bits of fabric in her ears to muffle the sound. It worked mildly well. Corinne would not complain and eventually, she fell back asleep.

The morning was hot, and the buzzing continued. The Platte nearby was low, only a few inches deep and looked still. They were back to straining the water for washing. Any clean water left in the barrels was used for drinking. No one wanted a repeat of the Cholera incident. Word passed along the trail from other wagon trains' scouting parties, that Cholera had killed almost a hundred people already this year. And it was only June.

After breakfast, the wagon train rolled out, hoping to outrun the evil swarm of biting flies and mosquitoes. A woman made her way through the maze of wagons, in search of Corinne. She found Corinne beside her own wagon astride Clover.

"My children got into some berries last night. They are hurting somethin' fierce today. Their bellies are rumbling. The berries look like under ripe blackberries. I don't think they are poisonous, but I was wondering if you have any way to ease their bellies."

Corinne grabbed her satchel and followed the woman. After a few doses of marshmallow root, and some water with a few drops of peppermint oil in it, the children were feeling better. She gave all the youngins a healthy lecture about being patient with summer berries, 'that they may look and smell good, but they need to be ripe to eat.'

She started to ride back to her wagon when she saw Lucas on his mount nearby.

"Are you following me Mr. Grant?" Corinne asked with a smile. He was a nice sight to see, even while swatting flies with his hat before placing it back on his head. ˙

"Well, I feel silly, but yes, I am. Chelsea says you came out this way, so I took it upon myself to check up on ye." He smiled so slowly that Corinne felt her stomach do a flip of its own. His dark green eyes were as friendly as ever.

"I never want to hear you call me Mister again though. We've been too many miles for that nonsense."

Corinne was at a loss for words for a second, then finally grasped at anything her brain could come up with.
"Well...thanks...Lucas." She added his name at the end, but she felt like a fool.

"I'm guessing you are using your healing skills for someone? Nothing too serious I hope," Lucas said. His hand gripped the reins and he pulled his horse up close next to her.

"Yes, a few under ripe berries made for some upset tummies. A little marshmallow root and peppermint will ease them for a while. I may stop back later to see if the trouble has fully passed. They are brave little ones and I do hope they don't suffer too long." She smiled wistfully. Her love of helping children was a deep longing. She harbored a few wishes for her own children someday.

"You are so good with the children, it seems you'd make a great mother." Lucas winked at her and smiled a bit mischievously. Corinne practically turned purple, to think he could read her thoughts so easily.

"Now Mr. Grant..." Corinne ran out of words, her mind a blank.

"I told you before, no more with the Mister. I shall have to think of another way for you to realize that we are friends now. The formality is unnecessary." He came nearer to her on his own mount, his shoulder almost touching hers as they walked along. Clover seemed completely comfortable with Lucas' mount so close, that Corinne felt a little betrayed. Corinne's heart was pounding as Lucas leaned near her ear.

"Please call me Lucas, Cori," he whispered.

He backed away just as she began to blush again. She wasn't sure if this one would not stay permanently. Something about him using her nickname was very pleasant. She meant to reply but stayed silent. She smiled his way and nodded as if agreeing to his suggestion. She sat there thinking how to continue this exciting conversation, but just then another rider joined them, and the private moment was lost.

<hr />

"Mrs. Temple, my mother would like a word with you. She's been feeling poorly today and is wondering if you can pay her a visit." Sidney Prince had a low smooth voice. His body was thin and awkward, it didn't match the grown-up voice.

Lucas and Sidney gave each other a nod. But for a brief moment, Sidney frowned while nodding. Corinne wondered for a split-second but then became concerned about his mother, Ellie, hoping she wasn't in pain.

"Of course, I'll go with you right now. Is she in her wagon or walking?" Corinne gave a wave to Lucas and followed the young man next to her.

"She is walking but feeling faint and dizzy today. She has tried drinking more water but that doesn't seem to help." Sidney was riding slowly next to Corinne, watching her intently.

They plodded their way to the Prince outfit just in time for the wagon boss to call the train to a stop for lunch.

After looking over Ellie, she identified a few infected bug bites. Corinne took her into the wagon and tried to painlessly drain the small amount of puss that gathered in the wounds. She washed and dressed the bites with oils and fresh bandages. Corinne ordered Ellie to ride in the wagon, if possible, today. Corinne would redress the wounds later. She took infection very seriously.

Sidney served Corinne some bread and cheese as she exited the wagon. She washed her hands in the wash water and gladly accepted the noonday meal.

"I have heard the whole wagon train talking about you," Sidney said, starting the conversation after she had taken a few bites.

"I do hope you have heard good things." Corinne looked at him sideways to see what kind of rumors he meant.

"I heard about you getting gifts from Indians and taking out bullets. It seems everyone thinks you are a savior to the wagon train." Sidney blushed and then added, "I guess I just saw you as a beautiful girl. Now I know you are much more than that." He seemed shy on the surface, but he knew when to be bold. Corinne was surprised, what a day she was having.

"Mr. Prince you are very kind. I just do what my mother and grandmother taught me. I learned at an early age how to use plants and herbs to help the human body. My mom grew up with Indian and militia skirmishes nearby. She learned from a doctor in her town how to take out bullets. I guess I learned somehow, too." She hoped that explanation would keep his compliments at bay for a little while. She was at a loss how to react to him yet.

"You amaze me Mrs. Temple."

"You flatter me Mr. Prince but..."

"I know you are recently widowed. I just wanted you to know that you have a protector and admirer," Sidney shushed her, with his bold announcement. She just smiled and nodded. He was so sincere she had to let his statement stand. She ate her bread and cheese, as he watched her.

That night after she finished checking on all her patients, she pondered her strange day, so full of odd feelings and ideas. She hoped tomorrow would be a relief from the bugs, and from men and their confusing ways.

<hr />

The newest additions to the wagon train joined their tight-knit group. It consisted of the Grants, the Temple crew, and now the Prince family, as well as a few other groups who enjoyed their company. Along the journey, all their personalities seemed to mesh well. The daily habits were working like a dance. They seemed to know when to get water or wash the clothes, all in a non-verbal way of working together. As a traveling family, they sang and worked as one. A new family joined their midst in early June.

The bugs were losing the battle. Or, after the wagon traveled a few miles, the bugs were just staying behind. Corinne was thankful for whatever way that allowed the pesky creatures to nip at her much less constantly.

Corinne had a soft cloth sack containing extra cornbread that Cookie made that morning. The cornbread was still warm from Cookie's small oven, and the fresh butter they got from Chelsea created a luxury to savor. Lucas brought the butter over. He managed to find lots of little ways to be near her. She liked it. She would not let thoughts of his fiancé back east enter her mind this morning. She quietly smiled to herself as she headed over to meet the new folks.

A beautiful blond woman greeted her. A young pair of equally blond twins were holding onto her skirts. The young boys were truly as close to identical as Corinne had ever seen. She smiled a welcome their way, but they buried their heads further into their momma's skirt.

"Welcome to our train, just saying hello and sharing a treat," Corinne said, with a friendly smile.

The woman smiled big, saying nothing, and looked expectant.

"Jah," she said after a minute. Her smile was stunning, but she didn't seem to understand Corinne. Corinne tried again using gestures. She smiled and handed the bag to the woman. The woman accepted it and examined it, then started speaking in a language Corinne didn't understand. It was Corinne's turn to look confused.

Corinne pointed to her chest, said, "Corinne," and waited expectantly for the woman's name. It never came. The blond mother took the bag and showed the boys, then rubbed her tummy and waved. They all walked away from Corinne, heading to their own fire to enjoy the treat. Corinne felt dismissed. She turned around, and walked back to her own fire, laughing to herself. *So much for getting to know the neighbors,* she thought.

Today was going to be a busy day. The courthouse rock was visible in the distance. As much as Corinne wanted to see it up close she had other things she needed to do. Laundry was a tedious chore that mocked Corinne's best efforts. She felt her clothes looked dirty even after being washed in the silt water of the Platte. The edges of everyone's clothes looked dingy and sweat stained.

Rain and trees were a lovely memory of Ash Hollow but that memory was dimming with the reality of the barren landscape. There was plenty of low scrub brush and dirty sand. They walked through it, day after day. Corinne reached her wagon and after getting the wash bags, she began her daylong fight with the laundry. She felt grimy, but the luxury of clean water in which to bathe was not to be had. She hoped that she kept herself from stinking but knew she looked as travel worn as everyone else.

The hot sun was beating down on her face and shoulders as she scrubbed. Eventually, she retrieved a light bonnet to keep her face covered. She didn't want to burn and be miserable tonight. She was just starting to sleep better, the bugs having tormented her for the last several nights.

After hanging up all the relatively clean wash she strung on a thin rope between the two wagons, she decided to rest in her wagon. The men and the Grants left on foot or horseback to go see the landmarks. Clive had been gone for several days. He took over some scouting duties, after three of the scouts had died from cholera.

Corinne strongly felt his absence but knew he was good a good scout for their train. His wisdom would get them through it all.

That night as everyone filed back to their wagons, a festive spirit had everyone wanting to celebrate reaching the landmark. Near the wagons was a large flat clearing. After lighting some fires, a few chickens and rabbits gave their life for the cause, and a feast was laid out. Fruit preserves that had been held back were now opened and shared. Music was at its best and Corinne danced with many partners. She thought of her dear friend, Angela, and how much she would have enjoyed this time with her.

"Can I convince you to take a stroll with me, Ms. Temple?" Sidney Prince was by her side after dancing with his mother. "We will stay close," he added when she had a look of refusal. He offered his arm, but she nodded and took two steps ahead of him. She wanted to be his friend but taking his arm might encourage him too much.

"I'm sorry. I know you shouldn't take a man's arm this soon." His face was young, and his jet-black hair was slicked back. Corinne admired the kindness in his eyes but was afraid to be too nice to him. She knew he was harboring budding romantic notions about her.

"Mr. Prince, you honor me with your attention, but I want to clear the air between us." Corinne stopped walking and tried to look him in the eye before she let him down. She wanted it to be painless and friendly. "I would love to have your friendship, but beyond that, I have no aspirations of seeking romantic attentions from any man." Her heart did a flip at the thought of another man's recent attention that she enjoyed rather well. "Liar!" she whispered to herself.

"I have been three years away from the company of my Father. I wish to finish this journey, Lord willing, and spend some time with the only family I have left." Corinne took his arm then, as a friendship gesture. He took it gracefully and walked her back.

Within five minutes, Lucas came around and she was swept away on a fast jig. He didn't wait even a minute before asking where she had gone.

"Sidney took me walking, but we didn't go far." She felt ten times the liar for enjoying his gaze, as he danced with her. His medium brown hair was recently trimmed. His tan made his dark green eyes seem more intense than usual. Corinne tried not to notice too much.

"Well, Sidney is young, and I hope he realizes that the dark isn't safe. And I don't like him taking you away from your friends." Lucas had a possessive look that charmed her female senses. Though she wouldn't have admitted to it, she really enjoyed a man being a little bit jealous of her attention. She smiled to calm him.

"I took the moment of privacy to let him know that his attention was flattering. However, I have no intention of having any relationship with him other than friendship."

Lucas smiled his brightest smile of the day for that remark.

Corinne finished the dance knowing her favorite dance partner enjoyed her company. Inside, she ignored the question in the back of her mind. *What will he to do with his fiancé back in Kentucky? Should he be throwing his affection around when someone is waiting for him?* Corinne knew little of how to deal with these questions. She felt the smallest amount of guilt for passing off Sidney's sweet honorable attempts at courting, considering he wasn't spoken for but Lucas was. *When did this all become so confusing?* she thought.

She laid her head down at a late hour. She had been sleeping for a short time, when she awoke to banging pots and children's laughter. After listening to a few sentences, Corinne realized the Swedish family was still awake. Corinne sat up and lit her lantern. This reminded her of Andrew's early morning habits and she smiled. It is nearly one a.m. She extinguished the lamp, lay down, and tried to sleep, but the racket was loud. A male voice joined the speaking. Corinne imagined that was the husband. She absently wondered if he was blond, too. After thirty minutes of shuffling and finally, a bit of shushing from the mother, the family seemed to settle down. Then began a song of sorts. They all did it together, the children and the parents. It lasted a few minutes. Corinne had to keep from laughing at the silliness. *What are they doing?*

The chanting song ended and soon the entire camp got back to its slumber.

Chapter Twenty-Two
June 21, 1848

The first official day of summer. The morning started with a creek crossing. It was easy going but for a few breakdowns. Some wagons were taking a beating and many repairs later, still barely holding together. Corinne felt confident in the Blake boys and their care for her. The wagons had been excellent. Reggie and Cookie watched over her like brothers. *They are a great team,* she thought.

The air was dry, and the creek was refreshing. The women found a secluded place to bathe again. Everyone enjoyed the clean feeling, after a long while of dusty trail grime.

Corinne stayed away from Sidney and Lucas lately. She didn't like the feelings she was having. She thought the best course of action was to avoid those feelings completely. She kept her eyes on the landscape and her mind occupied with her own dreams of Oregon.

She had the image in her mind. The mountain behind her and the fields before her in purple splendor. She could see different trees blooming in the spring, maybe even citrus fruits. She drew a blank on how that would happen. She heard rumors that women could own property in Oregon, but she would not know until she arrived. There was also her father to think about. Would he support her dream of starting her own farm and understand what she wanted to grow? She hoped to make lavender and other oils, possibly be the first producer of some oils in the states. It would take time and many people to help, but maybe her prayers would see fruit.

After crossing that clear-watered creek, the climate turned toward dry. Corinne spent these harsh, arid days on Clover or on foot. Sometimes her handkerchief did little to block the choking dust from her nose and mouth. Her eyes were constantly coated with caked-on sand and a white silt substance that made her eyes tear and burn. Everyone was in this together. The summer was just beginning and they all suffered through the miles of endless rocks and sand.

The march was enduring and measureless. The daily routine engrained. The mile markers were the big landscape changes. These were the landmarks they read about and used to guide their steps.

The end was coming closer, but the going was painfully slow. Everyone felt today was the day. Corinne anticipated it. It was the high point they had all been waiting for. Independence Rock was ahead!

———◆·◉·◆————◆·◉·◆———

Corinne planned to carve her own name in the famous place. She forged ahead through everything and knew of untold trials waiting. Soon, the halfway point would be behind her. She dreamed of a roof and bed almost as much as her lavender fields. Oregon City began sounding like heaven to her, a land of milk and honey.

The wagons took a break. Men stretched their tired muscles and gave water to the animals. Corinne used a rag with wash water to clean her face and hands of the trail dust. Chelsea strolled over with Brody and made small talk. Brody even seemed excited about "pendance rock." The scouts said they should see it on the horizon today. The rocky hills were small and spread out. Everyone missed the sight of trees.

By late afternoon it had been spotted. A cheer rang out and wagons stopped for good. A line of people with homemade paint and brushes were marching out to a turtle shaped mound that stood out from the stark dry landscape. The air was full of joy as they battled the heat, a song on their lips. The journey was halfway done. They all secretly knew that the easiest half had been already accomplished, but no one said so today. Today, they celebrated life and the bright future ahead.

Corinne traveled with the Grants. They all took their turn painting their names. Corinne spent an hour looking for her father's name without any luck. The place was enormous, and she soon gave up and headed back with her companions. She found herself watching Lucas as he walked back with Brody on his shoulders. His eyes were smiling, and he treated Brody to stories and smiles. She found herself daydreaming about him sometimes, too. He was taken, but she felt that someday a man would come along for her that was like him, hopefully.

———◆·◉·◆————◆·◉·◆———

Food was spread out in a dazzling display of resourcefulness. People pulled out reserve stocks of canned fruit. Pastries and previously hoarded butter were stacked high on makeshift tables. Clive, with the help of another scout, downed three deer. Roasted venison steaks were also shared.

The land was barren, but the people didn't care. A feast and a party were now the order of the evening. Corinne had been learning some great cooking tips from Cookie. She helped him make enough biscuits to share with everyone. Corinne was proud of her growing list of skills. Her hands were properly calloused these days. She felt a growing sense of womanhood rising in her chest. She had her own goals and also had a taste of freedom that she would not abandon lightly.

Corinne enjoyed the meal. As soon as the dancing started, she actively danced with her friends. She stopped after the fourth dance to go back to her wagon. Her stomach was a little upset, so she put some peppermint in her water. Within minutes, she was very uncomfortable.

"Chelsea, I'm going to head in for the night. I am feeling poorly." Corinne walked over to her friends to let them know where she would be. She didn't realize that she would soon have company.

"Hello beautiful." A familiar young voice interrupted Corinne's thought regarding her churning stomach.

"Sidney, I am sorry I didn't get a chance to dance with you. I am feeling..." Corinne wanted to send him away so she could be ill in peace. Her stomach was getting hot and her head spun a little. Sidney interrupted her.

"I have wanted to talk with you for days. I have tried to stay away from you." Sidney looked so serious with his dark eyes full of young passion. He pulled her close. He was not paying attention to her distress.

"Oh Sidney..." Corinne groaned and grabbed her stomach. She wasn't even listening to him. Her stomach cramps grew in intensity.

Sidney suddenly realized his folly. He was trying to woo a sick woman. His frustration grew. His timing was always off. He took his large awkward hand and patted her back. He tried to find soothing words as she groaned and doubled over. Any moment, he was afraid she was going to lose her dinner on or near him. His stomach had never been one to handle that. If anyone was sick near him he usually would end up joining in. "Let me find you some help." Sidney didn't even get a glance from Corinne as he nearly sprinted away from her. He found Chelsea and sent her to rescue her friend. Girls knew how to handle these things. He would have been disappointed had he waited around another moment. The man whom he secretly disliked, was recruited for carrying the beautiful young invalid.

Corinne did indeed lose her dinner, a moment after Sidney left her company. She was glad he had left. His company was getting more and more pressing on her. He looked at her in an odd way, like he expected something of her. He would someday be a very handsome man, but his boyish actions prevented her from seeing him as anything but a sweet lad who wanted her attention. Right now, she just wanted to not exist, as she fought a dragon battle in her stomach.

Chelsea, Russell and Lucas came to her aid to settle and clean her up. Ten more people over the course of the night got severe stomach cramps. Though at first everyone was afraid of another round of cholera, they soon discovered that everyone who had been sick had eaten some fruit pastries. From a certain family.

The Swedish family had shared several fruit pies with everyone. Some of the fruit had been put up badly. No one could tell them, for none of them spoke English. This family was quickly making enemies, with many outfits tiring of their late-night loudness. And now sharing bad fruit preserves. The gossip about them the next day wasn't very flattering.

Corrine didn't feel up to doing much for several days. She hid in her wagon as they traveled but the rocking and jerking from the uneven terrain did little to ease her illness. She wished for rest and finally after three days of fitful sleeping, she felt a bit better. As the Sweetwater River revived the entire train, she began enjoying life again.

They passed the Devil's Gate in awe of its magnificence, but kept moving through, refilling water barrels and keeping a steady pace. The summer heat wasn't fooling anyone. Winter would come, and they knew they had to make every day count. They would be traveling along the route of the Sweetwater for almost a week. They would cross over the river several times before leaving it behind to head toward the South Pass. They knew it would be the easiest way to get through the difficult, wagon-crushing Rocky Mountains.

Chapter Twenty-Three
July 7, 1848

A daylight moon shown in the clear, cloudless sky. Corinne stretched her back while sitting on Clover. It was nearing noon and the train had been traveling all night. The heat was dry and scorching. The wagon boss decided to push on this morning, despite the protest of several ox handlers.

The animals were dying.

Mr. Walters reminded everyone of the contracts they signed, and they agreed to keep moving. Corinne heard the shout for the wagons to rest and she was certainly glad of it herself. They should have stopped hours ago. Corinne had a feeling tempers were going to get worse as the heat and the barren, waterless landscape tested them all. They filled their barrels after a difficult crossing on the Big Sandy two days ago. Many travelers wished to stop and camp near the water to allow the weakening animals to drink and rest. Mr. Walters and his crew ignored the requests and pushed on.

Corinne saw at least ten dead oxen that day and she heard rumors of many other ox handlers losing the battle with the heat. Every day the terrain grew more difficult for the animals to find any kind of sustenance. Many of the poorer families had no oats or feed of any kind left and those who had it, gave it sparingly when they shared. The women were getting nervous about the growing tension. Desperate men had short tempers.

Corinne was grumpy. She had several good reasons. Dirty everything. Face, hair, and clothes. A monthly cycle with the accompanying cramps in her belly and back, and an injured horse. A sharp rock got wedged into Clover's hoof. After removing the rock, Corinne was certain Clover was bruised. Corinne was gladly giving her mount a break from riding, but wasn't enjoying the walk much herself. Corinne shared her womanly grief with Chelsea and got the traditional female sympathy, but it didn't help her mood. She tired of the dreary landscape, the dry dirt she ate all day as she walked, and everything else this trail threw at her. There was no plant life to look at. No trees, just dry sandy dirt that swirled around, caking on her eyes, nose, and mouth. The evening was better when the temperature dropped but the celebratory atmosphere was gone with the last river crossing.

"There's my sweet girl." Clive rode up to Corinne as she was starting the fire for dinner. She could not help but smile a little when she saw him. He was like a cool breeze to her parched hot day. His white and grey peppered hair had grown longer around his ears. It suited him perfectly.

"Hello Clive, I have missed you," Corinne said, weakly. She just had enough energy to fail at sounding perky.

"You are looking peaked child. I have to say this is the hardest part of the world to travel through, I reckon, and it gets under everyone's skin. We git ourselves a few more weeks of this before the terrain changes and then it's just plumb difficult." Clive sat down next to her as she poked her fire with a stick." I am not doing well at cheering ya, am I?" He laughed at himself softly and put a gentle hand on her shoulder.

"I wonder if you'd like a chance to get away from the trains for a few days and ride out with me and Lucas to talk to some of the local natives. We need some hints for water spots, 'cause there's been a few dried-up springs. We were counting on them for water. You can bring some of your good oil and make some good trades again." He looked to her hopefully. She smiled but shook her head.

"My horse is lame and needs a few days with no rider." She went back to poking a stick at the fire. Her mood lifted at the thought of a small diverting adventure but dove back into the depths when she realized it was impossible. She felt like a four-year-old whose candy had been stolen. Tears were threatening to fall.

"Ah, well that's no problem. I have more than one horse on this trip. I have a nice ride for ya, no worries. I will bring him by tomorrow morning and you can see for yourself. Will ya come with us if the horse suits ya?" Clive was all cheeriness and Corinne nodded with a bigger smile.

"I'm sure your horse will suit me, Clive. I will come. How many days will we be gone? I'll need to pack my saddlebags." Again, Corinne felt her mood lift and she leaned over and planted a kiss on Clive's cheek. She looked up to see Lucas standing over them.

"I was coming to check to see if we are leaving tomorrow morning and I catch you kissing Clive. What does he do to deserve it, so I can try to get one too?" Lucas laughed as he approached the fire, his green eyes always teased her lately.

"I just told her about the trip and loaned her a horse, Lucas my boy. I'm sure you can think of some way to get a kiss if you thought hard enough on it." Clive stood and accepted a mug of coffee from Cookie who joined the group. Lucas gave Corinne a wink, headed over to the coffee pot and came back with two cups.

"Will a coffee be enough, my Cori?" He said low for her ears only, as he handed the steaming cup to her.

Corinne gave him a long slow stare that made him swallow hard and then found her voice. "I think you can do better than that, Lucas Grant. A man has to work to earn a kiss... unless he's the kind that goes about stealing them." She watched his eyebrows rise and she might have seen him blush a little under his tanned cheek. She was mortified at herself. Corinne had no idea why she said that. *Do I want him to steal a kiss? Would it really be stealing? Argh...* she thought. Her mouth had gotten ahead of her.

Her face heated up. She turned away from the group and Lucas's reaction. She made her way over to see what was cooking for dinner. She called herself all sorts of names as she walked away from the group.

She didn't see Lucas playacting with Clive behind her. He acted like she had shot him dead in the heart. He landed with a thud on the stool behind her. She turned in time to see Clive and Cookie laughing quietly at Lucas. Her face was calm now as she sipped her hot coffee, but her stomach was certainly jumping around still.

Chapter Twenty-Four
July 12, 1848

Corinne was up, dressed and packed before her alarm went off. She grinned as she thought of Andrew and his early morning habits. His memory was far away now, almost like she had never known him. Had he never made some of those hard decisions, perhaps her mind would have dwelled on him more. But even the pleasant thought reminded her of how Angela's road was shortened. Corinne prayed for her friend and for Andrew's parents, as she got out of her wagon and stretched. They would certainly be sad when she arrived in Oregon City a widow. She wasn't looking forward to that.

The sun wasn't up, but there was light nearby at the Grant outfit. They had their fire going and Corinne caught the faintest scent of coffee drifting by. She had never been a coffee drinker before this trip, but she surely was now. Three cups everyday if she could. It was a way of keeping her going. Clive and Lucas were sitting by the fire looking like they had just rolled out of bed themselves. They each brushed at their tousled heads when they saw her approaching, all bright and pretty in the light of the campfire. Her improved mood had also put a light in her eye and a little bounce in her step.

She was going on an adventure with two of her favorite people. She loved seeing them in their morning routine, a bit tired and sloppy, in that endearing sleepy state. Men seemed less powerful when their hair was tousled. Clive and Lucas looked a little vulnerable. They seemed approachable and Corinne felt comfortable with them. This trip would be enjoyable. She knew they would see to her safety and make sure she was well entertained with stories and sights along the way.

"Good morning men." She realized her voice was sing-songy and tried to remedy it quickly. Nothing was more annoying to her than a perky morning person. "I am usually never up this early unless forced. I cannot stay in bed any longer. I am more than a bit happy to be seeing new sights." With the smallest hint of a blush, she remembered Lucas's comment from last night, as she accepted a mug of coffee.

"Clive, do we have a plan as to where we are going today, exactly?"

"There is a Shoshone tribe west of here that I would like to visit. I have met up with them several times in the past and would like to gain some of their knowledge of the water system here. They will be able to help us. Lord willin'."

Corinne nodded and finished her coffee. They packed up their bags and were ready. Within a few minutes they were off. Corinne's black and white spotted mount was sweet and gentle. She had her own comfortable saddle and everything she would need in her saddlebags. They brought a packhorse, too, to hold extra supplies in case they were gone longer than a few days. Clive was always well prepared.

The early morning sky was soon bright as they trotted along slowly. Clive shared a few stories of his earlier trips to see this same Shoshone tribe. They were relatively peaceful, only having issues with some Comanche who thought that every few years they could hunt on certain grounds where the Shoshone hunted. It made for tense relations. "Though some intermarriage of the two tribes has helped it along," Clive shared, wiggling his eyebrows for effect.

He explained about the battles that sometimes happened between these people. Corinne thought it sounded like the great wars of Europe. Kings, queens, and their princes marrying for power and how there was always an undercurrent of dissent.

With the light of day, she could see the mountain range to the West. The wagon train dust trail kept visibility low but now she could make out wispy far off shapes. Like low-lying clouds.

"It's the Wind River Mountains. We'll be heading a bit north. The wagon train will be setting down on the planned route. We have time to get some good information about any route changes we need to make. Animals cannot go so long between good grazing grounds." Clive shared his information with her as an equal. She enjoyed knowing how things worked. She wanted to make sure he knew how much she appreciated it.

"You know Clive, I have always been treated as a child. My aunt never spoke of anything except frivolous things, and my father last spoke to me when I was fourteen years old. I feel suddenly thrust into an adult world and I enjoy being a part of it. I feel like I'm seeing many things in a new light." She felt more at ease as she rode along.

"I see wisdom in your eyes, Corinne. Your hands have healing in them. You have big dreams." Clive had a serious look for a minute then gave her a sideways smile as he rode along. The heat of the day was building. They needed to find shade soon and rest during the hottest part of the day.

Within a few hours, the heat was melting them. Clive led them to a large boulder that would shade them from the heat of the sun. He set up two tents there. Corinne protested at the extra work of setting up two tents, but he insisted. She stretched out in the shady tent and settled into a mid-day nap. She recognized Clive's snore before she dozed off, and it made her smile.

She wondered why Lucas wasn't talking very much. Maybe she would have to try and get him to open up. She drifted off while thinking up ways to bring Lucas into the conversation.

Corinne woke up confused. It was getting darker, but she didn't know what time it was. The nap threw off her inner clock . She worried for a minute that she was left alone. The crackling fire and Clive's tinkering with the coffee pot calmed her. Her fog lifted. They would eat dinner and then leave. She crawled out from the tent and shared a smile with her companions.

"I nearly forgot what day it was. I cannot get used to traveling at night yet," Corinne said, laughing at herself.

"I agree. I nearly panicked when I woke just now. I didn't know where I was," Lucas shared. He was skinning two rabbits near the fire. Clive sat on the ground, the coffee pot brewing on the grate over the hearty blaze. The larger fire seemed a little unnecessary, but the night would turn chilly later. There hadn't been clouds for a week and that made for cooler nights until late August.

"Can I help with any fixins?" Corinne rolled up her sleeves as she sat next to Lucas. He reacted a little, just a hint of a smile.

He silently handed her three potatoes. She cut out the eyes and peeled the potatoes with her own short knife. Clive had placed a pan of water on the cooking grate. Within a minute, she cut the potatoes into pieces and plopped them in. They were all quiet, but the company was pleasant like a family gets when they feel comfortable. Dinner was delicious. After a few cups of coffee they packed up and began the evening journey under a cloudless sky and a bright moon.

They traveled through the night with a canopy of stars twinkling overhead. Clive told them they would find the Shoshone within a couple of hours, but six had passed with no sight of any inhabitants. The land was mostly flat with enormous boulders, like miniature mountains jutting out of the ground. They all joked about how the rocks got there, they looked so out of place in the flat landscape.

It was near dawn when strangers on horseback approached. Clive and Lucas appeared on edge until Clive let out a whoop and a cawing sound.

As they approached, the two young men with long hair had big smiles for Clive. They called out several greetings and spoke animatedly to each other. They used the Chinook language when talking to Clive. Corinne watched them with interest. Lucas gave Corinne a bump with his elbow and a quick wink. Corinne could not help but enjoy the attention. The sunrise made the sky orange and pink all around them. It was a nice moment.

"Come along, we are a few miles out they say. This is Desert Cloud and his brother Black Hoof. They will lead us to their village. They are further north this year. Water is dry in several creek-beds." After he explained, Clive reined his horse around and followed the boys as they darted off. Corinne and Lucas picked up the pace to catch up with them.

The village was larger than Corinne imagined. The vast tepees and dwellings spread across the flat landscape. The early morning routine looked like the wagon train's, with many fires burning and women starting breakfast. Dark little faces peered out from the doorways of tepees. Corinne could not help but smile at the people she passed. The women had a welcoming look once they saw Clive in the party. Men, young and old, made their way over to the group to see the long-time friend of the Shoshone.

"They seem to love you Clive." Corinne was in awe.

"I have been a friend of theirs for many years. I trapped furs with them and fought beside them against the Sioux and the Blackfeet years ago. Chief Washakie is a good warrior and friend of mine. We have had many good talks. He is a wise leader that has peaceful ties with our government..." Clive pointed out the riverbed on the far side of the village. Corinne could see it was clear and a few feet deep. She rejoiced inwardly at the thought of bathing in water not muddied from a hundred sharing families, and horses and oxen stomping around.

They dismounted and were welcomed to a fire and shared plates of breakfast. Fish baked over hot rocks, were served with berries and nuts. The long night of riding gave them all a healthy appetite. Clive and the men carried on a friendly conversation. Lucas and Corinne enjoyed the kind faces around them.

"You are probably the first white woman ever to enter their village." Lucas gave her a wink and she rewarded him with a blush. The nearby children giggled as they caught the actions between the two. Children saw everything.

"Well I hope to leave them with a good impression. I brought some lavender to share with them. I hope to learn from the women and healers about any local fauna that has healing properties." Corinne missed the look of awe on his face, as she was giving a little child a silly face.

"Cori, you are a very special lady," Lucas leaned and whispered close to her ear. Every nerve-ending she had stood at attention. She turned and stared into his eyes until she was sure the world had stopped. His eyes showed respect and something else. Something she had never expected.

"Thank you, Lucas," she whispered, when she found her voice. She had forgotten what she was thanking him for, but it broke the spell. They looked away from each other and ate a few more bites.

"The women will help you get cleaned up after we have a chance to nap a little. I told them about your 'Good Medicine' and they all eagerly wait to see what you brought. Already five young men have offered payment to have you as a bride," Clive chuckled, watching her blush. He was more fascinated watching Lucas's response though.

Lucas' jaw was tight, and he took a protective lean toward her. Clive gave Lucas a knowing look and smiled. It was Lucas' turn for blushing, just a little.

Two women came and escorted Corinne away to rest in a tent. Soft furs welcomed her, and the warm earthy scent of the tent was pleasant. She was alone, and thought of Lucas for a little while before finding rest. His intensity was pulling her in. Honestly, he always seemed so calm and sweet natured, but now she was seeing another part of him. She slept heavily. Her dreams were of a land with many mountains and fertile valleys.

A few hours of rest were all she found. She climbed out of the tent when she smelled smoke. Venison or beef, she thought as she opened the tent flap. Two women sat nearby sewing beads on a piece of leather while another sat at a loom. The area was full of children and adults all going about their lives. A tall device was twenty feet away that Corinne discerned to be a smoker. The smoke made a thin haze around them, and the scent made her hungry. She nodded to the women and gestured about where to find her saddlebags. One woman directed her to Clive and Lucas who were sitting at a nearby fire. Clive was still talking to the men.

As Lucas looked up at her, Corinne's stomach did another little jump. She called herself a childish fool, trying not to react. Her whole life, every close relative and friend teased her for never being able to hide her feelings from anyone. *What makes me think I can hide anything from Clive and Lucas?* she thought.

"Corinne, we just woke up too. I hope you got enough rest." Clive welcomed her to sit next to him. "I was going to teach you a few words of Chinook to help you if you wish. Some simple hand gestures can make a big difference." Corinne promptly sat down on the ground and was given a very thorough lesson on communicating in the Chinook language.

Clive described the Chinook talk as 'an old language used by traders and Indians for several generations' and as 'a passable way to talk between trappers, tribes, and also the rugged men of the West, who shared this world with the many different tribes here.' Corinne was a quick learner and had already grasped a few phrases but was eager to learn more. If possible, she would be using her future time with Clive, learning this language to communicate with native people in Oregon, too.

Lucas and Corinne practiced the Chinook language skills they learned, until five women summoned Corinne. She nodded a goodbye to Lucas and followed the women to the river's edge. They walked along the edge to a well-brushed area where a large rock gave them privacy. With a quick glance to determine the level of privacy, she joined the giggling women and disrobed. The water was warm enough to be comfortable but cool enough to be refreshing. The women's beautiful brown bodies were playful in the water. Soon Corinne was welcomed into the play, splashing and giggling along. The water was deep enough to swim in and the freedom to do so was delicious. Corinne spent nearly twenty minutes just swimming and splashing before getting to the business of washing. She was pleasantly surprised with the use of a creamy soap and the help of a young woman Corinne later learned was named Bluebird. She was tiny and sweet, and Corinne saw a profound sense of humor behind Bluebird's eyes. Bluebird washed Corinne's hair with the sweet-smelling soap. It reminded Corinne of the milk baths she had enjoyed in Boston.

She was shocked to even think of Boston after her world had changed so much now. That was such a different life. She was bathing naked with Shoshone Indian women. Her heart was happy here, with these beautiful souls surrounding her. She climbed upon a nearby rock and with the other women, sunned herself dry. Bluebird was bold and held her feet next to Corinne's in an obvious comparison. The dark tan foot of Bluebird next to the milky white foot of Corinne was a stunning contrast. Corinne found the humor and was the first to laugh. Another darker foot came in beside Bluebird's. Corinne wondered why Bluebird's coloring was a bit paler than all the other women. She gave Bluebird a look that hopefully welcomed friendship. There was something about her.

Corinne felt welcomed by them and had bonded in a strange way. The bright sun soon made them warm, so they scattered to get their clothes and headed back to their jobs. Bluebird gave her a nod as she moved away.

Corinne spent the day with Clive and Lucas watching the lives of the Shoshone people. When the men came back from a hunt with meat and skins, the women were busy preparing everything from cutting out the bones to make utensils, to scraping fur off the buffalo hide.

That night's dinner was roasted buffalo with small potatoes. And great company. Corinne enjoyed their haunting voices as they sang to the honored guests. The Shoshone bedded down early but Clive, Lucas and Corinne had held strange hours and stayed awake talking quietly around the fire. A few young men wanted to talk to Clive, so Lucas and Corinne were then alone.

For a minute the silence was heavy. Lucas cleared his throat a few times then finally spoke. "Corinne, I just wanted to tell you, I see how wonderful you treat these people. I know many women who would never do what you did today."

"They make it easy."

Lucas reached out and took her hand in his. Corinne's arm felt on fire as he stroked his fingers over the top of her hand. He didn't say anything, and Corinne was certain she was coming down with some deadly fever from the slow, persistent, sweet agony he was doing to her hand and brain. It may have been a minute or an hour, but she began to think about sitting just a little bit closer to him. Lucas had the same idea as he nudged himself closer to her place on the ground near the fire.

"Lucas,'' she said softly, not wanting to break the mood. "I don't know what you want." She looked deep into his dark eyes and saw hope there.

"I just want to understand why I want to be near you. Why I am drawn to you?" He was still holding her hand and stroking it slowly with his thumb, driving her nerve endings to a slow roar inside her head.

"I feel the same Lucas, but what about Sarah Ballentine?" He had a pained look and stopped the torture to her hand.

"I never felt this way about her. She was pretty and pleasant. I was at Yale and she was taking courses in a sister school nearby. I was in the orchestra and so was she. Sarah sought me out. She was constantly around and a friend of hers finally forced the issue by telling me she was interested. Once I graduated, it seemed like the next step was to get married. She said 'yes,' but then, once I told her I was going to farm out west, she changed. I hope the best for her, but I am certain that our engagement is all but over." Lucas gave Corinne a boyish smile that completely made her forget what she was going to say. Suddenly, a sound drew their attention.

A 'kip-kip' sound echoed through the dark night. It resembled an animal noise, but it wasn't. Whistles followed it and a strange hush fell over the camp.

Without knowing why, Corinne's heart did that jump that could not be explained. A certain knowing that danger was near. She glanced at Lucas and felt the grip on his hand loosen, but then his arm was around her shoulders protectively. His face a wash of the same feelings she felt just then, an unknown fear.

Clive broke through the darkness slowly. His face was serious and his body tensely listening. He leaned in close to them.

"It's the Blackfeet. They have been threatening to raid for months, over the buffalo hunting grounds. Lucas, get her out, they cannot find her, or you, here. There is a great rock just on the north side of the camp. There is a deep crevice. You can hide there. Don't come out until it's quiet. Keep her safe."

Lucas and Corinne were on the move as Clive disappeared into the darkness. The kip-kip sound continued but Corinne was practically oblivious to it. Fear was pounding in her ears. This could not be happening. They ran by her tent and with a second to think, she broke her grasp with Lucas' hand, ran into her tent, and grabbed her saddlebag. Her mother's journal was in there. She would not lose it in a savage battle over hunting rights!

"Cori, where did you go?" Lucas said, in a savage whisper. She clasped his hand wordlessly and he pulled her along. Her eyes were still adjusting to the blackness, after staring at the fire so long. She was having little luck seeing anything. Her inner compass was aware that the river was around this area. Not wanting to spend the evening shivering, she whispered.

"Be careful, the river."

They moved quickly, weaving through the village. The small fires were down to embers that gave off little light. Corinne tried to keep her eyes off the embers, to not ruin what little night vision she had left.

The last tepee was soon a hundred yards back. They moved slowly now with no moon to guide them along. Corinne thought about Angela stumbling through the dark, then tumbling into a ravine. In this flat terrain, it was unlikely. She could easily trip though.

They stopped. Corinne reached with her free hand and felt the barrier of rock.

"Cori, this way." They scooted to the left, and then felt the edge turn. They nearly tripped on low brambles twenty times before they came to the crevice. It seemed wide enough for them both and they cautiously moved into the depths of this enormous boulder. It was clean and quiet. They sat down in the middle as it opened into a small flat area. There was a fire pit there, but fear made them cautious. Lucas sat with his back against the opening and pulled Corinne next to him. The night air wasn't cold but the chill of the situation drew them closer.

Savage screams broke the silent night. Whether in pain or to terrify, they worked on Corinne. Fearful, she broke down and began to weep quietly, holding her hands over her face.

"Cori, be calm. The Shoshone have many great warriors. This fight will not last long." Lucas held her as she calmed down, his chest catching any wayward tears as she slowly stopped crying. They sat, unmoving, but tried not to listen to the haunting sounds of battle. The grunting and yelling muffled through the rock.

"Why did Clive say they cannot find me here?" Corinne asked softly, to distract herself from the sounds of battle.

"Cori, you are far too precious to end up captured in a Blackfeet war party. All I can do now is pray and keep you safe. Thankfully we got out of the village before anything could happen to you." He held her face with a strong hand and gave her a quick blind kiss that penetrated her heart. It was over fast, but she thought about it for several minutes. On this dark night, he had shared much with her. His protection, his feelings and even a kiss.

As she sat in the dark listening to the sounds of war dying off she was thankful for the quiet company of Lucas. He was a steady strength when she needed him. She knew her feelings were new and unknown, but another part of her felt he was solid and already tied to her in some way. She didn't know how to continue the talk they had started tonight but she would find the right place and time. She was certain that she wanted to go slowly. She thought of Andrew. The day they married, the relationship started sour and continued until that last day.

The sound of hoof beats came and went. Corinne thought that the Blackfeet had gone. They sat still and waited. There was no need to act hastily and draw attention from anyone, if there was still danger lurking around. With the night air beginning to cool down, staying still within Lucas' arms felt warm and safe. Corinne smiled to herself a little whenever he moved in closer.

The sound of far off footsteps caught their attention. They both tensed and listened harder.

"Lucas, it's safe to come out. Or you can wait, I'm bringing a lantern." Clive's voice calmed the tension out of their shoulders. Lucas helped her stand. They heard Clive shuffling around outside then saw the light from the lantern coming closer through the cleft. He was within the circle in a few moments. With the lantern, they could see the inside of the boulder. It was an interesting place. This natural formation created a little hollow place. As they suspected, there was a fire pit. It also had a place on the wall to place treasures.

"Clive, are you hurt in any way?' Corinne's voice was quiet and shaken. Her hands checking him for any sign of injury, as soon as he was near enough.

"A few scratches, no need to worry Corinne. However, a few others did get more than scratches. The Blackfoot party was not a large one. They just seemed intent on stealing horses and today's buffalo kill. Two young warriors had the worst injuries. I am hoping they will allow you to take a look. Maybe you can prevent infection." Clive said, pulling Corinne into a protective embrace to calm her fear.

"The battle was short, as you heard I'm sure. The Shoshone warriors have the renegades under control. No women or children were involved."

They walked back to the village and Corinne was taken at once to see the injuries. Lucas was still carrying her saddlebags as she went to retrieve her oils and herbal kit. He stopped her for a moment after he handed them over.

"We'll talk again soon Cori." Lucas said simply.

Corinne had to look up to watch his eyes as he spoke. She gave him a nod and squeezed his hand before she let go.

"Thanks for taking such safe care of me tonight."

"It is my pleasure." His easygoing look was back, and he gave her a wink before leaving her to her business.

The young men had some cuts but no puncture wounds. Corinne could see they would need a few stitches. Clive translated to the women caring for these men that she had some healing medicine that might help fight infection. They welcomed her help. She was thrilled.

She spoke in English, in a soothing voice that Clive translated softly. She went through her kit and got lavender, eucalyptus and the precious small vile of Tea tree oil. She cleansed their wounds and then applied her mixture to the edges of the wound and to the needle. The women did a good job cleaning the wounds free of dirt and grime. Corinne briefly stitched the wounds. Then she reapplied her mixture and bandaged them. The job was completed quickly. She washed her hands and thought she would head to bed, when she realized that sleep would be a long time off. They wanted to know more about her medicines.

The elder women and a few prominent men of the tribe were talking animatedly about the medicines. Clive could not translate fast enough. They wanted to see her mother's journals and learn everything from her. Corinne was excited to share but also exhausted from the long day. After a few hours, Clive called the event closed and told them that Corinne was tired. Lantern in hand, he led her back to her tent and gave her a fatherly kiss on the forehead. She fell asleep as soon as she lay down. She had nightmares all night though, battles and injuries greater than the ones she had recently experienced.

The morning came late for Corinne. The whole village seemed to be moving slow after the long night. The young boys were talking of the battle, and in the way of young boys, they enjoyed reliving the fight. The sizzling food eventually brought everyone out of their beds.

Corinne sat at the fire and wordlessly nibbled on her breakfast. She was nervous to see Lucas today. What would he think of their time together yesterday? She wasn't sure what to think about it herself. The feelings inside her were swirling around faster than she could catch up with.

The day flew by when the women came for her, along with Clive, to talk about her herbs and oils. They had an idea. They wanted to send someone with Clive to Oregon City to learn the language and get trained by Corinne. She was very willing to do the training if they could keep both lines open. She wanted to learn from them as well. Corinne was excited to hear they were serious about their intentions. The women discussed who the most capable young woman was for the journey.

The Indians had given a map to Clive with lots of instructions about the location of water holes. There would be a few people traveling back with Corinne and Clive, tagging along to Oregon City with the Grant outfit. Corinne was thrilled when she found out that Bluebird was coming with them. She felt a strong bond with her and longed to breach the language gap between them. She knew Bluebird was a special girl with a keen intellect. Her dark eyes were filled with mirth and wisdom for one so young. Corinne guessed she wasn't even sixteen years old.

Before they left that evening, Corinne made a few good trades for her bottles of oil. She got beaded moccasins that were so comfortable, she was certain she would never again wear any other shoes. They also made her a full-length coat with heavy warm fur insulating it. The golden tan hide was delicately beaded with wildflower patterns. Corinne was touched to get such a beautiful and generous gift. They said the coat would keep her safe for 'the time of cold, mountain snows coming soon.'

She knew she would wear the coat in honor.

Chapter Twenty-Five
July 17, 1848

That night, Clive, Lucas, Corinne, Bluebird, and two men from their tribe set out, travelling in the cool evening. The tribe members would be guiding the group to some springs, on their journey through the South Pass and mountains ahead. Corinne didn't understand much of what they said, unless Clive translated, but she did enjoy their smiles and genuine warmth. She looked forward to traveling with them and knowing them all better as the journey progressed.

A few looks passed between Lucas and Corinne as they prepared to leave. She could read in his eyes that he wanted to talk more with her but the right time would come another day. She had a strange wish to be near him again like they were the night before. Cuddling against his chest had been lovely, and a bit frightening. She could not say why it was both, but now she seriously wished she had her mother or Angela to talk to. She may yet confide in Chelsea, but that was complicated. She was Lucas's sister-in-law. It could potentially create a strained relationship if she had questions about his sincerity or changed her mind about her feelings. *How did things get so complicated so quickly?*

They slowly plodded through the night, guided by the stars. The few night bugs chirped and hummed their songs as the group moved toward the South Pass. The wagon train would be close to that place soon. They were going to find a water hole ahead of them and then guide the train to it. Corinne had concerns that the loss of so many animals had already crippled the train's ability to keep going, but Clive explained that wasn't the case.

"The harsh reality is, that with the loss of life and supplies along the way, it is an unfortunate, but necessary, part of the journey. The strain of the journey will always mimic nature. The survival of the fittest is the rule. The wagons get lighter as they eat through supplies. The terrain gets harsher. People and animals get sacrificed to the demands," Clive said. "It's the hardest thing to see after so many years of traveling, but it's a brutal truth." He made eye contact with her as she thought about his words. "What we are doing

Corinne is harder than anything ever should be. When we get to our Valley, we will have 'seen the elephant'. We will have survived the trail. The great spirit of this land will be in us, and we will have conquered it." Corinne felt humbled by his speech and remained silent for a while. She could only wonder at how she had survived so far, when she had seen so many strong men and women fall.

***

"Come ride with me Corinne." Lucas rode near her and spoke loud enough for Clive to hear, too. Corinne glanced to Lucas' expectant face, and then to Clive who nodded and gave the smallest hint of a smirk.

They rode ahead for a few minutes and then slowed to a walk. Lucas kept looking forward. Corinne could see a serious look cross his features as he was thinking about what he wanted to say to her.

"I keep thinking about you," he finally said, daring to look at her. She wanted to smile but his serious look made her pause. She would let him talk.

"I know we have a connection, but you are right to ask about Sarah. I left her behind without truly letting her go. I believe in my heart that she is not waiting for me, but my integrity and honor is smarting from my actions with you." He looked away to say the rest. "The fact is, I entertained feelings for you while engaged to someone else. I do not regret having feelings for you at all. However, I cannot abide the dishonor upon you and myself, if I continue to act upon my feelings, before sending word to Miss Ballentine of our cancelled engagement."

"I will never doubt your sense of honor, Lucas," Corinne said softly. She could see he was struggling with his actions.

"Perhaps I am too harsh on myself, but I have to see myself as a just and honorable man. I cannot, in good conscience, play with anyone's emotions lightly." Lucas stopped his horse, and with such intense rawness, looked toward the sunrise before him. In that moment, Corinne knew she would never see him the same way again. He truly was a good man. That he cared for her at all, seemed a miracle. His integrity and honor were surely traits that made her proud to know him.

Corinne suddenly felt her heart drop. What if Sarah still wanted him? What if she had already written to him, telling him of her devotion and willingness to come to him? Was this just a mild feeling Lucas had? His honor would dictate him to wait for Sarah. And abandon his fledgling feelings for her. Corinne realized that she had no claim on Lucas, like Sarah had. He had accepted gifts from Sarah's family. In some cultures, that alone made the couple legally bound.

"You look worried, Corinne." Lucas's face was calmer now, like he had released some pressure off himself, and now was happier for it.

"I ..." Corinne faltered not wanting to admit she suddenly wished to keep him for herself. "I am at a loss. This is new to me. I cannot say how I feel, as well as you have." Corinne felt a foolish tear escape from one eye and travel down her face. She hated her stupid emotions that kept betraying her. Lucas rode up close to her, so he could wipe away the tear. She beat him to it, with a swipe of her hand.

"I just realize that you are quite a man, Lucas Grant." She stood up in her stirrups. Without pausing to think, she kissed him briefly, just as he had done the night before. "Now we are equals in this." She sat back down in her saddle and waited for his response. At first, he was surprised, then seemed pleased.

"I will bide my time for you, Cori." Lucas reached his hand to her face, stroking her chin. For a moment, she leaned in, accepting his comfort.

"If we are meant to be, it will be," she said simply. She felt a peace wash through her. She put this in God's hands.

They turned back and rejoined Clive and the others. They all settled soon, in a shady place, to sleep during the heat of the day.

Chapter Twenty-Six
July 18, 1848

The travel was slow. Clive checked his map and conversed with the Indian scouts that came along. Lucas kept busy with the men and Corinne stayed near Bluebird.

Though the communication between Corinne and Bluebird was limited, Corinne desperately wanted to get to know her. Bluebird's kind face and wise eyes beckoned her friendship. Corinne was certain Andrew and Auntie Rose would have hated her having any relationship with what they would have called 'a savage redskin.'

Clive said that Bluebird was the English translation of her name. Bluebird's real name was 'Doli'. Pronounced Doh-leh, Corinne practiced it a few times before she had gotten it right.

As they rode along, Corinne and Bluebird traded words. They went through 'hair,' 'hand,' 'horse,' 'foot' and each other's names, but tired quickly. The morning heat was escalating. They kept watching the men to see if they wanted to set up a rest area soon. Doli knew a few English words. She had explained, in very simple terms, that her father had been a trapper. Corinne was pleased to know a little about her. She looked forward to learning more as time passed.

They had been travelling for many hours. Water and rest were in order. Clive seemed engrossed in conversation, then gestured that they follow. Since they rose in the pre-dawn hour, it had been a habit to look for a good water source for the animals. They all knew finding a water source was of the utmost importance. Every time Corinne thought of her own thirst, she realized the wagon trains' would be even worse. She had her fill of fresh water back in the Indian village.

Clive led them around a group of low scrub bushes. A giant boulder jutted from the ground. Behind it was a shadow where the sun could not reach this early in the day. The Indian scouts jumped off their horses and began digging with small wooden shovels. Within a minute, the ground began to grow dark and water bubbled out like a deep breath. Everyone gasped and jumped down with their canteens. They all were laughing and drinking as they each took turns. The water was plenteous. Clive drank his fill of the sweet, cold, water then got busy with the map again. The scouts were pointing and talking. After several minutes, they all agreed they had the lay of the land captured. Bluebird pulled a satchel from behind her saddle and opened it near the water spring. She pulled out a brush and some powder. Adding a small scoop of water, she made a red, watery, paste. She went to the side of the rock facing east and began to paint a bright red circle with two wavy lines under it. It was large on the rock and would be seen from quite a distance.

"She is certainly a smart one," Corinne said to Clive, seeing him smile as he watched Bluebird paint.

"Yes, this will certainly help us get back to this spot. We will have her mark rocks on our way back, too. We should set up our rest stop here. We have some shade and the water will need to be dug out some more." He spoke to Bluebird and the scouts as they all began to work together on the tents.

Corinne and Bluebird were learning to work well together. Corinne looked forward to being able to talk with her. Clive told Corinne that Bluebird was sent to learn medicine from her and would then pass it along to their healers. Corinne was anxious to learn to speak Bluebird's language and to teach her English, as well.

The traveling party rested in short order. They woke to the smell of coffee and biscuits. They got to work quickly, digging out the water spring. This would provide easier access for the animals, in a few days. They had a great distance to travel to reach the wagon train, but they knew their efforts would benefit everyone.

Chapter Twenty-Seven
July 20, 1848

Corinne was excited to see the wagon train in view. Though the dust was an unwelcome part, she nearly ran to Chelsea as Corinne finally wove her way through the wagons. The hug was endearing. Several kisses for Brody completed Corinne's joy. The two women spoke until late in the evening. Corinne kept all romantic thoughts about Lucas to herself. It was confusing to bring Chelsea into this situation when they did not know what 'it' was exactly.

Clive took the opportunity to introduce Bluebird and the young men to the crew. Everyone did their best to make them feel welcome. They were very quiet when Clive wasn't around. Corinne was already working on her Chinook and few Shoshone words that she had heard. She was determined to make them as comfortable as possible.

The information Clive had gleaned from the Shoshone proved very helpful. With a small detour following Bluebird's painted rocks, they were able to restock water supplies and make it through the dry South Pass with fewer animal deaths. Water barrels were full of fresh clear spring water, and tempers cooled. Their water-hunting trip had been a blessing to so many. That day, every man, woman, and child breathed a deep sigh of relief.

Everyone thanked Bluebird and her two companions. Sharing the waterhole and its destination, had endeared them to all. The fireside chat that night was pleasant and the guests were treated with honor. There was no longer a class system here. Every man or woman was judged upon their merit, not by the color of their skin.

Bluebird and the two scouts stayed close to Clive, but quickly, a friendship blossomed between Chelsea and Bluebird.

Clive had taught Chelsea the Chinook language. Without a pause, Chelsea scooped up Bluebird under her wing and made her part of the family. Corinne was so pleased to see Bluebird and Chelsea communicating easily. It wasn't long before all three women were friends and sharing stories of their lives.

With the success of the South pass behind them, the wagon train moved forward. Corinne settled back into the daily routine, gladly wanting something to distract her from thinking about Lucas. Unfortunately, she failed nearly every minute.

Chelsea suspected there was something between them but only questioned Lucas.

"Corinne looks at you differently now." Chelsea was preparing dough for biscuits and glanced his way, as he sipped coffee near the fire. Lucas harrumphed, in the traditional way men expressed dislike at a topic of conversation.

"You try not to look at her at all. You don't always succeed," chuckled Chelsea as Lucas blushed a little.

"I have a deep respect for her."

"We all do Lucas. Just letting you know, I'm here if you need to talk." Chelsea watched him chug down the rest of his coffee, probably burning his mouth in the process. He was trying to escape her questions. What he didn't know was how much he communicated with his actions. Men were the silly ones, sometimes.

------◆◦◆◦◆————◆◦◆◦◆------

Fort Bridger was the next great milestone. Excitement abounded. The ability to send word to loved ones back East was on everyone's lips. A pony express post had been added. Nearly every wagon would be taking advantage of it. Corinne had several letters for her aunt and Angela, no matter the expense. She pondered the idea of sending word to her father. Knowing she was headed in his direction, it would be wasteful. She might arrive before the letter did. The visit to the small post gave everyone a little boost of energy. Corinne gladly handed over her coins to send off her precious letters. The line behind her was long and she saw many of her acquaintances with letters in hand. She said hello to Ellie Prince and was chatting with her when, out of the corner of her eye, Corinne caught Lucas passing behind her. He gave Corinne a small smile and continued walking. Had he sent a letter back east? She would wonder about that for days certainly.

Some local natives heard about the wagon train going through. They brought goods to trade. Locally caught fish and game was available, as well as some foodstuffs and dried goods. Everything was expensive. Several families had to go without refilling supplies, due to lacking funds. Things like coffee and flour were running low for many. Those wagons would have to learn to live without it.

The scorching summer days were going to be a memory soon. The mountains were ahead. Unforgiving terrain and snowy slopes would test and try them before the journey's end. Everyone had their own idea about how they would cross the mountains. Except for those who had already crossed and lived to tell, the rest secretly feared the unknown,

The hot dry weather had Corinne longing impatiently for the scenery to change. The weeks passed slowly. They all tried to keep their spirits up, but everyone was feeling the same sluggish, exhausting strain of the trail. The daily grind was interrupted one morning when Chelsea had an announcement.

"Well, I guess morning coffee is a good enough time for our news. I wanted everyone to know Russell and I are expecting another child." Chelsea was rewarded with a cheer. Everyone jumped up from their seats, sharing hugs and handshakes with the mother and father-to-be.

Clive gave Russell some good-natured ribbing about his being too busy on the trail for those sorts of shenanigans. Everyone laughed and loved the idea of another young Grant baby.

"Corinne, I can't wait to see you this way, someday." Chelsea said, winking over her mug of water at Corinne. "You will surely make an excellent mother." Corinne blushed and felt her eyes drawn to Lucas across the fire. His eyes locked on hers for a several seconds and she lost track of the conversation. Lucas' slow, dark gaze held her captive for a minute. He agreed silently with Chelsea. His eyes spoke volumes they shouldn't say. There was an uncomfortable silence. Corinne broke her gaze. She attempted to say something but was at a loss.

Clive broke the silence. His grin split his face in two. "She surely will be a great mother and she has lots of knowledge to pass on to her young'uns."

Corinne tried to stay engaged in conversation with Chelsea, but her awareness of a certain person was making her batty. She needed to remember that there was no reason to change her feelings at this moment, when the uncertainty of his current relationship was still unknown.

The subject moved on to lighter things as they discussed baby names and future plans. Soon, even that became part of the everyday routine. Chelsea was healthy and strong. She had few troubles beyond the discomfort of walking so much, and the wagon jarring when she needed rest. Bluebird was an immense help to Chelsea on this part of the trail. Chelsea repaid her by helping Bluebird learn English, and teaching her to read. Corinne was amazed everyday by how quickly Bluebird was learning.

The landscape passed by and everyone did their best to keep moving and survive. Corinne had learned so much already. She wondered what else the trail would teach her, as the struggle continued with each hard-fought mile they traveled.

Chapter Twenty-Eight
August 13, 1848

Sidney Prince came by the fire several mornings in a row. Corinne humored him but wondered if she needed to have another talk with him.

"Sidney, you are gonna make me choke on my coffee if you keep staring at me like that. It distracts me completely." Corinne put on her friendly smile, but she was annoyed. She endured his company, but was losing patience with his constant awkward compliments. She got sly looks from Cookie and the Blake brothers, every time he showed up. She always laughed, but the teasing from them was adding to the situational annoyance. As soon as she finished her coffee, she planned to escape to her wagon using some excuse to get away from him. Later when she walked along with Chelsea, she shared her feelings out loud.

"I am not sure why Sidney doesn't understand. I just don't see him in that way." Corinne said. Chelsea hugged Brody's warm little body as they moved along.

"See who in what way?" Lucas rode by and Corinne nearly jumped. They had avoided each other successfully for the last week. They hadn't spoken much at all since the trip back from the Shoshone village.

"Corinne has an admirer, Lucas. He has deaf ears to her rejection." Chelsea said, smiling. She winked in Corinne's direction, further mortifying her.

"I do believe she has more than one admirer. I've heard her praises being sung by many in the wagon train." Lucas gave Corinne a glance then dismounted. After removing the saddle and blanket, he tied his horse to the back of the moving wagon.

"Well this particular young man is making himself a nuisance," Corinne shared. She tried to keep her focus on Chelsea and not on the man behind her.

She blushed as Chelsea teased her a little, then got distracted when what sounded like a fight, erupted close by. Lucas ran toward the sound. Corinne and Chelsea stayed back. They were learning to keep out of the trouble. Corinne could tell that the wagon boss, Mr.

Walters, was the loudest of the men hollering. Something about oxen and boys...

Corinne and Chelsea jumped up on the wagon box to get a better look. Two teenage boys were being held by the scruff of the neck by Clive and another surviving scout. They all were unhappy. The yelling calmed to a harsh lecture. Soon the information was shared with the whole train.

"These two young men had the night watch for the herd last night. They were found this morning asleep. Not in the saddle, but on the ground, with blankets. They intentionally went to sleep. And now, more than twenty oxen and ten horses are missing." Mr. Walters was more than upset, and the angry crowd was joining in with him. The wagon train always herded the animals together at night, to keep them safe from harm.

How many people would be unable to move forward without their oxen? A few men from every outfit went to survey the missing animals. The Blake brothers came back a few minutes later. Two of their oxen were gone.

The women stayed behind as the men formed search parties for the missing oxen and horses. Corinne felt a little left out but decided to be calm. They had a good camp spot for now. The clear Boise River was nearby and with the men gone, the women took the opportunity to clean out the wagons and take time for themselves.

Corinne pulled out her mattress and gave it a good thrashing. A few spiders had made webs high in the bonnet. With a long stick, she cleared the pests from her wagon. A few leaky containers had made messes in Andrew's wagon.

Corinne tried to think of it as Reggie's wagon now, but she realized all of Andrew's belongings were in it. Corinne was determined that not one of Andrew's items would be left behind. With the hills starting to get steeper, Corinne knew the temptation to lighten the load would be great. She would throw out her own clothes, if necessary, to keep mementos for Andrew's mother and father.

While helping Cookie scoop ashes out of the stove, she got a visit from Clive and Mr. Walters.

"Pardon me, Mrs. Temple." Mr. Walters had been quiet around Corinne since Andrew's death, but Clive gave her a wink and cleared the air.

"Mrs. Corinne, how do you manage lookin' perty when you are covered in soot and filth? I do declare..." Clive reached over and gave her shoulders a squeeze.

"Well, actually Clive, it takes years of training in Boston. Society pressures a young lady to always look her best." She showed them a lopsided curtsy to be funny and was rewarded with laughter. "Well, Clive, I do believe you are due for a shave yourself. I do declare..." she said, in her best southern accent.

"Well, I was thinking of trying to grow my facial hair long enough to braid. Perhaps that may get me a new squaw wife. They do love them braids." Clive bowed and watched Mr. Walters squirm. "I apologize, I believe Mr. Walters has a chore for ya, Mrs. Temple."

Mr. Walters made a gesture for Clive to do the asking.

"Well Corinne dear, we've got a job for ya, if'n yer willing." Clive rubbed his jaw a second before spitting it out. "Well, the two boys caught sleeping are going to get their punishment and we are wondering if you will look in on 'em when it's all done."

Corinne paled a moment. "What's the punishment?" She was dreading the answer but knew the consequences of the boys' actions were dire for the whole train.

"Ten lashes each. If it had been accidental they may have escaped with five but the fact that it was intentional has to be reckoned with, " Mr. Walters spoke up. It was his place as the head of the train to lay down the law. Corinne knew she had no right to question it. She had never seen a man whipped before and wasn't certain she wanted to now.

"We need to teach the boys a lesson and show everyone the importance of doing their duty for the good of all, but we also don't want infection to hurt these young men either. The West needs good strong men of integrity. It's no good to teach them the lesson and then hey die from the wounds."

Corinne paled again but nodded. "I will be available."

The search for the oxen and horses continued with little fruit for the effort. The traveling party drew some attention and in a strange twist, some local natives offered their services to help find the missing animals. They wanted a hundred dollars and twenty shirts or blankets to find the missing animals. Their offer was politely refused. As the night wore on with no sign of the animals, Clive negotiated the price to fifty dollars and ten shirts. With handshakes and the deal settled upon, the leader of the small group of Indians yipped and yelled and left in a rush. After midnight, the Indians rounded a hill, crossed a shallow part of the nearby creek, and returned the animals.

The next day, Clive told Corinne he was certain the local Cayuse Indians took the oxen and horses when they saw the boys sleeping near the fire. They just wanted the money and shirts to trade at Fort Boise. The two Shoshone men laughed with Clive as they talked about the trick the other native people had played. Bluebird sat near the women and stayed quiet. She had been learning English from Chelsea, but she was a quiet girl. She had a ready smile for everyone and was willing help to any who needed it, but she was not one to speak unless she had something profound to say. Brody loved his new female friend and lovingly called her "Dolly," so close in pronunciation to her real name. Soon after, Bluebird made it clear that was what she wanted to be called.

Corinne had nightmares the night before the whipping. She woke up with dread, the boys' screams wracking her brain. She got up and prepared her kit before she even had coffee. She wasn't sure if she would need to sew them up, clean out wounds, or just try to prevent infection. She packed the best she could and then, said a prayer for bravery. In her young life, she had done a lot of things to help people, but usually it was after something had happened. She had never prepared to heal someone before they got hurt. Her stomach was jumpy, and she had sweaty palms.

Sidney was waiting by the fire. His young boyish face a wash of admiration as Corinne walked out to the fire. He had a mug of coffee in one hand and handed another to her. She accepted it uncomfortably. She did not know what to do to discourage his attention. She had already told him once she was not interested. Did she need to again?

"I heard, Corinne, that you are going to doctor the boys getting whipped today," said Sidney, sounding excited about the events. She felt a sudden disgust at the sound of his voice. *He is happy at the prospect of watching someone get punished,* she thought.

Corinne knew it was necessary for the boys to receive punishment, but she wasn't going to delight in anyone's mistakes or the pain they received for their actions.

"I am not a doctor, Sidney." Corinne took a sip of her coffee and with a free hand, called Reggie over to the fire. "I will try and prevent infection for the young men today as I would for anyone who has an injury of any kind."

"Well, Corinne, I must admit, after my ma's horse was missing yesterday morning I was about ready to beat those boys myself. My mother cried for hours, but when I found out they was getting a whipping I was happy. They caused a lot of trouble."

Corinne tried to ignore him, but she failed, commenting back before her better judgment stopped her.

"Honestly, Sidney. You are happy to hear someone is going to suffer agonizing pain?" Corinne asked him pointedly.

Cookie was nearby and coughed to disguise his laugh at the sickened look on Sidney's face. Sidney looked a bit like a guilty puppy.

"Well, no. Well, I mean the wagon train manifest says the punishment is a whipping, but I didn't know this would upset you so much." Sidney dumped half his coffee on her boots as he tried to back away from his current statements. "I misspoke Corinne. I am just lucky that I haven't fallen asleep on the night watch."

"Aren't you too young for the night watch? Isn't the age over eighteen for night watch duty?" Reggie chimed in, to make Sidney crawl a little more. His company every morning this week had been a nuisance. It was trying their patience, too. Cookie and Reggie shared a glance and were trying not to choke on their laughter.

"I turn eighteen in a few weeks, certainly man enough for the job now. We joined the train late and they had a scheduled rotation. I wasn't needed." Sidney sounded pouty and defensive. His thin boyish shoulders slouched dejectedly.

"I will gladly aid you if you have any needs today, or any day, Corinne. I will go eat with my mother this morning, but I will check in on you later." Sidney stood and was gone with a bound. Corinne didn't even try to wave because he never looked back. She had a feeling he was as resilient as a cactus. He would need no encouragement from her.

Clive and Lucas came by a few minutes after breakfast to escort Corinne to the front of the train. The boys were going to get their punishment before the wagons rolled out. Corinne was hoping to tend their wounds before they started traveling for the day. Treatment in a lurching wagon wasn't going to be ideal but she was willing to do whatever was necessary.

The boys were scared but stoic. The morning wasn't hot but they both were sweating a bit. Corinne could tell who the parents were by the stressed looks on their faces, a mixture of regret and fear pasted on their foreheads.

The sun was rising, with a yellow glow that should have put everyone in a good mood, but the first duty was for every man and woman to witness the punishment being carried out.

The first boy was led to an area prepared with two small trees serving as the whipping post. His wrists were tied one to each tree and his shirt removed. Then Mr. Walters announced the crime and punishment, while the man with a whip came forward. Corinne recognized the man as an ox wrangler but didn't know him. The whip was long and dark against the brightness of the morning. Corinne stared numbly at the boy's pale back.

The first crack of the whip settled with perfect accuracy across the skin. Corinne jumped at the sound. She stopped breathing as the second crack rang across the opening. The crowd watched unhappily as the welts multiplied.

Two, then four, then five.

The boy's reserve was lost. Screams began, he started to squirm, and the welts got worse. With one move, the whip lashed on top of a welt and blood started to flow. He yelled more, saying again and again how sorry he was.

Corinne was openly crying now, along with the majority of the other women there. Corinne felt a presence behind her and a hand upon her shoulder. She looked into the comfort of Lucas's understanding eyes. She leaned into him and pulled his arm around her shoulder and over to the other side. With his arm around her in a protective embrace, she could hide herself from the crack of the whip and the boy's pain.

Finally, the first boy was done. He was untied and taken to his parents. He had several open welts from squirming and would probably need a few stitches.

Now the next boy's turn came. He was shaking so badly he could barely walk. His father helped him with his shirt and even tied one of his wrists. The father spoke calming words to his boy before Mr. Walters read his fate in front of the crowd.

"Lucas, I don't know if I can watch again." Corinne felt fresh tears fall but didn't even wipe them away. She held her breath again as the first crack came down, jolting her with its crisp sound as it echoed. She watched as two more lashes fell on his back. She could not watch anymore. She turned and buried her head into Lucas's chest and whimpered, as the boy cried out with each lash, until his ten were received. Lucas pulled her chin up when it was over. He handed her a hanky and gently kissed her forehead. She wiped her eyes and reached around his middle for a brief hug, before letting go.

They didn't need to say a word. He was just there for her. She knew that for certain now. After sharing a silent look with Lucas, she stepped away. She was carrying her kit and herself wherever needed, when she collided with Sidney. He stared at her angrily.

"Corinne, I thought you were my girl." Sidney looked crushed but stood his ground. Corinne was worried and felt trapped. *Hadn't I told him already that I wasn't his, or any one's? Well, he likely witnessed the tender moment between Lucas and me.* She did not care. She was tired of his possessiveness and clinging. He had absolutely no claim over her.

"Sidney, I have never said I was your girl. I am not anyone's girl," Corinne said softly, trying to not make a scene.

"Why did Lucas just kiss you?" Sidney's eyes were red. His boyish emotions rising, tears threatening to spill.

"He kissed me on the forehead, Sidney. Stop being so dramatic. He is a good friend of mine and he was comforting me while I was upset. If you will pardon me, I have some mending to take care of." Corinne was losing her patience. She decided to push past him and let him deal with his own problems today. She was through coddling his childish behavior.

Mr. Walters led Corinne to each of the boys' wagons, and with help from their mothers, she got each of them stitched and cleaned. Corinne eased the families' fears and for the next few days she said she would check in on them every time the wagons stopped. Both boys were young and should heal quickly.

The wagons rolled out soon after Corinne finished. She walked back to her own wagon outfit, where Clover was saddled and ready for her. She thanked her crew and spent a quiet day on the trail alone. She was not in the mood for much company, beyond the occasional female trip for privacy and necessity.

The morning whipping had affected her. At first, the faces around her had been expectant. Some were even excited, like it was entertainment. Corinne felt nothing but horror. She prayed for the poor boys through the entire thing. She knew what they did was wrong, but the healer in her hated pain of any kind.

The noon and evening stops kept Corinne busy checking the status of her young patients. They both rallied enough to eat. This encouraged Corinne. Eating was always a good sign. She even got a weak smile out of Caleb, the first boy who was whipped. He was eighteen and a bit silly. But now, there was sadness in his eyes that would last a few more days. Corinne had been worried about the second boy, Charlie, until he decided to eat. He was a bit more sullen and embarrassed, but after eating, he sat up for a little while. They would both be sleeping on their stomachs for a few days, but they would recover.

The next few mornings the Temple outfit was quiet. Sidney had not made an appearance. Corinne secretly wished her harsh treatment had calmed his attraction to her. For several weeks, she tried to patiently endure his presence. Well, almost patiently. She was very grateful for the reprieve.

The wagons rolled out of Fort Boise within a few days. They embarked on the northern route along the Boise River and made great time. They were all eager to beat the mountain snow.

Clive and Lucas kept busy teaching the Shoshone some English and scouting the trail. Corinne heard whispers about the local Indians, but they all seemed friendly enough. They had a large enough train, that theft was only a problem if people got careless. The Indians were very helpful for getting the wagons across the rivers safely. As September was drawing near, they were becoming increasingly valuable in trading for new animals. The Indians had been trading oxen, mule, and horses with eastern travelers for several years now. They had healthy animals to trade to those whose animals had died or were too weary to continue.

Chapter Twenty-Nine
August 22, 1848

Corinne knew she was in trouble. She heard a loud crack and felt splintered shards of tooth float onto her tongue. It was two seconds, without breathing, then pain sliced through her jaw.

She decided to throw ladylike table manners aside. She spit out meat, buckshot, and bits of tooth into her hand. She got close to the fire, so she could see what happened.

"What is wrong Corinne?" Cookie and Reggie looked concerned. Corinne was certain she would be fine, so she shook it off.

"Just bit a piece of buckshot, no fuss necessary. So sorry to spit at dinner." She grinned, but tried not to grimace when a sharp pain took her by surprise.

"No trouble, my lady," Reggie said, chuckling at the joke. "You may spit anytime in front of me. I promise not to tell anyone."

"Sorry about the buckshot. Sometimes the hunting can get sloppy, with a few of our inexperienced scouts," Cookie said quietly. They were all still sensitive talking about the loss of the main scout party. It was a bad memory and would be for a long time.

Everyone, but Corinne, finished eating. She was fighting a losing battle. Her heartbeat elevated every time her tongue traveled to the source of pain in her jaw. The sharp edge of a jagged molar was her new challenge.

She waited until the dishes were washed, before heading to her wagon with a lantern. She rustled around in her trunks of extra oils and ointment. Finally, she found clove oil. She spent another minute looking for slippery elm bark but gave up in the semi-darkness. The lantern light was a warm, orange glow bouncing off the white bonnet above her. She stared blankly for a minute before starting the exploration in her mouth.

She conversed with herself while sitting in the wagon. With freshly washed hands, she applied a little clove oil to her pinky finger. *The key is to get the oil in the right spot,* she thought to herself. *Drat!* She missed and hit the roof of her mouth. Now her tongue tasted the overly-sweet cloves. The cloves had a strange numbing sensation that was unpleasant. Corinne bit back a complaint and began again. Fresh oil and back in, hopefully this time, with better aim. She reapplied the oil, and with a quick prayer, found the center of the gaping hole on the side of the rear molar. The clove oil instantly helped with a measure of the pain, but Corinne nearly gagged. She exited the wagon and washed her hands again. She walked over to Chelsea's wagon, and in silence, the two women did their necessary walk. She headed to bed without talking to anyone.

The moon was overhead when Corinne bolted up straight. Her mouth was open, and she was certain she had moaned or yelled, and woke herself. She tasted blood in her mouth and all the flavor of the cloves was gone.

She heard stirring in the camp and knew she would have visitors shortly. Reggie and Cookie greeted her at the side of her wagon.

"Corinne!" Reggie whispered hoarsely. "Are you injured? Is someone in there with you?"

"I am alone Reggie, I have a bad tooth. I am sorry to wake everyone." Corinne felt the fool as she climbed out a few minutes later, dressed in yesterday's clothes. She should have dealt with her tooth before bed, but she was a coward. She hated to admit that she was afraid, but she truly was.

"I am sorry," she said humbly, holding her left cheek. That didn't help with the pain but seemed comforting to protect the tooth. She wanted to cry when she saw all the adults from the Grant outfit walking up to them, lanterns in hand. Her night was complete.

"We heard Corinne yell. Is all well?" Clive asked first. His look of concern was as sincere as everyone else's. She was mortified but also felt loved.

"I am sorry," Corinne said, a little thickly. Her cheek was swollen, and she was swallowing a lot. "I broke a molar on some buckshot and tried to manage it on my own. I am sorry to wake everyone. I am a fool," Corinne said lamely. She was tired and in pain and hated to inconvenience everyone. She inhaled sharply as another pain shot through her skull. It was getting worse.

"Oh Corinne, you aren't a fool. I did the same thing a few years ago. I got a cavity from too many sweets and pretended I was fine for the longest time." Chelsea stepped forward and gave her a sisterly hug. "I got the worst fever and eventually had to own up to my problem. That tooth is gonna have to go!" Chelsea said with a pout.

Corinne nodded and moaned in agreement. Then she did a fake cry, a little pathetically. Everyone chuckled when she brought her head up with a lopsided smile.

"No one is gonna pull my tooth in the dark. Let's not get silly," Corinne said seriously then listened as the plan unfolded for her day. Clive came by with a quick solution for the rest of the evening, whiskey. Chelsea would administer the whiskey to help Corinne sleep. They would stay behind until there was enough light in the sky. Then, Clive would do the extraction. He claimed to have the most experience.

Corinne spent the next hour sipping whiskey, in medicinal doses, and putting clove oil in the proper spot again, to numb the pain. Chelsea was good company. She kept Corinne laughing, until they both lost their battle with sleep.

Corinne woke up several times when sharp pains took over. Corinne weathered the pain bravely and tried to fall back asleep.

"Are you ready?" Corinne closed her eyes and nodded. She held Chelsea's hand as Clive's supportive voice talked to her calmly. He used her own mother's surgical pliers and was ready to make quick work of Corinne's tooth.

The whiskey was again warm in Corinne's belly. It made her feel affected and loose muscled. She knew that would go away soon enough. She just didn't want to embarrass herself by screaming too loudly.

She leaned back and felt the tool enter her mouth. Clive's hands smelled like soap and the lavender oil he used to clean the pliers. He was as gentle as he could be, until the work needed to be done.

In a quick, masterful move, he grasped the offending tooth with the pliers. Corinne moaned a little from discomfort and felt her legs wanting to squirm. Russell held her head and shoulders as the pulling began. White-hot pain shot through Corinne's skull, but she barely moaned. She focused on breathing and not screaming, as the tooth fought its losing battle to hold strong. With the second pull, the tooth was free. Everyone sighed with relief when Corinne sat up and bit on a clean bit of cloth. She grinned weakly, and after the bleeding slowed, she muffled a thank you to everyone.

Reggie, Lucas, and Cookie joined them after the ordeal. They gave the group privacy but checked on Corinne to make certain she was truly okay. She was still a little affected by the whiskey and gladly laid down in her wagon for the remainder of the day.

Chapter Thirty
Fort Boise - September 3, 1848

Some hilly conditions made travel a bit difficult for a few days, but they were finally at Fort Boise. Fresh elk, flour, coffee, and some fruit preserves were purchased. Men shared ideas about routes and the local Indians. The weather was fine. The warm day and the fresh supplies put everyone in the mood for a celebration.

In addition to Clive and Lucas, Corinne made sure to dance with her two new friends, Caleb, and Charlie. After a few rounds, Corinne held Brody, so Chelsea and Russell could take a few turns around the camp. The music played into the night. Corinne smiled and waved to Sidney, who was dancing with a young lady from the camp. She was probably only fifteen, but Corinne thought they looked charming together. She hoped Sidney had moved on from his boyish infatuation.

As Corinne sat with Brody, she tapped her feet, watching Clive dance with 'Dolly'. Corinne kept her thoughts on the present. With the impossibly tall mountains ahead, she tried to keep worry from getting the better of her. Corinne's heart was longing to find a home again. Traveling life was not in her blood. Her thoughts jumped ahead to her father's home and hearth. She rocked Brody in her lap and dreamed of a new beginning. His warm heartbeat joined hers as they both enjoyed swaying to the music filling the night air.

The next day they crossed the Snake River. Corinne got across with her own horse and into a safe place. In the swift flow of water, a few unlucky souls lost their lives and wagons. Andrew's wagon was very nearly lost to the current, before some fast thinking men saved it. They were able to get ropes hooked on it, before it tipped. Corinne watched from the safety of the other shore, but seeing Reggie and Cookie so close to danger, shook up her nerves. These were her men, her crew. She said a prayer of thanks that her crew was safe.

Corinne was on the other side of the river when Clover heard a sound and bucked. Corinne lost her seating. She went flying, bumped her head, and rolled for a second or two, before she felt water splashing all around her. At first, she was dazed and saw stars.

Where am I?

The water was chilly, and under its surface, the gurgling current was loud. Quickly, the river swept her along. She broke the surface once or twice, gasping for air, but was pulled back under. She began to panic as her lungs started burning. Her head hit another rock, feeling a thud deep to her core. Kicking her legs, she cursed her skirts and petticoats for entangling her.

She grabbed at anything. Reaching out, she found a branch. With what little energy she had left, she used the branch to pull herself up on a rock. She laid there for a minute without moving, except to breathe and cough. By the time she had coughed up all the water that she had breathed in or swallowed in her panic, her lungs and throat were raw. Her head ached from hitting something underwater. She laid there thinking of Angela falling into the ravine, knowing that had been so much worse than what had just happened. Groaning, she sat up slowly and observed her surroundings. There were high rock walls on each side of the river. The crossing had been a good place. This was not.

It was dark and foreboding as she looked up, her head pounding. Near the top, the rocky cliff was ragged. With shaky legs, Corinne stood and tried to climb the wall but the edges near her were smooth and mocked her. There was nothing for her to grab. She looked down. The rock ledge she was sitting on was covered in slime, and a few mysterious spongy things that Corinne assumed were alive in some way. Head still pounding, she sat back down, ignoring the slime. Her dress and petticoats were now filthy and clinging to her legs even worse than they were in the water. Corinne sighed and looked up at the edge, hoping to see someone looking for her. At the wagon crossing, there was always a lot of chaos.

How long before someone notices that I am missing? she wondered.

She thought about yelling, but with the headache, she figured she should save herself some pain. She was not desperate enough to yell, yet.

She was glad the clouds were moving in a little, to block the hot sun. She had been sitting on the slimy rock for more than twenty minutes according to her pendant watch. She had shaken the water from it and it was still ticking. She pinned it back on her damp collar. She heard a few far-off gunshots and watched a torn-up wagon come around the bend, toward her part of the river. Corinne panicked a second but then saw the water pull it away from her perch, dragging its twisted, empty shell away. She hoped the family got out in time and said a prayer for whoever they were.

She was so focused on the errant wagon, she didn't hear the nearby voices. She pulled herself away from praying, looked up and saw Clive and Lucas smiling down at her.

"Well, you are a sight to see, my Corinne!" Clive yelled down. His eyes showed fear while his smile tried to chase it away.

Lucas didn't say a word but helped Clive with some clever rope tying. After twenty minutes of scheming with the ropes tied around a nearby tree, using leverage and a few loops, they got Corinne back on dry land. Filthy, damp, and bruised but sound. She rode back with Clive holding on to her protectively, like her father had when she was a child.

Chelsea had grief written across her face as Corinne and the men arrived. Russell was trying to keep her calm but failed. Tearstains on her cheeks, she ran to Corinne and held her close like a sister, for two solid minutes.

"I just don't want to lose you, Cori!" Chelsea was emotional, but Corinne didn't care. She would be just as upset if anything happened to Chelsea. Her heart was still sore from her experience with Angela. She missed Angela every day and now Corinne became very protective of those she loved.

She asked Chelsea to help her change, and with shaky legs and hands, Corinne climbed into the wagon. Chelsea helped her with the damp fabric and all the buttons. Corinne felt some muscles tighten up and thought she might have gotten banged up more than she realized. She could still hear the roar of the water in her head. She let out a shaky breath, finally letting herself feel afraid. She allowed herself the luxury of crying with her friend Chelsea, as they peeled her out of her wet things. Once her hair was brushed and she was dressed in a warm cotton frock, she exited the wagon. She saw the men watching for her across the camp.

They all fussed over Corinne's scratches on her forehead. She pushed their prodding fingers away, claiming she was fine. This day had started hard enough, without them worrying over a trifle of a scratches and bruises. She knew others were having difficulty on the rough and tumble Snake River. She didn't want the unnecessary attention.

Within hours, several more accidents claimed more lives and wagons. Hasty funerals were held. Corinne's crew and the Grants attended quietly. They were all thinking about Corinne's close call today. It could have gone so much worse.

Mr. Walters called the adults together. They discussed the next stretch and the routes they would be taking. Everyone was told again to lighten heavy loads.

The Blue Mountains were ahead. No one wanted a repeat of last year's infamous Donner party tragedy. Everyone read in the newspapers about those people getting trapped in the snowy mountains. Their unspeakable deaths and actions served as a warning to those who were ill prepared and unwise.

The mood was somber as they headed through another area of alkali water. There were rivers and then there were none. The weather was mostly fair as they headed toward Powder River. The road was difficult, and everyone felt the incline. The wagons stretched out and they camped on the incline. It was a poor place to camp, with shoulder height sagebrush. With little grass, the animals protested.

The early morning brought minimal relief. They rolled out, grinding their wheels against the tough incline, hacking through sagebrush, and choking on the flying loose soil.

They all kept their eyes to the top, as they could barely see the end of the incline. They climbed for four long, grueling days up Burnt River Hill. The weary animals were finally given a rest, on the fourth evening. Tempers were high. There was no relief from the lack of water. Campsites were barely functional.

Trying to cook over an inclined campfire proved nearly impossible. Even getting a stool to stay put on the uneven ground, made resting difficult. Corinne and everyone had gone to bed early. Corinne tossed and turned for quite a while, trying to get comfortable. She once flipped over with a frustrated jerk and heard the wagon creak in protest. There were wood blocks under the wheels to keep the wagon from rolling haphazardly back down the mountainside, but that creak had brought up a sense of panic. *Did I wiggle the blocks free?*

She didn't want to think about what would happen if her wheels broke free and she tumbled down the hill. She shuddered and laid still for a long while, even in discomfort, before her mind would allow her to sleep.

The next morning dawned with petty arguments and harsh words. The wagon boss had to remind everyone who was the law. Several men had been warned to shape up or get left behind.

Four more hours of hacking through sagebrush brought them to their sanctuary, the lush Baker Valley. Meandering the valley floor, the Powder River spread out before them, and a thick, green forest gave them a hint of the fertile land that soon would be called home.

Hope fluttered in Corinne's heart. After the morning sun brought the warmth of the day, the mist cleared. In the distance, the Blue Mountains peaked their heads up. Beyond, were valleys and green grass. A promise, full of dreams. The wagons ground to a halt and everyone took a moment to enjoy the view. They were so close to their promised land. Jimmy and Joe, in the way of twins, began singing a song at the same moment. Corinne was always amazed how well they worked together.

Corinne rode Clover while listening to the Blake brothers sing. Clover handled the terrain well. Corrine was still sore, mostly her back, from her mishap on Snake River. All the twisting underwater had pinched and pulled her muscles a bit. The horse riding and walking was not the most restful way to heal. Corinne never complained, but was quick to retreat to her wagon in the evenings. She hummed along with the Baker boys, to distract herself from the stiff muscles.

She escaped into her mind for hours, plotting and scheming about fields, herbs, and all she wanted to accomplish. She often wondered if a woman could ever be considered a sound business person. She spent too many thoughts waffling between doubting herself and dreaming of sharing her goals. It filled the many long days in the saddle. More than anything, Corinne wished to see her father and share her heart with him, after three years of being alone. But for now, her goal was survival. The mountains could not hold her back.

I have too much to live for, Corinne thought.

The terrain suddenly changed. The green grass was plentiful. The draft animals freely grazed, as they rested near the river that day. Stocks of fresh meat were restored, as elk and hare were shot for supper. The young children went into the forest with their mothers, gathering bags of mushrooms and wild berries. Suddenly, the world was new again. Spirits were refreshed. This was their start, the promise of the West. They could envision a future in this wild land. Corinne could see hers, too.

Chapter Thirty-One
Sept 9, 1848

After two days of rest, the wagon train rolled ahead. They kept close to the Powder River and crossed it the next morning. They crossed another fork again the next day. The terrain was tougher to negotiate but water and wood supplies were high. Repairs made to wheels and wagons kept every man and ox handler busy. Soaked wheels and used spares were a common sight. Corinne was so grateful for her crew and realized daily how lost she would be without them. Everyone was happy to be moving forward. Even if the trail led to hardship, they could face it. They had seen the worst, and they had survived.

After a few days of rain and rough terrain, illness began to increase. Corinne spent her day backtracking to stopped wagons, tending to the fevers and chills in several outfits. Some kind of fever was taking hold of families. Headaches, and sweaty, clammy skin were the main complaints. Feverfew tea helped, and Corinne gave fresh water liberally to those infected. During the day the sun was warm, but the nights were bitterly cold. The lingering drizzle caused the fever to keep more than twenty people moving slowly. Corinne used her last supplies of herbs and teas. Cookie and Chelsea along with others, kept busy making broth to aid the sufferers. Corinne joined with Clive and some of the older women on the train, to find ways to stop this fever. Everyone dug through their wagons, finding more feverfew and other helpful teas. Everyone survived. They kept moving through the rugged terrain, sick or well.

Though the hills were steep, the roads were specifically chosen to get the wagons safely through the mountainous terrain. They moved rocks and branches, and when necessary, used ropes and pulleys to get the wagons through. Every strong man spent his days either blazing the trail or forcing the animals forward. A few animals succumbed to exhaustion while in the yoke. dying where they had taken their last step. Broken limbs and pulled muscles became more common. Corinne did everything she could to help, but she was no doctor. Except for her oils, she had few supplies left to help anyone.

There was a heavy frost several mornings. Everyone began those days in warmer gear, only to later shrug off the clothing, after a tiresome day of travel. The rain and hail were brutal. The evening after the worst hailstorm, Corinne patched up those who had cuts from the pea-sized hail that had poured down on their heads.

The Blue Mountain crossing area had plenty of firewood, if only you could find any of it dry. Chilly rain fell almost every day. The nearby Cayuse Indians had fresh salmon, peas, and potatoes to sell or trade. They followed along the train and were quite companionable. They built ferries for the large rivers and streams, charging reasonable prices to help the train across. The ferries made everyone's lives easier. An occasional ferry tipped, but the loss was not great during the last half of the journey.

Their days in the Blue Mountains were ones of struggle, constantly adapting to the environment. They cleared trees, moved rocks, or found a better path around, as needed. They progressed favorably and made it safely to the Umatilla River. Not one person died during the mountainous journey.

Corinne had Jim and Joe trade with some of the local Indians. She needed to replace several head of oxen. A few had died, and two more were doing poorly. Corinne was concerned that their outfit would be left behind. Other groups had been, when their animals could go no further. Finding a good trade, at the right time, was important. Corinne was grateful to the animals which had taken them so far. She knew it was silly, but she thanked the animals, patting each of their rumps before trading them.

Corinne pushed all thoughts out of her head but survival. She kept her dreams in her pocket for another day. She told herself to focus on the moment and push the wishes of her heart to the side. She and Lucas regarded each other as friends, nothing more. When she fell into Snake River, he lingered close to her for several days, but Corinne kept him at a distance. There was no need to pine for a man who was taken. Her goal was survival. She laughed whenever a romantic thought fell into her head. Her hair was dirtier than it had ever been. Her clothes were like rags, tattered and stained. It had been months since she even looked in a mirror. The summer bugs had surely eaten away any skin she had, long ago. Now was not a time for romance. She had other problems to face right now.

Food stocks were running low. Yet Corinne, along with her crew of four grown men, had to be fed. She was grateful that she had set aside money for purchasing food from the Indians. They only had a few more days' supply of coffee. Instead of buying more coffee, she knew there were some people in the train who would gladly trade their coffee for paper money. She would help those folks out, giving them some much needed paper money. The wagon train was good at notifying everyone of each other's business. There were several families who had run out of funds. They all knew which families were struggling. They did not leave gossip behind, and like any good sin, a wicked tongue traveled easily.

They had been on the road, traveling together for more than five months. Everyone could feel the anticipation. Every mile they traveled was counted in their hearts. As they crossed rivers they sensed the nearness of the end. The lush valleys they camped in, reminded them why they had traveled. To be in this beautiful land and begin anew.

Corinne also longed for the fresh start to begin. This nomadic lifestyle had worn as thin as her clothes. She looked around her. These people struggled along the rocky roads, chopping through trees and thorns to get their families through. Their journey was almost over.

At Four Mile Canyon, the view of Mount Hood to the west was truly magnificent. The white-tipped peak reached the top of the sky, reminding and warning them of the last barrier before they arrived at their new homeland. Clive sent a few scouts ahead to tell the town about their arrival. They would also bring back any information of obstacles on the path. The new scouts had learned their job well. Everyone was grateful for all the work they had done to keep them moving, and for the hunting, providing necessary meat to keep their strength up.

<hr />

Mr. Walters called the group together. Decisions had to be made. There was a fork in the road ahead and each wagon outfit had to decide who would move in which direction. The decision was not an easy one.

Most were planning on taking the new southern road around Mount Hood instead of the Dalles Rapids river trip. Every year several people drown in the rapids while trying to cross. No one who had survived this trip thus far, wanted to watch another family member die in an unnecessary water crossing. Though it would be a few days slower, taking the Southern, safer option was a blessing to most of the travelers.

Corinne met with her crew the evening they camped on the John Day River. They discussed, at length, the option of The Dalles versus the new Barlow Road. The grueling temptation was to take the quicker Dalles choice. A day or two compared to a week of a rough mountain pass. Everyone agreed that the road was the better option. It wasn't worth more loss of life. But the mountain passes they had just survived were still fresh in their memory. The Blake brothers, Cookie and Reggie all had an equal say. Unanimously, they voted to go the Barlow Road. Corinne passed along the information to the wagon boss. They spent the evening preparing the wagons for the days ahead by soaking wheels and repairing axels. Chelsea came by to tell Corinne that their outfit was doing the same route.

Their friendship had blossomed on this long journey together. Corinne thought of her as the perfect example of a strong woman. Chelsea's relationship with Russell gave her a lot of positive visions of a good marriage. She could not help but look to Russell's brother and wonder if he would make as good a husband.

The next morning, they crossed the John Day River. They followed the map toward the next river crossing in two days' travel. The scenery was breathtaking as rock and river competed with the peaks, creating walls to the north and south of them.

Scouts and maps showed them the safest way through. More days of climbing hills pushed their animals and their bodies to the limit. Then, fighting inertia on the way down challenged them. When the way got treacherous, they got out the ropes and chains, easing stubborn animals and wagons down slowly. Again, muscles and tempers were tested often.

A cold rain started in the afternoon and continued during the night. There was no dry firewood, so most went to their beds with little or no supper. When the next morning dawned, some nearby

Walla Walla Indians sold dry firewood and fresh meat to them. Everyone ate a hearty breakfast, then the wagons rolled out. They made good time with food in their bellies. The oxen and horses did well, too, with plenty of plant life to graze on.

They reached the Deschutes River. The Walla Walla Indians followed them and offered to help. The Walla Wallas found a low point, an easier crossing ground for the wagons and animals. The current was strong, however, and the rocks gave more than one wagon trouble.

The sight of the Columbia River reminded them of the choice they all had to make in one day's travel. The Dalles were ahead!

Chapter Thirty-Two
Sept 18, 1848

The wagons rolled out, frost still on the ground. The sky above was overcast, and the train members smelled more rain in the air. They wanted to get in as many miles today as possible before the rains hit. By noon, the wind and rain left everyone soaked and cold. The gusty wind furthered the situation from annoying to miserable. Animals pushed against the wind and the miles were hard-won. By mid-afternoon, the dark sky opened. Suddenly the sun burst through, just as they came upon the fork in the road.

The Dalles stood straight ahead and the great Columbia River was showing all her glory. Only five wagons stayed put deciding to camp there and ferry their way to Oregon City.

With determined hearts, the remaining travelers turned south to get a few more miles of road behind them before camping for the night. Mount Hood was the next obstacle and they all watched her throughout the evening. When they stopped to camp that night, Corinne noticed everyone was quiet. There were no more words to say. Bodies were bone weary and thin. There was no more gossip or fun to be had until they reached their destination. The goal was within their grasp. Just a few more days. Just a few more days...

Corinne spent the early morning preparing biscuits with Cookie. Many families were struggling without food stocks. Tempers rose, as some who had food complained about those who had run out. Some families chose to suffer in silence. Others were very vocal about expecting help from others. Corinne would not get involved with any of the negative hearsay. Instead she chose to act. She knew their outfit had plenty. They had rationed carefully with the help of Cookie and Reggie. Throughout the night, they took turns preparing food on the sheet iron cook stove, to give to those without. She recruited Chelsea and Brody and a few Grant tagalongs to distribute biscuits, bacon bits and potatoes. After nearly a hundred hugs, Corinne realized she had made a few life-long friends. Other folks could be angry all they wanted. She preferred a good deed done, instead of always having to express opinions. It was the way she was raised.

⚬

That day, the steep hills were treacherous and deadly. A resident of Oregon City, Sam Barlow, had traveled this trail several years back. With a few friends, he cleared a path to Oregon City, so wagons could bypass the expansive and dangerous Dalles area. Sam Barlow's Road was the result. But this road had dangers, too.

After struggling on the choppy terrain for two days, Corinne was devastated when her own horse, Clover, stumbled. Corinne didn't like riding her horse on the steep incline. She was proven wise when Clover fell about ten feet down the hill. Corinne gasped, watching her horse's body roll and twist against the trees and rocks along the edge. Clover's roll slowed, and she jumped up to a standing position, quickly. Corinne ran to her to carefully to assess the damage.

Clover's body was sound, but her legs were scratched up and bleeding badly. Corinne unsaddled Clover. She sought advice from Clive and Russell when they reached the camp later in the day. Corinne cleaned the wounds, removing any dirt and debris. Clover still had a limp but did not have any noticeable breaks or muscle tears. Clive and Russell agreed that the injury was superficial. Perhaps, without a rider, Clover would mend perfectly. If she could survive the terrain.

The Barlow Road was not without other incidents. Several weak oxen perished the first day on the road. A few more the second. The uphill climbs were brutal, and the road not always perfectly cleared. Corinne received more cuts and bruises than she ever had in her life. As a child, she had fallen off a horse a few times, but that was nothing compared to the aches her body felt now.

For five days, they struggled on Barlow Road, with the forest and steep hills around. Mount Hood led them to a pleasant sandy bar next to a clear flowing river bank. The night had fallen. The way ahead seemed simpler.

Clive told everyone they would arrive the next day. If anyone had one ounce of energy left, they would have continued. But the animals could go no further without rest and feeding. Corinne suspected the same for the people, too.

That night they ate small meals and headed to bed early, but not without a group prayer and a few minutes to thank God for how far they had come. Lucas pulled out his violin, played a sweet melody and then Amazing Grace. All shared tears of exhaustion and joy. It was a beautiful moment.

Chapter Thirty-Three
Sept 24, 1848

The air was crisp on her face as she walked along. Clover was tied to the slow-moving wagon, as they climbed the shallow hills that morning. Her heart felt squeezed within her chest. She knew it would be hours before she would get a glimpse of the town. Still, her heart raced to think about where she was.

A few wagons ahead of Corinne's outfit had already climbed the hill. She kept glancing ahead to see signs of homes, farms, or anything that looked like a town. Her heart jumped when a shotgun boomed in the distance. She was already on edge, but when she heard the cheers around her, she nearly jumped out of her skin. She looked up at Jim Blake who sat in the wagon box and had a better view.

"Some people up ahead. They aren't part of the train." He smiled big and Corinne's heart began its own race again.

She picked up her skirts and walked faster. She reached the top of the hill within a minute. The flat valley before her looked like a farm. She covered her eyes from the bright sunlight. She saw a house in the far corner and a path that could pass for a road nearby.

A road...

Her heart thrilled at the sight.

The Blake brothers reached the top of the hill within a few minutes and began hooting themselves. Chelsea was behind Corinne and caught up after hearing the shouts. They shared an embrace and tears, and continued walking. They had no words, just joy shared between them. As they followed the wagons ahead of them, they noticed what looked like a gathering in a cleared field. As they drew closer, they saw buggies and horses tethered there.

The wagons stopped, and everyone piled out of wagon boxes. They walked together, leaving their animals in harness to graze along the grassy road. A gathering was waiting for them.

Corinne walked toward the group. She saw a sea of happy faces. She did not recognize anyone yet.

"Corinne!"

She heard it. Like a yell across a canyon, but it was there. She looked to her right and stopped moving. Her hand blocked the bright sun distorting her vision. She saw a man in a black suit. He headed her way, his hat waving about as he called out again.

He was there, it was him!

Her dear father ran toward her in his own reckless way. His black hair, his beaming grin. As he approached and barreled into her with a bear hug, she saw her own eyes looking back at her.

"My girl, my baby girl."

His tears fell as freely as hers. The fears, and pain of the past melted away with a new love and acceptance of each other. She hugged him back as she remembered his smell. Her childhood memories of his warm hugs rushed back to her. She was safe and loved.

He pulled away and laughed. "You got taller, a little," he chuckled, as he away wiped a few tears.

"You look good father. I missed you so much." She started crying again and reached for another hug. "I am so sorry Papa." She sobbed, and he just held her.

"Now don't you say it again. We have both made our mistakes. We are together again, at last. I just love you and am glad you are safe. You don't know how much I prayed that this was not a mistake. I wanted to see you so badly but knew the dangers. Oh, my girl, you are safe."

Part Three:

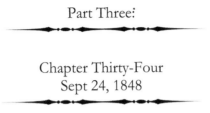

Chapter Thirty-Four
Sept 24, 1848

"Where is your husband, Andrew? Back at the wagon?" His voice was so warm and loving but his words stopped her heart. They were walking toward the wagon. "His family is so eager to see him, too."

Corinne stopped and took a deep breath. She had been having nightmares about this for months. She dreaded breaking the hearts of his family. "He died nearly four months ago, of cholera." Corinne wanted to keep the story simple but saw her father's face fall. He looked like he wanted to say something but kept silent.

"It was horrible, father," Corinne continued, feeling so weary. "Can we find his family? I want to tell all of you." Corinne held herself together. She walked arm in arm with her father back into the crowd.

He waved a couple over and Corinne saw the resemblance at once. The tall man had Andrew's blond curly hair, cut short just the way Andrew wore it. His mom's smile looked so much like the smile Corinne rarely ever saw. She was no taller than Corinne and seemed very sweet.

"Is this your Corinne?" The dark blond woman spoke. Her smile was huge as she reached forward to share a hug with her daughter-in-law. "I've been dreaming about meeting you for eight months." Corinne accepted the embrace but knew she had to break the news to them soon.

"I am so sorry, Mr. and Mrs. Temple. I have bad news that cannot wait... Your son passed away four months ago, of cholera." She watched Mrs. Temple go from confused to devastated. She buried her face into her husband's chest. Corinne watched them accept their loss, while reliving the awful night in her mind. She realized she was crying again.

"I am so sorry. I know this is not how you wanted to meet me." Corinne was certain she was handling this all wrong. "I kept all of his belongings. They are yours whenever you are ready." Corinne felt overwhelmed and exhausted. She barely knew these people but felt so wretched for meeting them with such horrible news.

"Let's head back to my home and we can absorb all that has happened. I'm sure your crew is ready to rest." Her father took charge and organized everyone in quick order. They met the crew. The Temple family awkwardness was only short-lived, as everyone was exhausted and just wanted to finish their traveling and find shelter.

Wagons rolled out, following Corinne's father in his buggy. The Temple's followed behind. Corinne rode next to her father, wordlessly. He finally broke the silence.

"I know this is hard for you, you have been through so much. To have to help them mourn the loss of their son must be difficult as well. I am so sorry you had to endure this trip alone."

Corinne smiled faintly. She had survived the trip, but she had never felt alone for long. Good friends were there for her. The Blake brothers, Reggie and Cookie, then the Grants and Clive. She smiled when she thought of Clive and knew she would have some introductions to make once everyone was rested.

"You just smiled a little, what are you thinking of?" John Harpole asked. Seeing her grin had warmed his heart.

"Clive." She just shared one word.

"Who the heck is Clive?" John laughed.

"Clive Quackenbush is an amazing scout, and now a personal friend and secretly adopted grandfather." She truly wished it so. "He was a guardian angel to me. You will meet him soon."

"Quackenbush... There is a Mercantile in town that is owned by a Quackenbush."

"That would be Clive's business, well one of them. He also consults with the government, is a scout, a trapper, and Indian negotiations expert. I have learned so much from him." Corinne smiled a little more but then found herself overwhelmed and tired again. "How close is your home?"

"About three more miles. We are on the southern edge of town. We have a great spread. The Temple's live nearby. We set up the property that way. Our homes are on the edge, so we will have close neighbors in case of trouble. This land can seem big when we are all spread out. Having a close neighbor is good." John looked thoughtful for a few minutes. Nothing ever happened the way he expected it too.

"I have another surprise that you won't be expecting. I recently got married, to a widow in town named Marie." John smiled but saw the shocked look on Corinne's face. "I had thought it would be such a pleasant surprise but now I realize it may all be a bit much to take in. She is a sweet woman and her son is wonderful. He is six years old and well... you will just love him."

Corinne was spinning with the information but wanted to have something to say to her father. "I am happy that you are happy. It is a lot to take in, but honestly after some rest everything will seem a little easier too. I feel so beat up and dirty. I have dreamt of a real bath and a real bed for eight months now. You get me those and I will be in heaven." She leaned back in the buggy and closed her eyes for a minute. She never heard his reply, as she fell asleep. She slept the rest of the way.

———◆•●•◆———◆———◆•●•◆———

They reached the cabin. John got the crew to park the wagons behind the house. They would unload the next day. He woke Corinne gently as they neared his property. She was upset with herself for falling asleep, but he calmed her down. He remembered the exhaustion of the journey.

"We all thought you would be staying with the Temple family with Andrew. They added a large section to their cabin to give you and Andrew your own private living area. I think for now you, should stay with us. We can discuss your future another day. I have plenty of room."

John gave directions to the crew to go downtown. The boarding house had arrangements for all the men to have luxury rooms, dinner privileges and free baths for the winter months. They were also treated to payment packets. They received a healthy bonus for bringing Corinne home safely, having taken such good care of her during the journey. They would be having a harvest party in a few days and the crew would be welcome at the Harpole ranch for the festivities. Until then, they were dismissed to rest and recuperate. The men were grateful, indeed. Corinne gave them all a weary hug and promised to see them soon.

Corinne grabbed a few articles of clothing before heading into the cabin. Corinne was impressed by its size. It had several chimneys and good-sized glass windows. Wooden shutters were open and painted a dark green. This cabin looked so welcoming. Her father carried her few articles in for her. She wearily followed her father into the cabin and saw the inside of her new home. A beautiful blonde, with a sweet smile and curvy figure, greeted Corinne enthusiastically.

"Oh, you beautiful girl!" Marie was pure kindness. "You must be exhausted. I made the trip two years ago and remember... Glad I never have to do that again. Why don't you come with me? We'll get you settled in your room." Marie had large caring eyes that were the color of dark honey. Corinne could not help but like her.

Corinne's room had a westward facing window, with views of beautiful fields and mountains. Corinne was so relieved to see the bed, she nearly wept. A roof and walls were something she had long taken for granted in her earlier life. Now they equaled heaven.

Marie ran off to prepare a bath for Corinne. Her father had brought in the cumbersome tub, setting it in the corner of Corinne's room, Marie was in and out filling it up. Corinne sat on the bed, a bit dumbly, watching everyone scurry around her. Soon, more water was heating in her fireplace. From outside, a young boy peeked through the window to ask if more water was needed.

"Are you my new brother?" Corinne had enough energy to ask.

A sweet face peeked over the windowsill again. He had brown hair just as dark as her own. He grinned and said, "Yep!"

"I think tomorrow will be a good day to get to know each other okay?" Corinne reached through and took the bucket of water that he lifted.

"Yea, my ma said you'd be tired today. Do you like fishin'?" His brown eyes were excited at the prospect of someone new to fish with.

"I sure do. Ya know, I don't even know your name." Corinne laughed at her own comment a little too hard. She was punchy.

"I'm Cooper but some people call me Coop. Somebody else called me something else but the teacher took a strap to him for callin' me that." He was a storyteller for sure! Corinne giggled, as she guessed possible strap worthy nicknames.

"Well Cooper, you and I will do a little fishing tomorrow if we can. I am so glad to meet ya." They shook hands through the window then he ran off for a few more buckets. His mom gave instructions to leave them on the windowsill from now on without peeking in. He promised.

Corinne took a long leisurely bath. She washed her hair three times to get all the trail dust and grime out of her long brown hair. Marie brought in a cream rinse, smelling of honeysuckle. Corinne felt pampered and revitalized. After putting on a soft robe, she sat in a rocking chair by the fireplace. She brushed her hair in the warm air to dry it. Her father brought in a tray and she dined on fresh fried chicken and green beans. The glass of milk was cold and refreshing. With a full belly and dried hair, she barely lasted long enough to get into her nightgown. She thanked her family briefly. Then even before the sun went down, she crawled into her cozy bed.

The next morning Corinne slept in well past the breakfast hour. Hungry, she finally crawled out of the soft bed. After dressing, she was surprised by a breakfast plate waiting for her.

"I heard you moving around, so I hurried and made you some eggs and bacon. It is no worries, don't bother apologizing." Marie made a sweet picture standing in the kitchen, Corinne was happy her father had found a companion who made his home so warm and cozy again. Marie seemed like she was a good woman. Corinne would sort out any complicated emotions another day. Right now, she could smile and eat her breakfast at an actual table.

"I was hoping to spend some time with Cooper today and maybe clean out the wagon. I will have to find some of the clothing I packed away in Boston and never wore. All my traveling clothes are a disgrace." Corinne ate her breakfast and felt her energy returning. The sleep had done her wonders.

"That sounds like a fun chore. Will you want some help or is that something you want to do alone?" Marie was very accommodating, sensing her needs.

"Actually, a partner will make it go quicker. We can spend the time getting to know each other." Corinne washed her own plate in the wash bucket and dried off her hands. "Just let me know when you are ready."

The morning passed pleasantly as they conquered the wagon's contents. Corinne and Marie lugged the two largest chests to the edge, and then managed to find a ranch hand nearby to lift them off the edge, safely to the ground. The rest was easy to handle, and the women took care of it all. There was a shed nearby where they stored all of Corinne's dried plants. Marie had an idea for the glass bottles that held Corinne's special oils. Shelves in Corinne's room were suggested later, as John and Cooper came to the house for lunch. It seemed, Cooper spent the morning shadowing his stepdad. He was all grins and full of stories about the horses and the barn... His smiles were infectious.

Corinne was pleased that her stowed clothes lasted the trip so well. The lavender packets in the trunk had done their job keeping the bugs away. With a day or two to hang and air out, the clothes should be good enough to wear for the upcoming harvest party.

Corinne helped Marie prepare dinner. After dinner, Cooper and Corinne spent a pleasant hour at the nearby creek. A fallen log made a comfortable seat. They talked about nothing more important, than the silly things you talk about while fishing. They caught nothing, but they bonded nicely. It was decided that sisters 'ain't so bad,' and she agreed that brothers were keepers.

After another early night to bed, Corinne felt whole. She was ready to face her new life head on.

The morning sun streamed through the glass windows. There was a chill in the morning air that the warmth of the kitchen stove chased away. Corinne dressed sensibly. She sat at the breakfast table with her family, when the Temple family arrived. They came bearing gifts. Corinne could see Mrs. Temple still wearing her grief some. Her embrace was sincere when Corinne stood and welcomed them.

Corinne's father quickly found a few chairs for them.

"We didn't come by to be a bother, we have already eaten. We just wanted to make sure that Corinne was rested and well. We have gifts to share with her, and I felt ready to come over. I do hope this is not too soon for you, dear Corinne." The woman was so considerate and sweet.

"Of course not, I am glad you came." Corinne felt awkward at what to say next. She was relieved when a package was thrust into her arms.

Corinne opened the brown parchment paper and found a silk shawl. *The delicate lace on the edges rivals any lace my Aunt boasted about,* Corinne thought.

"Mrs. Temple, this is so breathtaking! Thank you." Corinne looked her in the eye. Mrs. Temple bravely grinned through her tears. It was all she could handle, at the moment.

"The other gift is outside," Mr. Temple said, with a scratchy throat. He was struggling in his own way too. Corinne could tell that he was a quiet one. So far, Corinne could not see where the gruffness of their son had come from.

They all followed the Temples outside. Two gleaming wood cabinets stood waiting next to the door.

The cabinets were identical. Each one had more than ten drawers, and stood almost five feet tall. The carving and detail on each drawer and edge was amazing workmanship. Each little metal knob was a work of art.

"I do not know what to say. I will treasure them." Corinne walked over and touched the smooth wood, every edge fine and flawless. The dark gold finish was waxed and oiled, shining in the morning sun.

"We know of your love for medicines and herbs from your father's stories. We thought this would be useful for you. We do hope they are a blessing to you," Mr. Temple spoke softly, holding his wife's shoulders.

The Temple's excused themselves shortly after that. Corinne continued to admire the cabinets. Their leaving did something to her heart. She felt sad and empty.

Such a strange way to feel, Corinne thought.

Andrew was a short part of her life that she'd rather forget. And here he was again, sneaking into her mind in another way.

"Did you care much for Andrew? Was his passing difficult for you?" Corinne's father joined her. Corinne looked around and saw that Marie and Coop had left them alone to talk.

"His passing was difficult, but not in the way you think." Corinne stood quiet for a minute, gathering her words. It was tough to talk about anyone who had passed. If they were missed, it was tearful. If they acted badly, it felt wrong to tarnish their reputation.

"Andrew and I were not romantic at all, in any way." Corinne did not want to, but looked him in the eye when she said the last part.

She forced herself to continue. He nodded slowly to let her know he understood.

"His plan was an annulment when we arrived," Corinne said plainly. Their conversation felt stilted and awkward. The last time they spoke seriously was when she was still a girl in braids. Now she felt differently. She had done something that had stretched her beyond her childish thoughts and had changed her forever.

"I do hope he was kind to you Cori." Corinne's father spoke softly, fearing the worst.

Corinne said nothing, but the look in her eyes and a small shake of her head told her father the truth.

Corinne looked away, facing east, as the sun rose and peeked through the mountains.

"This journey has done something to me, Father. I can feel it in my bones. It has taught me about what is true, who God is, and what love really looks like." Corinne looked back at her father. His face was a wash of emotions. She held his hand, and for a while, together they watched the sun rise.

Chapter Thirty-Five
Sept 26, 1848

Corinne's first trip to town was exciting for her. She had dreamt of arriving for so long. She imagined many times, for many miles, what it would look like. She was expecting a few small buildings, a lumber mill, and maybe a crude church building. She knew towns weren't built overnight. She had no grand illusions that some elaborate society had blossomed, in the few years since Oregon City had developed. She was pleasantly surprised by the booming town, as she rode through. Her father was a good guide and told her about every building they passed. There were lumber and wool mills that used the waterfront property. There were logs floating down the river and men standing on rafts guiding them.

Their buggy came to a stop at an opening which gave an unobstructed view of the waterfalls showing off upstream. There were rock islands midstream with carvings of dissected circles.

"What do those symbols mean?" She pointed to the carvings.

"The local Clackamas tribe said those have been there for hundreds of years. They said other tribes lived here before them." Her father had a good grasp of the city's history. Corinne was eager to know everything about it. It was her home now. The falls and the river gave it a coastal town feeling, but Corinne knew the ocean was some ways off. She hoped to visit the Pacific Ocean someday, after coming this far. She would love to have traveled from sea to sea.

"You are so much like your mother, Corinne. Thirsty to know about everything around you. She would be so proud of you." The statement made Corinne a little teary eyed, but they continued the tour. Cooper sat in the front and pointed out his favorite places, too.

They reached the mercantile and Corinne asked if they could stop. She had a few things she wanted to buy, and wanted to catch a glimpse of Clive.

The Harpole family climbed out of the buggy and walked into the mercantile. Corinne and Marie headed to the fabric section. Corinne wanted to get few personal things made. Many items in her wardrobe were ruined on the trip. She had a few fancier pieces, but

Corinne wanted to be practical too. After a few minutes, she settled on a navy-blue print that went well with her features. Marie loved sewing and enjoyed the idea of having someone to sew for again. Corinne could easily say that sewing wasn't her gift. At best, she could only mend.

Corinne asked the clerk at the front counter if Clive was in. She was disappointed. Corinne tried to hide her distress, but felt Marie slip an arm around her shoulder. She wanted to see Clive and have her family know him better.

"I believe the Quackenbush family has been invited to the Harvest party this weekend. We can see them then. I will also invite them to another dinner sometime," Marie said, reminding Corinne gently. They left soon after with the fabric, and a few items her father and stepmother purchased.

She brought most of the left-over trip money, wanting to deposit the funds in the town's small bank. She was surprised to learn her father had already set up an account for her.

"Your mother and I set up these funds for you over the years. This is your inheritance." He patted her on the shoulder as her eyes misted over. The sum was greater than she expected, and was dumbfounded that her father had already taken care of that. She was overwhelmed, and still a bit emotional about all the changes that had come about so quickly. She came west to find a bit of independence. She had gotten everything she wanted. She thought about Angela, who was still likely recovering from her injuries. She prayed so often for her. But now, she prayed more fervently for her friend to heal and to receive everything she desired. If God willed it, Corinne was determined to help Angela to find her way west.

Having completed the tour through Oregon City, the wagon got them back home via a picturesque journey. Corinne took in the sight of the mountains and fields, soaking it all in. This was her new home, and she felt it in her bones.

Later that evening, she visited Clover in the stables. Her horse was healing nicely. In a day or so, she could ride Clover around the pasture. Corinne gave Clover a good brushing and an apple. For a while, she talked to Clover about how good she was on the journey and how Corinne had counted on her the entire trip. After a few extra love taps on the rump and a nose rub, she left Clover. Corinne went inside to wash up for the family dinner.

They were all talking about the upcoming harvest party. There would be games and prizes. Since they were hosting it at the Harpole ranch, there were lots of last minute things to do, over the next few days. Corinne ate dinner and halfheartedly listened. She was excited about the celebration but was thinking about her friends from the journey, missing their company, too. She longed to know how Chelsea was doing, but mostly she wondered about Lucas. Had he sent word to Sarah? Did he still think of her since the Wind River Mountains? She spent so much effort pushing him out of her mind. But now, he occupied her thoughts all the time.

She enjoyed the family but could not help but think of her own dream, her own lavender fields. She knew they were just dreams, but this valley seemed a good place for dreams. Corinne went to bed early feeling scattered and tired.

***

The next day, the Temple's invited her to dinner. They kept to themselves for a few days to mourn and go through their son's things. Corinne guessed they wanted to talk about what had happened. Corinne wasn't looking forward to reliving Andrew's last days, but knew it was important to share with his parents.

After spending the day helping her family prepare for the harvest party, she took the path to the Temple's house. She carried some freshly picked flowers to give to Mrs. Temple. Corinne felt so confused about what to expect that night.

Mrs. Temple loved the flowers. She welcomed Corinne into the cheery cabin where the table was set with blue and white china dishes. The two women chatted about the dishes and other small talk, until Mr. Temple arrived. The Temples had planned out and built this cabin well. The windows, like in her father's cabin, were glass paned and open. The cabin had a generous kitchen, and a fancy bread oven built into a brick wall. They had spent a pretty penny to get fancy bricks sent from back east, certainly. This was no crude frontier cabin. Corinne took it all in, wondering what could have been. If Andrew and she had had a real marriage. It was so difficult to imagine.

"Please sit and we can start dinner before it gets cold." Mrs. Temple pointed to the table and Mr. Temple pulled out the seat for Corinne.

Dinner was a wonderful spread of roast chicken, vegetables, potatoes, and fresh bread. Since ending her journey, Corinne savored the plentiful food. Cookie did a good job, but home cooked meals were really something to treasure now. There were much fewer bugs, dirt and other things trying to sneak into your food while exposed to the elements.

"Mrs. Temple, this dinner is amazing. I am still getting used to eating food not prepared on a campfire or sheet stove." Corinne smiled politely to her hosts. She was hoping to make them feel more comfortable than she was.

"Please, call us Henry and Linda. I am hoping we can call you Corinne."

"Of course, I am sorry to be so formal. I just want to make sure that you understand how sorry I am that we had to meet in such a terrible way." She saw tears starting to form in Linda Temple's eyes, but Corinne continued.

"Your son and I weren't married long before he died. I have had four months of hard road to accept what happened. You have had only days. I know the hope you carried around in the long months of our journey must have been like mine to see my father. I am truly sorry it did not happen that way for you." Corinne felt a lump in her throat watching the woman mourn. This was not easy.

"We just wanted to get to know you better, in person. We have read Andrew's journal. Reggie brought it by a few days ago. He told us about Andrew's death and how hard it was on you. How much you tried to save him. We can't thank you enough for trying. We have seen cholera ourselves and know how quickly and painfully it can take someone." Linda brought a small bound book out of her apron. Corinne was guessing it is the journal they mentioned. Corinne had no idea Andrew had even kept a journal. She wondered what horrible things Andrew had written about her.

"After reading the journal we can see how much respect Andrew had for you and wanted to make sure you know that he thought you were an incredible woman." Henry Temple spoke up. Corinne could not be more shocked. "He brags for pages about how you made your own medicines from plants and helped everyone on the train with burns and illnesses. And even took an accidental bullet out of him! I can't imagine you doing all those things, seeing you, just a tiny beautiful young woman. It boggles my mind."

Henry reached over, grabbed her hand, and looked to his wife. She nodded and looked at Corinne.

"I know it's not our place to ask but we were hoping perhaps you were with child." Linda did a quick look down to Corinne's obviously flat belly, did the math, frowned a little, and shook her head. "No, I can see that you are not. It's just a silly wish that a part of Andrew was still alive."

"I am so sorry to cause you any pain," Corinne said, and reached out to hug this woman so clearly hurting. She did not want to expound on the kiss-less state of their marriage. It was not the appropriate time, and it may never be.

"We will survive, sweet dear girl. You took care of my son when he needed you. For that, I offer you everything I have. Please come to us if you ever have a need and drop by for dinner often." She stood from the table and gave Linda a hug. Henry surprised her by embracing her, too.

Corinne walked home, her mind spinning. Andrew had written good things about her, and his family was so warm and welcoming. Had being away at college so long had jaded Andrew? Was he just not ready to be married? Corinne wrestled with her memory of Andrew. During the whole journey, she constantly questioned herself about his actions. Now perhaps she would wonder about him her the rest of her life.

She walked into her father's yard to see Sidney Prince talking with her father. His mother Ellie and a man that looked like an older version of him, stood with them. *From one awkward meeting to another,* thought Corinne.

"There is Corinne now. Dear, I was just telling them about how you were having dinner with the Temple's. I am so glad you didn't miss the Prince family. You and Sidney take a short walk, while we old folks talk inside for a spell." Her father's voice was cheery.

Corinne wanted to groan, but instead she smiled politely and accepted Sidney's arm.

"I missed you, Corinne." Sidney stared at her as they walked. Corinne could feel that strange feeling in her stomach again, the pressure of being nice when you just wanted to scream. Like a boiling teapot.

"Has your time at home been restful?" Corinne asked politely, as they walked together. The dusk was beautiful with the sun going behind the mountains, and the sky above them glowing orange and red. Corinne was certain that even the sky was pressuring her into an unwanted romantic moment.

"Yes, our two-story home in town is much nicer than I expected. I can tell you honestly, I was never more grateful for a bed in my life." Sidney was being genuine, and it made Corinne smile.

"I agree whole-heartedly. That and eating at the table without bugs buzzing around you, is nice too," Corinne said with a chuckle.

He laughed, and they shared a minute of quiet.

"Corinne, I know you have doubts about me. I can see it in your eyes, but I want to say something to you and I hope you will hear me." He stopped and gave Corinne a serious look. Corinne let him talk. He would certainly hear her better, if she gives him a chance to have his say.

"I am in love with you! I have asked your father's permission to court you, but I want so much more." Sidney didn't wait for a response and boldly grabbed her shoulders and kissed her fervently.

Corinne's anger grew fast as she realized how possessively he held her. She was forced into an embrace she did not want and couldn't get free of it. He held her tightly but after a few long seconds he relaxed his hold on her. Corinne quickly escaped and smacked his face so hard her hand stung.

"How dare you! I never gave you permission to kiss me. I am your friend only, Sidney." Corinne wiped her face unconsciously. She was spitting mad but not sure how to tell him.

"I am not in love with you Sidney. I don't want to be courted by you." She saw the hurt finally penetrate his eyes and though she didn't want to hurt him, he needed to know.

"You are so beautiful, I have to have you Corinne. My father taught me to take what I want. I want you." His eyes were angry now.

"I am not a possession Sidney. I am a woman." Corinne's voice was calm but her brown eyes were still angry and confused by the young man's actions. "I don't want to hurt you Sidney, but I don't care for you in that way. I never will."

"I don't think I can give up on you, Corinne," Sidney declared firmly.

"You don't have a choice." Corinne started walking alone back to the cabin. She didn't trust him anymore.

Sidney followed her silently and waited outside for his family. Corinne said her polite salutations to everyone, then headed to her room to collapse and not think. She heard the Prince family leave a while later. She was certain that Sidney wasn't going to give up. She would have to make it clear to him that she wasn't his!

Chapter Thirty-Six
Sept 29, 1848

The Harvest party was starting soon, and Corinne had taken a lot of trouble with her appearance. It was the first time she had dressed up since leaving Boston. She enjoyed looking pretty, without the pressure from Aunt Rose to be perfect. Those days felt so far away. The mansion on 12th street, the marble floors, and the oppressive high society expectations. Corinne chuckled, thinking about the silliness of those days. She had to remember to write to her Aunt using the new stationary she bought in town. A nice, long letter. Describing the trip, all the trials, and…all the grime! Her Aunt would be having fits for days.

Marie styled up Corinne's long brown hair beautifully, with curls and braids just as fancy as any Boston society debutante. Marie had a special recipe for lip rouge that she learned from her own mother. It gave her lips a natural looking, soft pink glow. Men liked to believe that good women never wore any type of make-up. That simply wasn't true. Wearing make-up was a well-kept secret by women. Corinne remembered all the cream blushes and powders that her Aunt had used and had even bragged about. Aunt Rose would gain favors from her Boston society friends by sharing her lady's maid's creations with them. The key was subtly. If someone could tell that you were wearing make-up, then it was too bold and you were considered a tart. But with a light application, a woman could enhance her features. Corinne remembered well, all those speeches from her Aunt. It felt like a lifetime ago.

The dark burgundy dress Corinne had worn only once in Boston, was pulled from her trunks and pressed. It was stunning, according to her father. Corinne glowed at his compliments. Corinne's brown eyes sparkled in anticipation of seeing her traveling companions. Corinne's father had run into Russell and Clive in town. They promised that they would all be coming tonight. The whole town was talking about this event.

At fifteen minutes past four o'clock, the guests started arriving. The host family's job was to greet folks and make sure everyone felt welcome. So, as the crowds grew larger, Corinne wandered through the guests. She pointed out the drink table or explained where certain events where going to be. She was well prepared for everything, with one exception.

The Grant's arrival...

She nearly squealed when she saw Chelsea, who was starting to 'show' in her pregnancy. Corinne glided towards Chelsea as quickly as her dress would allow. She wanted a quick hug from her friend. Corinne would have to grow accustomed to wearing her hoops again. Cumbersome though they may be, fashion was to be followed, even here. Their embrace was fierce and wonderful.

She cried, holding Chelsea for a minute before they laughed and then hugged again.

"You look so good Chelsea. I've been missing you." Corinne wiped a joyful tear from her friend's face.

"I was thinking of you too dear. Are you and your father getting along well?" Chelsea's honest eyes were searching her. Corinne knew that real friendship and concern were behind her gaze.

"Yes, wonderfully. He is re-married, and I have a stepmother and brother. I am so happy that he has found a good companion."

"Well I have stolen you long enough. Point me to the drink table, for I crave some lemonade. I think someone else wants your attention." Chelsea glided off in the direction of the drink table, her husband at her side. Corinne's heart did a flip when she looked up at Lucas. He was waiting patiently by the cabin. His dark suit was nicely tailored, and he looked every bit the Yale graduate. He leaned on the wall so casually, Corinne thought perhaps he didn't feel as knotted up inside as she did. A moment later, as she drew nearer, she saw that she was wrong. He had been anxiously waiting for this, too.

"Walk with me down to the creek," Corinne said, as she grabbed his arm.

"I missed those brown eyes of yours," Lucas said, before he started walking. He pulled Corinne along through the grass and they sat down on a fallen log near the water's edge. A strange, sweet fear mingled in her middle as she dared to look into his eyes.

"I missed you, too," was all she had the courage to say. All the thoughts and dreams she had, flew out the window and she felt like a dewy-eyed female.

She would try again. "Actually, I have been thinking about you a lot."

She missed his face, his strong chin competing with a grin that spoke of a boyish charm.

"Well I was hoping you would say that. I have had too much time to think since the last time we really talked. The waiting to come to you nearly killed me." He grinned and grabbed his chest dramatically. Even when being serious, he had a way of making her smile.

Corinne put her hand over his heart in a joking way. She laughed at the way he play-acted dying.

"I wanted to come to you, as I have today, completely unattached and free to honorably court you. I will tell you everything I am feeling, but first I must make it clear to you that I have been released of my previous engagement. Sarah Ballentine is no longer my fiancé, but a married woman now. I had a long letter waiting for me when we arrived. It seems her letter made it faster than I did." His laugh was charming. Lucas relaxed when he saw Corinne drop her nervous shoulders, her cheeks betraying a slight blush. But, her smallest hint of a smile was his undoing.

"If you give me a word or a nod, or even a swift kick, I will run to your father and get his permission to court you." Corinne grinned and gave him a big nod. Without another word, he kissed her soundly then bolted back toward the cabin. Corinne laughed at his antics but enjoyed how a grown man could be everything she wanted. Strong and safe, but still someone who could surprise her.

Corinne made her way back to the party. Her time with Lucas was exactly what she needed to unwind her nerves and enjoy the festivities. Within a few minutes, she saw Clive. She gracefully ran to him for a grandfatherly hug. He looked grand in a suit, and with a haircut that took years off the "old-trapper" look he had on the trip. He looked the proper businessman. Bluebird was with him. Though the party overwhelmed her, she had learned a few English words and impressed Corinne completely by saying "hello."

Clive was brought over to see Corinne's father, as they were re-introduced.

"Father, here is a man I greatly respect. He has started teaching me the Chinook language. He took me to a Shoshone village, and saved me from treacherous river crossings. He is a hero of mine." Then she introduced Bluebird to her whole family, as well. Corinne would be sharing with Bluebird all her knowledge about medicines. Once Bluebird knew more English, she would reciprocate to Corinne. For now, Bluebird would be staying with the Grant family.

The Indian girl shocked everyone when she clearly stated, "Please, call me Dolly." Her brown eyes were intelligent, and she looked everyone in the eye as she shook their hands. Cooper was fascinated and had a hundred questions for Corinne's Indian friend. Everyone could see that his brain was spinning with curiosity. As he bombarded her with questions, Dolly laughed and just shrugged her shoulders. Corinne gently informed him that Dolly would soon be learning more English. He was disappointed. The questions would have to wait.

After the introductions, Corinne's father pulled her aside and wanted to ask her a few questions.

"I can't help but notice that you have two men interested in courting you. I gave them both my permission, as long as they both came to dinner. Is that reasonable? I know you are a widow but are you ready for a new relationship?" he paused. Corinne could see how much he cared. "They both seem to be pleasant," Her father smiled a little, trying to hide a bigger one meant to tease her a bit.

"I do have interest in Lucas Grant, father. He has been there for me in many ways. We are good friends. I am hoping for more perhaps."

"Oh, my girl, I am glad you have found someone. I will look forward to getting to know him. Can we talk later, sweetie? I guess I have spent so much time with this party and helping you get to know your new stepmother, that I never did ask about anything from the rest of your trip." He grabbed her hand and gave it a squeeze. "What about the Prince boy? He seems very interested."

"Sidney is a boy who is infatuated with the idea of me. I have told him repeatedly that I am not interested in being more than friends. He is persistent, and he has pushed his luck with me." Corinne remembered his unwelcome kiss and her anger stirred again.

"That is good to know. I trust your judgment. We can figure out how to shake the unwanted suitor."

Her father led her back to the Grants. He invited them to share the meal at his table. Lucas' place was somehow next to Corinne and her father. It worked well, giving them all a chance to communicate. Marie was enchanted by his sense of humor. He even got Coop's attention. Lucas was promised a spot on the special fishing log, a few days out.

After the meal, the party events started. There were races for the young people, and fresh ice cream for everyone. Her father and a few people from town that Corinne didn't know yet, judged the pie-baking contest. She recognized some people that had been in the wagon train and visited with them. She invited Lucas along and enjoyed his company. He was great at making small talk and his hand on her arm was very pleasant. She was now allowing the idea to sink in that Lucas and she were courting. It made her heart feel light and sick at the same time.

At one point, she saw Sidney with his family, but conveniently kept at Lucas's side. Sidney left her alone. She somehow knew that he would still have to be dealt with, but for today she just wanted to enjoy herself.

Once the sun started going down, the party got louder. All the musicians, except Lucas, were on stage. And for once, Corinne was able to enjoy being with Lucas when he wasn't playing the music. They danced quite a few songs together. She also danced with Clive, Russell, and her father, too. Though Corinne thought Lucas and she were being discreet, somehow the whole town picked up on the sparks flying between them. The townsfolk seemed to approve of the couple. Tongues were already wagging about her being too young to stay a widow.

Sidney approached her for a dance toward the end of the evening, but Corinne's father saved her from the awkward moment of saying no. Her father stepped in and claimed that he was to have the next dance. Sidney backed away and didn't come forward again. He left the party with his family, early and angry.

Corinne said goodbye to her friends, as the night got later, and everyone started going home. Lucas promised to come by in a few days after taking care of some business. He kissed her on the hand and said "goodnight." That night, Corinne floated to bed and had sweet dreams.

Chapter Thirty-Seven
September 30, 1848

The next day, Corinne had errands to run. She wanted to talk to Clive about ordering some bottles from California. She was running low on some of her specialty oils and wanted to know about his contacts in California. She spoke to her father in the morning, borrowed a horse, and rode into town by herself. It was only four miles and she wasn't going to be buying anything today.

The horse was a sweet palomino, with a great temperament that enjoyed Corinne's easy pace. She was seeing the world with fresh eyes today. Lucas had missed her and had spoken to her father. She was in heaven.

The fall colors were just beginning to show off, with shades of gold and red tips on the trees. Further up the hills, and on Mount Hood, the colors were taking over, as vibrant warm hues splashed against the dark evergreens. The artistry of God's paintbrush was truly magnificent.

She made it into town and headed straight to Clive's mercantile. He told her the night before that he would be there. Clive was talking with his clerk, when she walked in. He immediately called her to his back room where they could talk some 'turkey'.

After an hour of talking, they both had an idea of what was available. She shared her plans with Clive, her dreams of being a lavender grower, and creating a supply of American made medicinal oils. She had never really shared her dream with anyone, besides mentioning it casually to Chelsea and Angela. She was surprised at how well he responded.

"I had no idea you had aspirations like that, my girl. You can't be beautiful, talented, and a brilliant businesswoman. You are gonna make us mortals look bad. Does your father know your plan?" Clive said, with a wink.

She blushed and shook her head.

"No. Honestly, you are the first man I have told. I just have a fear that men will think it's a silly thing to pursue. I know the power within these flowers and plants, but many do not. I guess I fear judgment for growing something like flowers, when people think food is more practical. Every good wife knows about lavender from their mothers. What they don't have, is access to its medicine, in the strongest form. I am hoping to change that." Corinne's eyes shone with passion. And right then and there, her dream came to life.

"If you want, I can help you make a business plan. Hmmm..." He grabbed his chin and scratched it a second. "I coulda swore I saw you holding hands with a handsome farmer boy I know. Maybe I was dreaming it, but he will be a good person to talk about this business with. He did study agriculture my dear, in case, you had forgotten." His voice was teasing but he had a point. She had kept her dream so close, that she failed to share it with people who would perhaps not find it so silly.

"You are right, Clive. Sometimes I let my own fear of people's judgment keep me from speaking out. I know I have support. I guess, some days I'm too foolish to use it," admitted Corinne.

"Now, it isn't meant to beat you up, my dear. But some advice from an old coot can help sometimes. Just remember, a good idea can never do any good, if it stays in your head." Clive started to write out a few ideas for her and she listened closely, as he shared his thoughts.

Within a few minutes, the back door swung open and Lucas popped his head in.

"Hey Clive, I got a problem," he said, before he saw Corinne. He grinned, but the smile didn't reach all the way to his eyes.

"Come sit young man, let's talk out this problem." Clive gave the table a smack and he pulled out a chair. He gave a wink to Corinne that made her blush.

"I can go, Lucas, if you need privacy. Clive and I are just talking about some dreams and wishes." She smiled and stood up to go. She really didn't want to interrupt, or assume she had any rights to hear his business.

"Actually, Corinne, you can stay. I may need you and your father's help too, as character witnesses." Lucas regained his worried look, Corinne sat and listened to him explain.

"I went to the land claim office today. I wanted to get my land papers in order and get the paperwork started. I know that all land claims here are decided by the land council. You can ask for a specific plot of land, but the council will have to approve it. When I went to the land office they were nice to me, until I told them my name. They said they refused to file my paperwork, because I am an outlaw. They would not talk to me about it further and threatened to call the sheriff if I didn't!" Lucas was very stressed as he spoke.

"An outlaw?" Corinne gasped. She would never in a hundred years believe him to be a criminal. "That's impossible!" She could not help but grab his hand to comfort him.

"You've only just arrived, Lucas. You haven't had time to cause trouble yet," laughed Clive.

"You laugh, Clive, and I want to as well, but we need to figure out why the land office thinks I'm an outlaw. We need to get this cleared up, so I can plan out my future." He slipped a glance over at Corinne and they shared a moment.

Clive harrumphed when he got uncomfortable. "I will head over there myself and see what's the hullaballoo." Clive stood up. "Corinne, why don't you head home. If this is more serious than mistaken identity, we may need to talk your father and find out who is on the committee. I was gone this year and missed the election for new members."

Clive handed her the notes on the business plan and walked her to her horse. Lucas gave her a kiss on the cheek and said he would come by later. She rode home quicker than before. She didn't stop to enjoy the scenery, but instead, spent it praying and wondering what the mess in town had been about.

Her family noticed her quiet presence at dinner and asked what was troubling her. She just told them she was thinking about something. They gave her the space she needed.

Around dusk, Clive and Lucas rode up on horseback. Corinne had been right and watched her father praise Lucas' big black stallion. The conversation was cut short though when Clive asked John Harpole for some help for Lucas.

They all sat at the dinner table to hear the story. Once they brought John Harpole up to speed, they continued.

"I went to the land office and got the same information that they told Lucas. But I pressed them about who I needed to talk to about these accusations. They sent me to talk to the sheriff." Corinne sucked in her breath, at the thought of Lucas being jailed. "The sheriff was informed by the land committee, that Lucas Grant may be an army deserter from the war in Mexico. He said several character witnesses came forward with the information just this morning, after seeing him at the harvest party. They said that they are doing their civic duty to not allow riffraff in the town. The sheriff said no charges can be made without proof, but he will be sending out inquiries, and should hear back from the US army by next spring."

"I would like to set the record straight that I was never in the army. I was an Agriculture student at Yale until last year, before joining my family on the trip West. These accusations are completely without any merit." Lucas was concerned that this was going to ruin his chances with Corinne, and deny him the ability to earn his living at farming.

"I am not sure what the cause is behind people trying to smear your name Lucas, but I believe you. We will attempt to find out whom we need to talk to drop these charges. I need some paper, Corinne." Corinne ran to get some paper from her father's desk.

John began to write down all the land council members but stopped mid-word.

"Do you remember them all?" Corinne asked, as she saw him struggle.

"Yes. I may have the answer to the problem, but I fear this could get ugly. The name that stands out to me is the newest member of the land committee, Jedediah Prince, Sidney's father," he said.   .

Corinne groaned aloud, and instantly all eyes were on her. She had no choice but to share what she dreaded sharing.

"The other night when the Prince family came by, I tried unsuccessfully to convince Sidney that I wasn't interested in him romantically." She was struggling with what to say. "Well, he grabbed me... and I smacked him and made him leave me alone." She saw the horrified look from all three men and realized they would want to know more.

"He didn't hurt me, but he was trying to win me over with a very unwanted kiss. This is so uncomfortable..." she sighed, then continued. The room was getting warm suddenly. "He said he would never give up, until he had me for his own. I walked away from him, after I told him it would never happen." She ended her tale hoping they would not ask any more about that situation. They discussed a plan to clear Lucas's name and talk with the other committee members. After a while, Lucas asked Corinne to walk with him before he left. She gladly escaped into the dark evening with him. At first, they said nothing, but held hands and strolled along.

"Corinne, thank you for believing in me." He turned her around and looked at her in the bright moonlight. "If you didn't, I would be lost."

"I am just so sorry if I brought all this upon your head. I am just a girl after all, hardly worth all this fuss." Corinne felt so guilty. She felt that if she had just communicated to Sidney better, they would not be facing this situation.

Lucas grabbed Corinne by the shoulders, and though she acted shy, he held her chin until she looked fully into his eyes.

"Not worth the fuss?! Corinne, you are worth everything. I feel so lucky that you even allow me to hold your hand. The fact is, I want to spend the rest of my days reminding you how worthy you are. Cori, I love you, I have never loved anyone else." Lucas bared his soul and Corinne rewarded him by throwing her arms around his neck. She just held on, saying nothing, just sniffing a little. She knew that this man was a miracle.

"Cori, we will work through this together. I just hope to share in your dreams and wishes, like you did with Clive today. I want to know everything you dream. I think you may be surprised that they match up with mine." He kissed her softly and held her for a long moment before he felt Corinne let go.

"Lucas, I believe in you, and I love you. I may sometimes doubt myself, but I will never doubt what I feel for you."

She pressed her head against his chest. It fit perfectly.

Chapter Thirty-Eight
October 2, 1848

Two days of talking to committee members had proven unsuccessful. No one was willing to believe without proof. John Harpole finally decided to pay a call on Mr. Prince at his home. John came home deflated and broke the news to Corinne before heading out to Clive's home to tell the Grants.

"He will not back down. I believe he has threatened the land committee, to refuse special pricing for government building deals on lumber." John's forehead was creased from the stress of the day and he sunk into a kitchen chair as they sat at the table.

"They have been planning the courthouse to be built for five years and finally he agreed to help with the cost of the lumber, for his spot on the committee." He took a moment and drank some coffee that his wife brought him. "The next part is hard for me to say, for it reflects poorly on a few people who are manipulating the situation. Mr. Prince said his son would be willing to negotiate with Corinne, if she would give her consent to marry him… I am sorry, but I laughed in his face. It was a preposterous suggestion. I told him to go back to the Middle Ages."

Corinne laughed despite the seriousness of the situation. He continued, "I will go over the county by-laws but as far as I can see, the committee is the only means to get land. I think Mr. Prince would block any future attempts made by Lucas, as retribution for you withholding your affections from his boy." She made a sour face at the thought of marrying Sidney as she watched her father leave.

Corinne realized that Lucas might not be able to settle here. She wanted to weep. She followed her father out of the house and informed him she was going with him. The trip took longer than the trip to town. The path to Clive's house was uphill toward Mount Hood. It was a three-room cabin. Tight quarters for all the Grants and Clive, but it looked like they were making it work. The front porch was spacious. Chelsea stretched out in a rocking chair holding hands with Russell, while he sat in his own chair. Lucas sat on a stump next to Clive, who seemed content to read a book.

"I think they are waiting for us," John said.

Corinne agreed.

They jumped up anxiously when they saw Corinne and John dismount. John quickly informed them that the news wasn't good. That government buildings were being held hostage if they didn't go along with the blackball of Lucas's land grant. Everyone accepted the news graciously. After they all talked about other possibilities, Corinne pulled Lucas aside.

"Lucas, I am giving you permission to find land where you can. If we can't do this here, I understand. I desperately want to plant roots with my family and yours, but most of all, I want to be with you." She kissed his cheek and watched him blush.

"You got back with your father, after years apart. I can't be the one to separate you from him again. Perhaps, we can wait it out. Sidney may eventually back down or fall for another girl." After he said it, Lucas doubted that would happen.

"Lucas, unless you don't want me, I go where you go." Corinne sealed the deal with a kiss that promised everything in her heart.

"Right now, I want to forget this mess and tell you my dreams, Lucas." He nodded, and they did just that. She told him about her thoughts on medicinal oils and explained about what she learned from her mother and grandmother. He told her about things he learned at Yale, which might be useful. They sat on the porch swing and watched the sunset to the west.

"I dream of lavender fields, almond groves, and you by my side." She shared a smile with him as he tried to picture her dream.

"Yes, and there's more. I want to be the first American supplier of medicinal oils." His eyes got wide as he realized the scope of her dream.

"I should have known my girl would have the biggest dreams. I just have my one dream, too. Marry me Cori, and we can build our dreams together." His green eyes told her everything she wanted to know.

"I will Lucas. Just don't leave me behind. Where you go, I will follow."

Sitting alone, hand in hand on the swing for a while, they talked about plans for their future. Afterwards, they went in to share their news and get the families blessing. A blessing which was heartily given.

Chapter Thirty-Nine
October 4, 1848

News of the newly engaged couple spread, as they were seen together at church and other social events. Everyone heard amazing stories about the young woman who was so talented, that she earned respect from the Indians and took care of the medical needs of an entire wagon train.

Then the townspeople heard about the generosity of the Grant and Temple wagons, sharing food with those on the journey who had run out of supplies. As a couple, Corinne, and Lucas were becoming the talk of the town.

The rumors that Lucas's name was being slandered because the young Prince boy had a crush on Corinne, set the town's gossip wheel spinning. They were everyone's favorite story to talk about. The newest buzz was that the young couple was soon to be married, and potentially moving out of town, in search of land in California.

Corinne and Lucas were oblivious to the talk around town. They had their own adventure planned with their families.

The Harpole's and Grants enjoyed their Wednesday on the Pacific Ocean. They needed space away from the trouble in town. They had taken a ferry to the coast, where they stayed with a friend of John Harpole. The cabin was vacant and quite large. Cooper, Brody, and Corinne shared the upper loft. Marie and John were in a bedroom. Chelsea and Russell in another. Lucas found a spot to tie up a hammock, and they all made it work. Corinne was amazed at how well everyone got along. They spent a few nights there. It felt like a holiday and they all cast all worries aside, and just enjoyed the fresh ocean breezes.

Marie and Chelsea packed a picnic. The gusty winds challenged them constantly to keep their bonnets and scarves on. But the water was magnetic, and the craggy shoreline was a beautiful site. With gritty determination, Marie and Corinne recruited the men to help them gather bits of seaweed that had washed up on the rocks. The men laughed as they watched the women balance precariously on the rocks. The ladies' voluminous skirts made it tricky getting to the pesky seaweed.

"The many benefits of seaweed..." Corinne's voice was lost in the sound of wind and waves, but Lucas could not look away. His mind was made up. He had to marry this woman. The future would bring what it may. They would face everything together.

After the seaweed gathering, the exhausted group sat and watched the waves from a safe distance. The seagulls and other large birds skillfully gathered clams. Flying high, they dropped the clams with precision, on to the rocks below. They would dive quickly and snatch the soft meat from the broken shells, before other prey would try to steal their food. It was a fascinating ritual to watch.

Cooper was certain he saw dolphins a few times, off in the distance. Everyone humored the lad, but no one could say for certain what was leaping out of the water, so far offshore. Clive told him stories about gray whales he had seen a few years back. Cooper was determined to see a whale someday.

A ferry took them back to Oregon City after the holiday. One early morning, Clive gave Corinne a special treat bringing Dolly by. Every time Corinne met with Dolly, they bonded closer. Dolly's grasp of English was remarkable. Corinne secretly wondered at this young woman's intellect. Dolly was astounding. Corinne was so pleased she had this chance to know her.

"I was going to take Dolly to the longhouse, downstream. The surviving Clackamas tribes are there," Clive explained. Corinne ate a quick breakfast before they left on horseback.

"I can't believe that hundreds died. Tis such a terrible shame." Corinne mourned the loss of any life.

"The white man brought sicknesses they could not fight against." Clive had his own feelings about these things. No one nation could lay claim to the destruction alone. In addition to the Indians, trappers from France, Britain, Russia and many more countries had profited from this land. The land was fruitful. Man would try to tame it. Disease was just another way the land tried to hold man back.

Clover was well enough again, and Corinne found joy in her ride to the longhouse. Dolly was getting her voice slowly. While she seemed willing to talk to Corinne, she was shy with others yet. Corinne was eager to learn from her.

There was a pit in Corinne's stomach about moving from Oregon City. Her father and Clive lived there, but she knew Lucas was her soul mate. She prayed that, over time, her troubled heart would learn to be patient. Perhaps they could own land nearby, and not have to travel so far to find their dreams.

Corinne took a few herbs and oils with her, to show to the Clackamas people. Their faces were friendly. Because Clive had earned their trust, she was welcomed. They ate fresh salmon and potatoes straight from the fire. A few tribesmen spoke a bit of English. When they left that evening, Corinne was pleased that relations had started so well. She looked forward to being friends with them, if she stayed nearby. She wished better living conditions for them but had to let that go. They had their way of life, and she had hers. She knew better than to interfere with the way a person wanted to live.

Lucas was at the barbershop nearby and Corinne was visiting with Chelsea at Clive's store. They were discussing baby names as Chelsea patted her belly affectionately. Just then, the bell over the door tinkled to announce a new customer. Chelsea was watching the counter that afternoon and went to welcome the customer. Suddenly, Corinne heard herself gasp.

"Mr. Prince." Chelsea said it first. Corinne thought Chelsea was trying to form the word 'welcome' but was having trouble.

"Hello Sidney," said Corinne quietly. Her voice was low and crackly. Forced civility.

Jedediah and Sidney Prince walked in, tall and pompous. They strode in unison to the counter, their boots loud on the wood floor.

"I want to pick up my order for coffee and flour." Jedediah spoke low and smooth. Corinne didn't suppose he had lost a wink of sleep over any of his dealings with Lucas.

"One moment."

Chelsea was usually never that stiff with a customer. Corinne wasn't sure what to expect. Part of her wanted to leave and another part wanted to hold her ground.

"Hello Corinne." Sidney's voice squeaked a little. At least he was nervous.

"I am not going to do this Sidney. We do not get to be friends, if you will libel the character of and maliciously lie about Lucas, like you both have." Corinne said it a little louder than she meant to.

"I told you, I have to have you." Sidney stood to his full height. It wasn't changing her mind.

"I am through with you Sidney. Please don't address me again," Corinne said firmly.

She turned her back and ignored her heartbeat loudly drumming inside her chest. She hated this kind of confrontation, but knew it was necessary. She had to burn the bridge between them. Or, he would never give up.

She waited, her back turned away from Sidney, until their order was purchased, and they left the store. It felt like an eternity. Chelsea and Corinne both talked nervously after they left. It was troubling knowing that someone in your own hometown, was now your enemy. Corinne was now going to be nervous every time she went into town, for she didn't want to see them again.

The town boasted of two churches. Corinne was selfishly glad to hear the Prince family attended the other church. It would make things awkward to share a pew every week. She could forgive them easily, everyone makes mistakes. Forgetting though, was sometimes easier when you did not have to see their face too often. Corinne would work on it.

Chapter Forty
October 15, 1848

Corinne and Marie were rolling out piecrusts for an after-dinner treat. The Grants were coming for dinner and everything else was well in hand. The air outside was crisp with a light drizzle of rain, but the kitchen was warm with soup on the stove and hens roasting over the fire.

There was knock on the door. Marie opened the door to see Linda Temple. They all shared small talk for a few minutes while Marie poured some fresh coffee from the stove.

"I am going to come to the point. I came with some news for you, Corinne. I want you to hear me out before you say yes." Linda held a look of excitement as she spoke. "My husband and I are leaving the valley." She reached out and clasped Corinne's hand. "We bought this land to get a start for Andrew and to have a place he could come to. But, we have no reason to stay now. Henry and I are thinking of California, as a place to live out the rest of our lives." Corinne and Marie both nodded. Everyone had heard about the pleasant weather in the California territory.

"In the southern parts, the sun is warm, The weather will be pleasing to our old bones. We have read through our copy of the county by-laws. We want to give away our land." Corinne felt her heart do a triple beat.

"You are our legal daughter-in-law and we have already had the deed signed over to you by the judge. We went by the sheriff's office, too. We informed him that this is now your land. In this territory, it is legal for a woman to inherit land from her in–laws, or to be given land, in this case. I have heard that you are now engaged to a good man, and we are so pleased. You are too young and full of life to remain a widow. Andrew would not want it that way and neither do we. According to the courts, you now own the land next door, Corinne." Linda Temple looked pleased as she reached out and hugged Corinne hard. Corinne was shocked and visibly shaken. Her eyes teared up a bit, but her heart was happy also, as she let any stray tears fall.

224

"I can't accept such a gift. You built a house and broke ground. You don't realize what you are giving away." Corinne looked at the deed on the table. It did indeed have her name on it.

"We can afford it, Corinne. Let us do this for you, for we cannot bring our son back, but we can bless you and your life. Be happy and fill the place with love and children. That is all we ask in return." Corinne cried and hugged her back. She would accept, she had to. Her father and the Grant families were so dear to her, she had to accept help from the most unlikely people.

"I cannot thank you enough, Linda. I have to go, I have to tell Lucas." Linda stood and laughed, knowing how young love was.

"We have been packing all week. We will be moving into the boarding house in town for the winter and leaving for California in the spring. The house is yours next week. Go, take your deed. Be blessed Corinne." Corinne took the deed. She paused in a moment of surprise, and with shaky hands, read the proof again. She gratefully kissed Linda Temple on the cheek and said something barely recognizable to her. Then she leapt for the door.

Corinne took the papers, put them in her saddlebags, and rode over to the Grant house. She was determined to not break her neck as she galloped on the pathway.

The family was inside when Corinne arrived. She ran into the house, grabbed Lucas, and kissed him in front of everyone. They all whistled and cheered as she dragged him out to the front porch.

"I have land!" she said breathlessly, as he stood next to her on the porch. He looked pleasantly confused.

"How do you have land?"

He smiled slowly, his boyish look showing as he looked at her face intensely.

"The Temple's deeded their land to me. They are leaving," she said, just above a whisper. She thought, if perhaps she had said it louder, then it wouldn't have been true.

She explained the Temple's plan, and the action that they took. They even by-passed any objection the land council could have had.

Lucas broke a wide smile.

"I have been praying unceasingly, since that morning when I was labeled a criminal," he started. "I petitioned God to clear my name and to allow me to stay here in this valley." He took a deep breath and sighed. "I am not one to share my thoughts on God. I have always been a quiet believer, I try to be a good man. But this whole situation shook me. It challenged my ability to trust God. To know that He had a plan for me, for us." He reached out and touched her arm. Corinne knew he wasn't finished, so she gave him time to speak. "I had to trust. If traveling across the country taught me anything, it was that we have no idea about what God is capable of. I knew if God had settled the issue with Sarah Ballentine so well, from across the miles, that He could handle the Oregon City land council. But the faith was hard to come by some days," he admitted.

"I know." She nodded, She also had struggled many times over the last weeks.

"Finding love, the complicated way we did..." He sighed again, searching for the words. "God has shown me what His love means. I am not certain how to express it."

He leaned down and kissed her on the cheek. "I know that loving you was part of God's plan. I am in awe of how it all worked out. It still must settle in my heart. God found a way."

"He did," Corinne said. Her eyes well up with overwhelmed tears.

They stood together holding hands. Without even planning it, they prayed. For the first time, they prayed together, thanking God for seeing them through. It was the first of many prayers.

They sat down on the rocking chairs and looked over the land quietly, reverently. Perhaps understanding, in a fresh way, how much God had done for them. Lucas reached over for her hand again.

"I think we should get married right away. I can't let anything else try to come between us," Lucas said, as he held her. Corinne could not help but believe his idea was brilliant.

That night, they shared all the good news with their family.

Sunday, October 29, 1848 - Oregon City

The small church was full for the Sunday service. The air was brisk and the snow on the peaks was bright white against the craggy rocks. The sun shown a yellow gold, for the wedding day of Oregon City's newest couple. Corinne and Lucas exited the newly built church as husband and wife.

Everyone headed to the Harpole ranch again, where Corinne's father had a wedding party planned. The sky was clear. And even though the air was crisp with a fall chill, the festivities commenced.

Clive stood up after the meal to share a story about the bride and groom.

"The day I met Corinne, I knew she was something special. When I saw the sparks flying between these two, I knew one day I would toast at their wedding." Clive lifted his glass, and everyone cheered. He took a drink and kept right on talking.

"We all know what these young folks went through to survive and be here now. What we all had to do to survive. To have the courage to 'See the elephant' will give us all the strength to tame this land. We have laid our claim. Let's build it into a fine state." The crowd cheered again, and Clive hugged both his young friends. He could not be prouder if they were his own kin.

Chelsea and Marie had been decorating the cabin for Lucas and Corinne. It had been the Temple cabin. A few days before, Lucas and Russell used chisels and paint to create a wooden sign to post near the road. So, with the preacher's declaration of man and wife, the cabin was now Grant's Grove.

The dinner party celebrating the young couple's wedded bliss, continued until the sky turned to dusk. The young couple escaped the crowd, made their way the short walk, to their own home that waited for them. The smoke curled from the fireplace and welcomed them. The candles and a lit lantern made the cabin glow with warmth, as they went inside and shook off their coats.

"Did I tell you at least once today, how beautiful you look in that wedding dress, wife?" Lucas hung up their winter coats. He reached for her and welcomed his wife into an embrace. The way he said 'wife' was much different than her previous husband.

"You mentioned it a few times, husband."

"I cannot tell you how adorable you were in the desert, with sand in your hair and sun burnt." He held her close and she threw a playful punch at his shoulder. "I love my brilliant, talented, and beautiful wife. You have changed and saved my life forever," Lucas said slowly, looking at her seriously for a second.

"I love you so much, but I never saved your life, Lucas." Corinne was getting used to him exaggerating.

He grabbed her chin.

"Oh, yes you did."

His green eyes were honest, and finally, she believed him.

~The End~

To continue Corinne and Angela's Story
Book 2 – Angela's Hope
Never miss a book release...

Sign up for newsletter at http://www.leahbanickibooks.com/

The Wildflowers series is now at 9 books. Curl up and read as much as you like.

———◆•◎•◆———◆•◎•◆———

Thank you so much for reading my first book. If you could leave a review, I would be so very thankful. Word-of-mouth is priceless for an Indie author. Thanks! – Leah Banicki

Wildflower Series

Book 1 – Finding Her Way
(also on Audible)

Book 2 – Angela's Hope

Book 3 – Daughters of the Valley

Book 4 – The Watermill

Book 5 – Love In Full Bloom

Book 6 – A Kiss in Winter

Book 7 – The Namesake

Book 8 – A Song for Sparrows

Book 9 – Down the Mountain Path

Work in Progress... Book 10 – Beside the Still Waters

Work in Progress... Book 11 – (Currently – no title)

Runner Up – A Contemporary love story,
Set in the world of reality TV.

IMPARATOS Series:

Book 1 – Aurora

This is a young adult contemporary series,
full of action and adventure.
I do plan to continue this series, in the next year or so.

https://www.facebook.com/Leah.Banicki.Novelist

Please share your thoughts with me.
leahbanickibooks@gmail.com

The self-publishing world is very rewarding but has its marketing challenges. Please remember to spread the word about my books if you like them. By using word-of-mouth!
You can help to bless an author.
Like – Share - Leave a review

Thank you, Leah Banicki

My Biography -

I am a writer, wife and mother. I live in SW lower Michigan near the banks of Brandywine Creek. I adore writing historical and contemporary stories, facing the challenges that life throws at you with characters that are relatable. I love finding humor in the ridiculous things that are in the everyday comings and goings of life. For me a good book is when you get to step into the character's shoes and join them on their journey. So climb aboard, let us share the adventure!

My writing buddy is my miniature poodle Mr. Darcy, who snuggles at my feet while I write until he must climb onto my chest for dancing or snuggles. My beagle Oliver is more concerned with protecting the yard from trespassers – squirrels and pesky robins.

I love hearing from my readers and try to answer every email personally.

I am always on Facebook and let my readers know about how the next books are coming along.

I have a slew of books in the works and plan on releasing a new series soon. Keep your eyes peeled for news!

My health does not always allow me to work as fast as I would always like but I am so thankful for every day that God lets me continue to do this work that I love so very much.

I plan on continuing the Wildflower Series for many more years.

https://www.facebook.com/Leah.Banicki.Novelist

http://www.leahbanickibooks.com

http://www.leahbanickibooks.com

Mr. Darcy – my writing buddy!

Made in the USA
Columbia, SC
19 August 2022